PRAISE F

"*Sips & Strokes* by Sarah Skye is utterly charming. Featuring a fake relationship plotline that quickly ventures into curl-your-toes territory, it is such a yummy read. You'll fall in love with Lily and Calder too!"

— Rosanna Leo, author of the *Handymen* series.

Sips and Strokes is sweet, sexy, and heart-achingly tender. Sarah Skye delivers a scorching romance that deftly balances characters you root for with the journey of finding the inner strength you need in order to ask for what you truly want. The story is an absolute delight at every turn. I can't wait for more books from Sarah Skye!

— Lindsay Landgraf Hess, author of *Storysinger*

Sarah Skye make fake dating sweet and fun in this entertaining novel. Lily and Calder are a perfect match!

— Charish Reid, author of *(Trust) Falling for You*

SIPS & STROKES

SARAH SKYE

Anti-Belle Books

Created with Vellum

To our Pride, Prejudice, and Pastry ladies. Stefanie, Sonia, and Sandy, we love you to bits.

1

CALDER

I'm a surgeon. It's a very important job. I'm definitely about to go in and save someone's life because I've got a stethoscope slung around my neck. The cold metal brushes my bare chest, but I won't allow myself to shiver. My green scrub pants are slung so low on my hips that my v-cuts are almost indecent.

Slowly, I reach for my mask. My eyes flash, my gaze full of angry intensity and unbridled lust that no dying patient can distract me from. These scrubs are going to have to come off, stat.

"Perfect, Calder, hold that look just another second... Now, let's lose the mask—yep, just like that, don't move." Moments later, the photographer lowers her camera and grins at me. "Fantastic."

I relax my expression and laugh as I yank the stethoscope off my neck. "If this thing hits my nipple one more time I'm going to break out in goosebumps."

"No problem, I'll take that. We're all set on this one. Take a quick break and change. I think it's the baseball motif next. Let's have fun with it, make it less smoldering and more playful, okay? The author is coming in to watch, by the way. She's excited to meet you."

"Brilliant, I'll be right out. She can tell me how to play with my bat if she likes." I laugh and wink, then head to change clothes.

While I'm stepping into the polyester trousers, I check my email to confirm the details of this afternoon:

Hey, Cal,

I bet you're stacked with jobs, but I've got an emergency and I've got to leave town. My regular spot as a form model at the local community college is set to begin this week. I know how you appreciate art—you're basically the only one in the business I could think of who'd say yes to a gig like this. The professor, Lily Maldonado, is fantastic. I'd hate to leave her in a lurch. It's 1:15 every Thursday through December. Think you can help us out?

Xoxo, Morgan

Morgan and I had done a few shoots together. She was always a sport. Even though most of our work involved us wearing underwear and tangled in bedsheets, she knew my devotion to the craft and appreciation for the beauty of the human form. How could I say no?

I close the email and check the time. Nine already. Damn, this baseball set better wrap quick, or I'll be late. I grab the bat and put on my best smile, ready to meet the author of the book and make all her design dreams come true.

2

LILY

"I just can't understand why you don't want to go, Lily. It's a wedding. Weddings are fun and romantic."

"Mom." I squeeze the steering wheel with both hands and pause to take a long, cleansing breath before addressing my phone, which sits on the dashboard of my car. "You really can't understand why I don't want to go to my ex-boyfriend's wedding? Seriously?"

Pursing my lips, I slowly and quietly breathe in and out again while merging onto the freeway. I can't sound too annoyed on this call. If I do, Mom will lecture me on my attitude, which will lead to an argument, and I don't have time for that. I'm already running late on my commute to work. My muscles are tense as I weave in and out of traffic. The last thing I need is to arrive at my classroom agitated right before I teach twenty college students about life drawing.

"Oh, Lily. You're being dramatic," she says. "It was years ago that you and Marco broke up."

"It was one year ago actually," I say, careful not to grit my teeth.

"Fine. Yes. One year. Whatever."

I roll my eyes at her dismissive tone. There's a loud typing noise on her end. She must be at work already, at her computer in her spacious home office, the headquarters of her high-end interior design business.

"I expected more from you," she says against the tapping sound. "Your dad and I raised you to be a mature young lady who can handle any situation with grace and poise, not someone who refuses to attend an important social event just because you are fixated on the past. That's very immature for an almost-thirty-year-old woman to act that way."

When she exhales, I can picture her disappointed expression as clear as day in my mind. A frown mars her perfectly made-up face. Those high arched eyebrows of hers that look like two perfect slopes of dark brown are furrowed. And her lips, which are undoubtedly shellacked in Chanel lipstick, are pursed so tightly that the muscles in her mouth are twitching slightly.

I scoff. This time I don't bother to hide the sound.

"Scoffing, Lily? Really? While I'm lecturing you on maturity?"

I bite my tongue to keep from saying anything more, to keep from reminding her of the actual reason Marco and I broke up. Because even if I do—even if I lose my cool and remind her for the millionth time what exactly happened to end my two-year-long relationship with the guy my parents spent my entire life hoping I'd marry, it wouldn't do any good.

They thought I made the biggest mistake of my life when I left Marco—even though he hurt me in the worst way. But I shouldn't be surprised. They've been disappointed in me ever since I dropped out of law school to become an art teacher. It didn't matter that I hated law and dreaded the thought of becoming a lawyer, or that art was my life-long passion. It was just one more mistake, one more way that I've fallen short of their expectations.

"Lily, are you evening listening to me?" Mom's shrill voice emanating from my phone snaps me out of my rage-sadness stupor.

"I'm listening," I lie.

Just then my phone buzzes with another incoming call. A number I don't recognize. I normally let calls from unknown numbers go straight to voicemail—it's usually a robocall or telemarketer or scammer. But right now I'd happily talk to any one of them if it means I can end this conversation with my mother.

"Gotta go, Mom. Important call on the other line. Call you later, okay?"

I answer the other call before she can say anything. "Hello?"

"Hi, is this Professor Maldonado?"

My chest squeezes at the low, growly voice spoken in an unfamiliar yet very sexy accent.

"It is. Who's calling?"

"It's Calder. Your new model."

"Oh, Calder! Hi!" I wince at how pitchy and excited I sound.

Morgan, my best friend and the form model I've worked with for the past few years for the figure drawing community college course I teach, left the state last week to live with her grandmother. She had major surgery and needs someone to help take care of her for the next few months. She thankfully found a replacement—a model by the name of Calder Ross.

I've never met him before, but I don't care. Morgan recommended him and since I don't have a backup option, that's good enough for me.

As I pull into the faculty parking lot of the community college, I search for an open spot and check the time. Five minutes until I'm due to meet him.

"Thank you again for taking on this job last minute," I say.

"It's my pleasure." My stomach flips at his clipped, blunt accent. It's British for sure, but I can't place it. Northern England, maybe?

"Just one thing, Professor Maldonado," he says.

"Please call me Lily."

"Lily." I can tell he's smiling when he says my name. It makes me grin. I can't remember the last time the sound of my own name made me giddy. But this dude could say anything in his sexy accent—the local weather report, a random phone number—and I'd be grinning until my face hurt.

"Well, Lily," he says. "If you insist."

"I insist." My cheeks are suddenly hot. Damn, is this really all it takes for me to blush these days, a hot male voice paired with an even hotter accent?

I clear my throat and refocus on the conversation.

"I'm running about ten minutes behind this morning," he says. "I apologize."

I'm taken aback. As a professor who's used to taking meetings with perpetually late students and faculty members, I can't remember the last time someone called me to let me know they'd be running late.

"No worries at all. Thank you for letting me know," I say. "I appreciate the head's up."

"It's the least I can do. Looking forward to meeting you in person, Lily. Very soon."

"Likewise."

We hang up just as I slide into an empty spot and throw

the gearshift in my car to park. I'm about to walk out of my car when my phone rings once more. I sigh when I see it's Mom again. I contemplate letting it go to voicemail, but she'll just keep calling until I answer. Like always. I may as well finish our earlier conversation now that I have a few extra minutes before I meet Calder.

All the muscles in my neck and shoulders tense when I answer. She dives right into a list of why it's important for me to go to Marco's wedding. Our families have been close since I was born. His mom is her best friend and his dad is Dad's best friend.

"Just imagine what people will say if you don't come," she says.

Instead, I imagine what people will say if I *do* show up, no date at my side. Ever since our breakup, I haven't had the energy to date, let alone attempt another relationship. I'm certain there will be endless pitying stares aimed in my direction during the ceremony and reception.

"Did it ever occur to you how I feel in this whole situation, Mom? How would you like to watch one of your ex-boyfriends get married while everyone around you throws you looks of judgment and pity?" I hate how pitchy my voice sounds, but I'm desperate for her to understand...for her to just for once empathize with me instead of trying to get me to do whatever she wants.

"Lily. You and Marco practically grew up together," she says, ignoring my question. "We've spent vacations and holidays together with his family. It's one thing that your relationship didn't work out. We can all learn to live with the choice you've made. But to just blow off his wedding like it means nothing? We raised you better than that."

Like a reflex, my mind goes back to the day that I ended it with him, the day he hurt me in the worst possible way. I even told my parents about it...and they didn't care. Why should they care about my feelings now?

I hunch over in my seat, shrinking into myself as I shove the painful memory of what caused our breakup in the back of my mind.

"You haven't spoken to Marco ever since you ended things with him," Mom says. "I know your relationship with his fiancée is...difficult."

"That's an understatement," I mutter.

A month after we split, Marco rebounded with my childhood bully Harmony...and then got engaged to her three months after that. I press my eyes shut, hoping the burning sensation doesn't cause any tears to fall. As tough as that was to process, that's not why I'm on the verge of tears. What's cutting me deep is that to my parents, maintaining appearances is more important than the happiness of their only child.

"It's like you're cutting him out of your life," Mom says. "How do you think that makes him and his parents feel?"

"I hate that you care more about other people's feelings than your own daughter's feelings. It makes me feel like shit." I cover my mouth as soon as I say it. Cursing in front of my parents has always been a no-no, but I can't take her badgering any longer.

"You watch your language, young lady."

I bite my tongue, my face heating instantly.

"I will not stand for this temper tantrum you're throwing," she scolds.

Closing my eyes, I lean my head back against the headrest. "I have to go, Mom."

I'm about to hang up when her tone turns gentle. "*Anakko*, please."

I soften and stay on the phone. *Anakko* used to be her go-to Filipino term of endearment for me when I was young and obedient and did whatever she and dad wanted me to. She hardly ever uses it anymore. It makes my chest squeeze to hear it again after all this time.

"Just come to the wedding for your dad and me. Please?"

Inside I deflate like a balloon. I know why she's saying this now...to soften me into saying yes to something I don't want to do. My shoulders hunch and I shrink into myself. The sad part is, I'm pathetic enough that it works. I'd rather drink shampoo than go to Marco's wedding, but if it'll make my parents happy in this moment, after a million moments of disappointing them, then I'll do it.

"Okay," I say quietly, slouching in my seat.

"Thank you. It means a lot to your dad and me."

Closing my eyes, my throat tightens. Another moment in my life where I didn't have the guts to tell her no.

We hang up, then I climb out of my car, purse and laptop in hand, and walk across campus to the fine arts building where today's class is held. All the while, the dread of Marco's November wedding hangs over me like an invisible cloud. In two months I'll have to attend in all my pathetically single glory, accompanied by my parents, while I watch my loved-up ex publicly declare his love for the girl who made elementary school hell for me.

I walk into the classroom and stand for a few seconds, taking in the empty space just to give myself some time to let my thoughts settle. I scan the empty easels and stools, the massive window that takes up almost all of the far wall, that filters in the perfect amount of natural light. I walk over and open the windows, inhaling the scent of fresh air and trimmed grass, then go and sit on the dais in the center of the room.

When I take another breath, I start to feel the slightest

bit settled. At least here in my classroom, nothing can faze me. I'm calm and in control—in my element. I'm surrounded by my students and my passion. I don't have to worry about my parents pushing me around or having to put on a brave face in front of my ex and his gorgeous new fiancée or bracing myself for the most awkward wedding ever. In this space, I can be happy and free.

I take another breath, hoping that today's class with this new model will be enough to take my mind off the impending disaster in my personal life.

3

CALDER

The shoot runs long. I'm practically hopping into my jeans as I hurry out the door to my car, trying not to run late for this afternoon's art class. On the drive over to the campus, I call to say I'm running late, but Professor Maldonado—Lily—is nothing but accommodating. Still, I don't want to be that person. I gun the engine and skirt the traffic as best I can. I'm nearly there when the phone rings again; it's Stella, my agent.

"Is this about Sonce?" I ask in greeting as I swing into the parking lot.

"Hello to you too, darling. But, yes, it sure is. Well, that and I've got a boxer-brief shoot for you on Monday if you want it."

I shift into park and fist my hair. "For the love of god, not more underwear right now. What of Sonce? Let me hear it."

"Fine, fine. It didn't go as warmly as I'd expected, I'll say that. They had a lot of questions about your portfolio and social media. Said they'd be in touch."

I groan. "You mentioned the connection, right? You told them I knew Nate Wallace, the owner, right? And that I learned the difference between a sherry cask and a rum barrel before I had my first kiss because I lived and breathed that distillery growing up? That Nate and I were best mates as kids and I'd already contacted him about how I'd be a perfect brand ambassador here in the U.S.?"

Stella laughs. "Of course I mentioned it. Come on, Cal, give me some credit."

"Ah, Stell, I'm sorry. I just need something different, and I think this is it. Know what I mean?"

Her usual cajoling tone softens as she says, "I get it, hon. This means a lot to you, and yeah, you'd be a perfect face for a new whisky label. But you've already made such a name for yourself. I don't want to see you put all your stock in one opportunity."

I glance at the clock, and then out the windshield at the small brick building a few yards in front of me. "Right, fair. I'll take the underwear gig, just text me the details. Got to go for now—be in touch if you hear anything."

"You know I will. Take care."

"Cheers."

A yellow visitor tag sits on my dash; a similar sticker is affixed to my shirt, somewhat ironically given my purpose here. The campus is a typical university, with trees and greenspace and students walking here and there. Inside the squat brick building, I'm sure the classroom is bland, with a linoleum floor and chairs in a circle. Just thinking of it melts a little of my frustration. There will be nothing flashy, no bright lights or people rushing to greet me, and yet this is my favorite kind of job.

I enter the classroom expecting to find Ms. Maldonado already there but stumble to a stop as soon as I'm inside. There is no middle-aged professor dressed in a long skirt and cardigan. Instead, there's a young woman seated on the pedestal in the center of the room. Her legs swing idly as she stares up at the sunlight streaming in from the windows close to the ceiling. An overstuffed blue velvet armchair sits on the pedestal, providing an interesting backdrop for her.

Her serenity, the graceful ease of her posture, and the faraway expression on her face make me wish I had my camera. It's a moment, absolutely beautiful in its simplicity.

Shame no one's capturing this.

She blinks and hops to her feet when the door shuts, her gaze focusing in on me. Her dark eyes give me a full-body scan, brows rising as she goes for round two. She shakes her head and swallows hard. "Oh, hi. Sorry, I was just having a moment."

"I hate to interrupt. Are you modeling for this class too?"

Her lips curve as a blush sweeps her cheeks. My attention snags on her mouth. Her full, pink lips are fucking lush. She's got the kind of mouth that women kill for and men daydream about. I'm not above daydreaming a bit myself, and with the way that blush makes her skin glow—

"I'm sorry, what?" I shake my head, sure that I was too distracted to hear her correctly.

"I said no, Mr. Ross, I'll save everyone from that horror and stick to teaching, thanks."

Well, fuck me running. This stunner in blue jeans and a white t-shirt is Ms. Lily? Where is my buttoned-up professor? I look around, taking in the space. The linoleum is there, sure, but this room is a proper studio. The walls are draped in warm cloth to enhance the soft lamps glowing in the corners. Easels are at attention around the dais with a teacher's desk off to the side, but everything about this place has been set up with creativity in mind. *Impressive.*

I stick out my hand and abandon all presumptions I'd

had about this gig. "It's Calder, please. And I am sorry to interrupt, but I'm also sorry I'm a bit late, Ms—"

"Lily."

"Ms. Lily."

She laughs as her hand slips into mine. I'm hit with a double whammy of sensation. First, the warmth of her soft skin sliding across my palm and then the muted sound of her mirth, which she hides with her free hand.

Her eyes squint as she shakes her head. "Just Lily. If that's what you're comfortable with."

"I could be very comfortable with it."

The words I'd meant to keep in my head tumble out without warning. *What the fuck is with you? Is this amateur hour? Pull your shit together and be a professional for a second.*

Lily's blush deepens, so I release her hand and flash an easy grin. "No need for formality in my opinion," I clarify.

She exhales and nods, and I take that as a decent recovery. I watch her go to her desk, shuffling a stack of papers as she says, "We'll start with some short gesture poses if that's good for you?"

"Of course." I tug off my tee as I head to the pedestal. Once I hop up, I drop my sweatpants and toss everything on the armchair.

"Great, so if you need any suggest—oh!" The papers flutter to the floor as she turns and looks at me. "Oh my god, you're already naked."

My brows knit. "Just getting comfortable. Was I meant to wait for a specific moment?"

"Well, I just, I mean class hasn't started and we—or, no, but it's just that you're... so naked." Her eyes dart around the room, landing on me at regular intervals as a blush paints her cheeks all the way down her neck now.

I bite the inside of my lip, glad I'm not the only one off their game today. "You could get me a robe."

The obvious suggestion makes her palm her forehead. "Oh, of course. Gosh, I am so sorry, I don't know where my brain is right now."

She hustles to the cupboard in the corner and fetches a burgundy robe. I drop down and cross to accept it, but this seems to be the wrong move, too. Her eyes go round as she freezes mid-stride, the robe thrust away from her body.

"Are you alright?"

"You're just so naked," she breathes.

I laugh. "It's an art class, isn't it? Is this unusual for you?"

"Well, no, but... but..." Those dark eyes sweep me again, and I have to think of cricket and my grandmother's knitting to keep this professional. I accept the robe and throw it over my shoulders.

She swallows hard and rolls her eyes once I've got it cinched. "I'm a mess today, Mr. Ross. Please, don't mind me."

"Calder."

"Sorry."

There's a note of defeat in her tone that erases my amusement. For whatever reason, I want to ask her what's wrong, but obviously I don't. Instead, I nod and go back to the pedestal.

Students begin to filter in shortly after, and that seems to snap Lily out of her fluster. As she greets them, she's relaxed and smiling, quick with replies to their questions and feedback as they set up their space. I sit cross-legged on the dais and wave at the students who throw me intrigued glances. When they're all ready, Lily begins the lesson by reviewing their objectives and explaining how we'll warm up with gesture drawings.

While they nod along, I run through a set of potential

poses and decide on a logical succession of four. By the time she says, "Okay, so if our model is ready, we'll begin," I'm in my professional headspace, game face on. I toss the robe on the ground and get into position. There's a palpable pause in the room as I drop into a runner's lunge, but then the whispers of pencils on paper begin.

Lily calls time after a minute, and I rise and shake it out. "Is a minute okay, or should I cut it to thirty seconds?" she asks me.

I grin and strike a new pose. "What, you think this is my first rodeo?"

The class laughs as they resume sketching. Without moving, I slide my gaze to see Lily's look of surprise melt into a giggle.

"If it's not your first rodeo, can we assume you'll be striking a bull-riding pose next?"

"Planning to straddle this armchair first chance I get."

"I'll see if I have a cowboy hat in the cupboard. Time!"

All the students are laughing as I drop the pose and allow myself a chuckle too. Then, I do indeed throw one leg over the back of the armchair and raise a hand into the air as if I'm on a bucking bronco. Every one of them loses it, but it's the melodic sound of *her* laughter that my ears pick up best. I can't begin to erase my grin, although I do a hell of a job keeping still for the minute.

She's left my line of sight when she calls time, but when I relax, she says, "Let's try that one again, only now with a prop."

I turn to see her holding a cowboy hat with a ridiculous ostrich feather jutting out of the brim. A cheeky grin purses her lips, and I laugh and scratch the back of my head. "Sure, why not?"

She waves the hat at me, but I shake my head. "No

ma'am. If I'm to wear that awful thing, you better come arrange the scene."

I have never flirted with an employer. Not even when I was eighteen and full of piss and vinegar did I have the balls to be anything but completely professional on a job, but there's something about this room and this woman that is just so damn fun. It's harmless, of course, and something about her tone when I walked in makes me suspect she needs this, too.

Or maybe not. Lily freezes, the smile slipping quick. "Oh, um, well I…"

"Do it, Ms. Lily!" one of her students shouts and is seconded by everyone in the circle.

She casts her gaze around at all of them, eyes narrowing. "I hate all of you," she growls with no malice, then huffs and stomps to the pedestal and clambers up.

I cross my arms, grinning again, and await instructions.

"Um, the chair." She points.

"It is a chair, yes." I've lost my mind, but I want to hear her boss me around.

"No, um if you could… straddle it."

She's instantly red, and I'm again needing to think of all the most boring things in life as the word straddle slips from her lips. I throw my leg over the chair again. Lily nods, fiddling with the hat, and then takes a deep breath and walks to me.

The class applauds as she sets the hat on my head and arranges the positioning, but her black-brown eyes are locked with mine, and for a moment I forget we're not alone. Her light, sweet scent hits me and makes my mouth water. *Fuck, man, calm down. A woman like this has got to be married. The last thing you need right now is to get a rep as a skeevy prick on the job.*

I throw her a wink to assure her this is all just good fun, and a spark lights her eyes. That cheeky purse returns to her mouth, and suddenly I'm half blind as she tips the brim low over one of my eyes and hops off the dais. "I'm setting a three-minute timer this time, Mr. Calder. I trust you can handle it."

"Yee-haw," I reply, getting another round of laughs.

The hour flies by. As I rise from my long pose—seated in the chair, that silly hat still on my head—the students begin to pack their things. I've just stepped into my sweats when Lily speaks.

"Thank you so much for being our model today, Calder. Before class ends, do you mind taking a minute and telling us about yourself?"

Shit. Didn't see that coming. My throat closes a bit as everyone looks at me. I plop back down in the chair and unconsciously dig my thumbnail into my pinkie cuticle. Biting your fingers is nasty, but tearing them is a habit I've had since childhood and cannot manage to break. I've tried everything short of hypnosis.

So I tear at my skin and try to come up with something to say. Sitting naked in front of 20 people is no big deal. Speaking to them? Another story. "Erm, well, not sure what you'd want to hear. I'm Calder Ross, been modeling since I was about eighteen. Mostly do underwear and romance novels. I do a lot of naked things for a living."

There's a burst of laughter, which eases my nerves the slightest bit.

"You, ha, you can check me on social media if you want."

Plenty of them are already nodding, clearly familiar with my profile.

"Erm, anyway, I love beautiful things. Art is one of the finest things people are capable of if you ask me. And it comes in so many forms. Whatever's created out of human passion and inspiration can be art, if you ask me—shit, sorry, said that bit already, huh? But yes. Art is incredible, and I think all of you are tremendous for developing your craft. Happy to be working with you this semester."

I'm mentally kicking myself for rambling so badly, but they're all smiling and nodding. Most importantly, the lovely Lily has a shine in her eyes that makes it hard to care about sounding like a fool.

"That was beautiful, Calder, thank you for the introduction," she says softly, then clears her throat. "Class, I'll see you Tuesday, when we'll work on analyzing the pieces we did today."

They all thank me and hurry out of the room. I toe into my shoes and take the hat over to Lily's desk, where she's sat on the edge.

She tosses the hat on her chair. "Thank you for being such a good sport."

"I don't usually laugh so much on a job. Hope it was what you wanted."

"It was better than what I wanted. It was fantastic."

"Yeah, it rather was, huh?" Relief loosens my shoulders.

Lily nods. "Honestly, I was having a terrible day before this. So, um, thanks for turning that around."

She bites her lip, and I want to sit beside her and ask if she wants to talk about it, but here's nothing to indicate she wants to elaborate. She must have a host of friends to unwind with and a good bloke at home to rub her feet and let her pour out her day later.

Instead, I flash a commiserate frown and take a step backwards. "Well, glad it helped. I'll see you next week, then."

A tiny light extinguishes in her gaze, but she nods

silently and waves as I take another step and turn toward the door.

My phone is full of notifications when I check it on the way to the car. Most I can ignore since they're just noise from social media that I don't need to respond to. Fans send me everything from selfies to phone numbers to fire emojis. I'm used to it.

More importantly, I've missed a call from Nate Wallace, my childhood friend and the man who holds my ticket to a huge career shift. I drop into the car, ready to tap the contact despite the adrenaline clenching my gut, but before I can, a text pops up.

Lucy: *Rumour has it you're looking to partner with Sonce. The town's buzzing. I want the details.*

And then a gif of some creep peering through hedges. My sister closes every text with a gif so perfectly chosen that I never fail to laugh out loud.

Me: *No details yet. Trying to do business now, but you're bothering me.*

Lucy: *What's a little sister for? Tell Nate I say hiiiiiii ;) :P*

Me: *He's married, you pervert. And don't you have a boyfriend?*

Lucy: *Oh look at that, Mum's shouting for me. Gtg, byeeeeee!*

And then a gif of Forrest Gump running away.

I quirk a brow, shake my head, and refocus on the business at hand as I return Nate's call.

"Calder Fucking Ross." Nate laughs into the phone on the second ring. "I was sure I was dreaming when I got an email from you last month. How in the hell are you, mate?"

"Looking for a bit of a change of pace and hoping you're hiring. Congrats on taking the label international. You must be very damn pleased with yourself." Already I can hear my accent getting heavier just talking to someone from back home.

"Aye, we are for sure. Heard you interviewed with my partners this afternoon. Wanted to be the one to call you back, didn't feel right otherwise, but, ah, sorry to say they don't think you're the person for the job."

I slump in my seat, every last bit of amusement from the class long gone in my mind, and gaze blankly through my windshield. Lily appears, striding out of the building with a bag on her shoulder. A line creases her brows as she stares down at her phone, but I barely register the image. I'm too busy having my goals wash down the drain.

There's no sense in going down without a fight. I clear my throat and sit up a little straighter. "I've been modeling since I was a kid. Since I came to the States, my client list has—"

"You don't have to tell me any of it. It's not that you're not good at what you do. It's that you're a little too well known. You're practically fucking Fabio of the modern age, Cal. That's impressive, no doubt, but Sonce's target market is trendy millennials, parents just starting a family. There's a certain prejudice against sexy Instagram playboys who grace the cover of every newest Fifty Shades of Whatever."

"That's a punch in the balls."

"Not meant to be. Just the truth. We need someone with a chicer and more wholesome image. Looking for the sexy dad, if you know what I mean."

"I can do that." I'm practically shouting, but I don't care. "Don't know how I can borrow a baby, but—"

Nate laughs. "Don't kidnap anyone for Christ sake. Listen, the contracts aren't done for a few more months. I'd love to give you this chance, but I don't have a leg to stand on with someone who's oiled up half the time and partying with C-listers the rest."

"That's not me anymore, hand to god. I'm revamping my image, have been for a while now. I've settled down, I'm dating someone, and... and she wanted me to grow up a bit, you know? That's why I thought this would be great. We're already talking about family in the future, and it just seemed to fit so well with Sonce that I thought..."

I trail off and let the silence hang between us. *What the fuck did you just say?*

"That makes things a bit different," Nate murmurs, so whatever I said mustn't have been as crazy as it sounded to me. He exhales. "That's a good bit different. Cleaning up the image, huh? Already got some new jobs that aren't underwear or condoms? That could change their mind. Listen, this is what we'll do. You shift that image, and I'll get your foot in the door at promo events just as a guest. We'll see what we can do before it's all signed and sealed, alright?"

"Perfect. Swear you won't be sorry."

Nate laughs. "Either way it's no skin off my ass, mate. Sounds good, though. See you soon. Oh, and of course—bring your girlfriend."

"Of course."

The phone goes dead. It takes several minutes of sitting and staring into space before I can fully comprehend the level of bullshit I just shoveled.

"Well," I say to the empty car, "so much for that dream."

4

LILY

A collective "aww" echoes around me. Harmony holds up yet another fine china set from where she's sitting in the party room of the local country club.

Her glossy pink lips stretch into a grin. Her blue eyes sparkle as she glances at the woman sitting at the table next to her. "Brittany, you shouldn't have. It's too much."

A soft wave of chuckles and more "aww" sounds follow. A handful of gloved servers drop off tiered silver trays of flavorless finger sandwiches and pots of tea at the tiny table I'm sharing with Mom. I try to shift in my chair, but I can hardly move in this floral cap-sleeve shift dress that I dug from the back of my closet. I bite the inside of my cheek to keep from groaning. This must be what hell is like.

There are a million things I'd rather do on a Saturday afternoon than attend the bridal shower of my ex-boyfriend's fiancée. Get a pelvic exam. Stand in line for hours at the DMV. Get run over by a bulldozer. But alas, Harmony's bridal shower is where I am because I can't say no to my mother.

My phone buzzes in my purse, and I quickly grab it.

Morgan: *Are you surviving?*

Me: *Ha. Barely.*

Me: *If you were still here, you know I would have dragged you to this.*

Morgan: *And I would have gone kicking and screaming...but I still would have come with you ;)*

Me: *How's your grandma?*

Morgan: *Okay overall. Still having mobility issues, but I think she'll be okay with some physical therapy.*

Me: *So glad to hear that.*

Me: *On an unrelated note, WHY THE HELL DIDN'T YOU TELL ME YOUR REPLACEMENT MODEL WAS THE SEXIEST MAN ALIVE?*

A loud throat clear makes my head pop up. Mom is flashing her disappointed stare at me, so I put my phone away and focus on the scene happening at the front of the room. There Harmony sits in some plushy upholstered chair opening up a designer luggage set.

Mom smiles as she looks on, then leans over to me. "Thank you for agreeing to come today," she whispers. "I know it means a lot to Harmony since you missed their engagement party this summer."

"Right." I fiddle with the microscopic slice of finger sandwich on my tiny plate, recalling how Mom texted me right after I agreed to attend the wedding while I was busy teaching class, insisting that I come to Harmony's bridal shower.

"When I told Harmony the good news that you'll be going to the wedding, she texted me and asked that you come to her shower," Mom had said over the phone while I walked through campus to teach my next class.

"Did she really?" I said. "Um...that's a surprise."

"Why is it a surprise? You two have known each other since you were kids."

I had to bite the inside of my cheek to keep from going off yet again. As kids, Harmony bullied me for a million random things. Sometimes it was for the gap I had between my two front teeth before I got braces. Sometimes it was because of my thick-rimmed glasses. Sometimes it was because my last name was hard to pronounce. And sometimes it was for being biracial.

Her biting words from long ago flash to the front of my mind.

Lily, what even are you? You're too pale to be your mom's daughter, but you don't even look like your dad. Are you sure some other family didn't take one look at you when you were born, freak out at how ugly you were, and then dropped you off at your parents' doorstep?

Laughter would always follow her taunts. Never once did I say anything in response. I was too embarrassed and scared of her. She had a gaggle of friends with her always. I was quiet and shy and wanted to blend in with everyone to avoid calling attention to myself. So I just ignored her whenever she said anything to me. When it got to be too much, I'd run to the girls' bathroom and cry.

I never told Mom and Dad the worst of it. I didn't want them to know what a loser their only child was. And Harmony was always an angel around other people's parents, so they never suspected a thing. The most I ever said were vague comments about her having a mean streak.

Thankfully Harmony went to a different high school, so I didn't have to deal with her as a teenager. But then by some weird twist of fate, she started dating Marco right after we broke up.

"You and Harmony were friends when you were kids, right?" Mom asked the other day on the phone.

"Nope. She was pretty mean to me in elementary school, actually. Remember?"

"Well, it's nice to know that she grew out of that stage and is being a mature adult," Mom said pointedly. "I think it's wonderful she's going out of her way to invite you to her shower, Lily. What a nice gesture."

I scoff into my water glass as Harmony opens another lavish gift. Harmony might be nicer now, but that doesn't erase how awful she was to me. I swipe a scone from one of the silver plates on the table and take a bite, wondering why in the world Harmony Daniels cares to be nice to me now after all this time.

The servers walk back into the room carrying bottles of champagne. I flag down the one closest to me and hold up my empty flute. "Fill it up. All the way to the top please."

The young server nods, a focused look on his face as he studies the pour, careful not to overfill.

I quietly thank him, then down the full glass, coughing softly as the bubbles hit my nose. Mom frowns at me before smoothing her hand along the slicked-back bun she sports. I turn my head away, ignoring the judgment in her deep brown eyes, and immediately ask for a refill.

"You guys don't have something harder you can serve, do you?" I ask him quietly.

He flashes an apologetic smile. "Sorry. The future Mrs. Woodruff wants to stick to a bubbles-only service for her shower."

There's a soft murmur to my left. When I glance over, a couple of the women sitting there immediately stop whispering to each other and look away from me, their faces red.

I grit my teeth and down my next glass, then dig a

twenty out of my purse and hand it to the server. "Leave the bottle at my table?"

His polite smile turns into a full-fledged grin. "You got it."

I thank him and fill my glass once more. Mom's dissatisfied sigh hits my ears, but I don't care. Everyone who's not currently watching Harmony open a plethora of expensive gifts is probably watching me right now, wondering to themselves and each other why I'm here.

Sitting quietly as your ex's fiancée basks in the joy of her impending wedding while everyone quietly gossips about you is a whole new level of discomfort. I deserve every drop of champagne I can get in this hellfire of a situation.

"Pace yourself," Mom whispers to me while staring. Her brows knit in annoyance.

Just then a tall, slim, and smiley blonde I'm pretty sure is Brittany stands up while tapping her champagne flute.

"I'd like to make a toast." She turns to Harmony, who's still sitting in the plush chair-couch thing that looks more like a throne the longer I look at it. Brittany raises her glass. "To the beautiful bride and my best friend in the entire whole wide world."

As Brittany drones on and on about Harmony's endless incredible qualities, I tune her out and guzzle more champagne. I'm very much not in the mood to listen to what a saint my elementary school bully now is. I look back at my phone to the message that Morgan sent me.

Morgan: *I thought it would be a nice surprise. You walk into class and bam! There's a hottie as my replacement ;)*

Me: *Seriously, he is the dictionary definition of hottie*

Morgan: *Well, the least I could do after ditching you for a whole semester is to leave you with some eye candy ;)*

I tuck my phone back in my purse before Mom can passive-aggressively scold me again.

A light buzz hits from all that champagne and my mind starts to wander...to Calder—even though I know I shouldn't.

But I can't help it. He was insanely charming during our first class together the other day, and he's been on my mind ever since. Yes, that's creepy. It's probably even creepier that I searched him online. But I *had* to look. I was very, very intrigued at his "I do a lot of naked things for a living" comment.

And boy oh boy was he right about that.

I blink, and a million images from his Instagram account collide behind the darkness of my eyelids. There's Calder standing on a deserted beach at sunset, his back to the camera and his perfectly sculpted naked ass the focus of the photo. There's Calder lying in a hammock with zero clothing, a linen sheet draped over his naughty bits, that killer smirk tugging at his mouth. There's Calder smiling in a kilt as he holds a glass of whisky to his lips, his eyebrow raised. There's Calder's chiseled chest and abs on the cover of a romance novel I remember seeing at the grocery store months ago.

The simple act of mentally running through these images has me sizzling from the inside out. I take another sip of champagne, but it doesn't cool me off, not even a little bit. Because from my online stalking, I've learned that Calder is a famous Instagram model and romance cover hero who's got millions of adoring fans...and I get to work one-on-one with him for the next four months. I get to see him every week, naked in my classroom, showing off that perfect physique of his. I get to ogle him on the reg for my job.

It's more than just physical appeal, though. Even though he's nude in all of his photos, they're not gratuitous or in your face. Every shot is beautifully composed. Lighting and setting are artfully done in each frame. It's like he employs an artist's eye to create his very deliberate aesthetic: sexy but also inspired.

I'm gulping water from my glass when I catch Harmony standing and thanking everyone for attending. I silently thank Calder. Thinking of him made that last chunk of the shower fly by.

I start to grab my purse so I can leave, but then the door flies open. Gasps echo around me. When I look up, I see the last person I ever want to see standing in the doorway.

Marco.

Another wave of "awws" follows. Harmony cups her hands over her mouth. She runs over and pulls him close by the lapels of his gray blazer. When she finishes kissing him, she smooths his dark brown hair, then strokes a dainty hand over his clean-shaven cheek.

My arms and legs instantly still. It's a weird kind of shock to see him after a year of zero contact. Like a punch to the gut.

Someone at the next table leans over and says something to Mom about it being a tradition for the groom to make an appearance at the end of a bridal shower. I would have loved to know that. I wouldn't have come if I did.

A second later, the whispered murmurs start.

"God, can you imagine seeing your ex with someone new right in front of your eyes?"

"Poor girl. I'd be in tears."

"Can you believe she broke up with him?"

"And she's going to the wedding! I wonder if she has a date."

I frown at my purse in my lap, digging for nothing in particular. Anything to keep from looking up and having to see three dozen pairs of eyes staring at me, pitying me, silently shaming me.

"You should say hi before you leave, Lily. It would be the polite thing to do," Mom says.

When I glance at her, I notice the faintest hint of shock in her eyes. She probably wasn't expecting Marco either, but she's all about keeping up appearances.

"I think I'll pass," I say before pouring the last of the champagne from the bottle into my glass and taking a long sip.

"That's enough for you," Mom says as she slides my glass of water closer to me.

As everyone chats and mingles around me, I eye the door, which is just a few feet away from where Marco and Harmony stand as they bid guests farewell. Maybe I can slip out of here while everyone is preoccupied.

While Mom chats to the table next to us, I stand up. I'd rather wait for her outside than spend another minute sitting here.

I'm on my way to the door when the sound of my name halts me mid-step.

"Hey, Lily," Marco's deep voice calls behind me.

I freeze and bite the inside of my cheek. There's no way I can ignore him and continue walking. Everyone will see.

I slowly turn around to face him. "Hey, Marco."

"You're looking well."

The way he says those words combined with the quick once over he gives me makes me want to spit in his face. His future wife is standing a handful of feet away from him. He absolutely shouldn't be looking at me like that.

He flashes that trademark dazzling grin of his, the one

that displays all of his perfectly white and straight teeth. It used to make me weak in the knees. Now it makes my skin crawl.

"It's been a while," he says.

"It has. Fortunately." I purse my lips and cross my arms, hoping my defensive body language broadcasts just how much I'm hating this forced small talk.

Marco's deep brown eyes dart away from me when I say nothing more. I'm guessing my "fortunately" comment rubbed him the wrong way.

He frowns the slightest bit. "Still doing that art thing?"

I bite down at his dismissive tone. "If by 'art thing' you mean to ask if I'm still working as an art teacher, yes. I am."

"Glad to hear you're still *surviving*."

I cringe inwardly at the way he emphasizes the word "surviving." To anyone who happens to overhear this conversation, what he says sounds benign. But I know better.

That word triggers a painful memory. The day I walked out on Marco flashes in my mind like a sad highlight reel.

I met him at his house so we could go to dinner. When I followed him to his living room, I noticed his fireplace mantel and shelves were barren. All the sculptures and sketches I had made for him as gifts for holidays and birthdays were gone.

"What happened to all the artwork I gave you?" I asked, my head pivoting around the room.

"Huh? Oh, that. I sold them."

"You what?" I barked, whipping my head to him.

His gaze was glued to his phone. And when he finally looked at me he shrugged, like he couldn't have cared less. Just thinking about it now cuts me right in the center of my chest.

"Here," he said, before showing me the screen of his phone. It was an online account with a balance listed in the thousands. "I sold your art and used the money to start a retirement fund for you."

"You did what?" The volume of my voice jolted him so much that he stumbled back. He looked like a surprised Ken doll.

A second later, he reined in his expression. "Come on, Lily. Don't be mad. It's the sensible thing to do."

"You sold the gifts that I gave to you—the artwork that I put my heart and soul into for you—to start a retirement fund?"

He tilted his head to the side before ruffling his short-cropped jet black hair. "Lily, listen. I know your parents are well off. I know they'll help you out if you ever needed it. And I'm sure you're going to get an inheritance when they pass someday, but until then it's time you took some financial responsibility for yourself. You're an art teacher. We both know your job doesn't pay a ton of money. On a salary like that, you're *surviving*, not living. We both know just how little you've got in your long-term savings. I was just trying to think of that—of your future. Can't you appreciate that?"

My blood simmered like lava on the cusp of eruption at his condescending tone and the way he sighed. Like he was exhausted and annoyed that he had to explain any of this to me.

All those times that he smiled and nodded along when I explained to him my love for my job, how art was my passion and I couldn't imagine doing anything else for a living...all those times I told to him why it was important for me to forge my own path independent of my image- and money-obsessed parents...all those times he said he admired me for my conviction and my willingness to strike out on my own...he didn't mean any of it.

That's when a whole new realization took hold of me. In that moment, Marco showed me just how little my passion, my art, my heart and soul, meant to him. In that moment, he showed me that he didn't give a shit about anything if he couldn't assign a monetary value to it.

Tears flooded my eyes. And then I blubbered, "I don't want any money from you. We're over" before walking out of his house.

When I told my parents, they were upset that I broke up with him.

He was just watching out for you, Lily. He wanted to help take care of you financially. It's kind of sweet and romantic when you look at it that way.

I can't fault a man for thinking in such a fiscally responsible manner.

Just then Harmony walks up to Marco. She swipes her perfectly barrel-curled long blonde hair out of her face, then clutches his arm.

She eyes me, her smile tight. "Thanks again for coming, Lily. And thank you for your gift. Marco and I will put that gorgeous crystal wine decanter to good use."

"Thank my mom. She picked it out." I'm careful to keep my tone from turning too exasperated. I don't know how much longer I can keep up this proper facade during the world's most awkward post-bridal shower conversation.

"You'll have to help me pick out a bottle of wine to christen the decanter this weekend."

"Sorry, what?"

Harmony shifts slightly, the full skirt of her white lace knee-length dress swaying with the movement.

"My bachelorette party. We're going wine tasting at that

really cute vineyard just outside of the city, then doing a bar crawl downtown. You're coming, aren't you?"

My heart races in pure panic at the thought. Spending an evening binge drinking with Harmony and all her friends? Dear god, no thank you.

My head spins as I try to think of an excuse not to go. "I don't think I can. I've got a ton of work to do."

Harmony frowns, then sighs. Then she glances up at Marco, who looks like he'd rather be just about anywhere else than observing this conversation between his fiancée and ex-girlfriend.

Harmony turns back to me and reaches to gently touch my arm. "Look, Lily. I know we weren't besties back in the day. And I know that you two haven't had the easiest history." Her eyes cut to Marco, who's staring at the ground. "Why don't we start over? Forget what happened in the past. We're all adults, right? Let's commit to being better."

Her speech has my head spinning. Sure, it's nice in the theory to start over, but for her to just gloss over all those times she tormented me in school makes me want to scream. I need something more sincere—like an apology—before I can agree to anything more.

I open my mouth to speak, but just then there's a hand on my other arm.

"Lily would love to go to your bachelorette party," Mom says.

Before I can turn to Mom and tell her that I can make my own decisions, Harmony claps her hands once, squeals the word "yay," and spins around to join another conversation.

"Marilyn. It's good to see you again," Marco says, flashing that winning smile to Mom.

She holds her hand out for him to kiss. They chat briefly

about nonsense, Mom chuckling every few seconds. I turn away and roll my eyes while huffing out a frustrated breath. Marco could set fire to an animal shelter and she would still fawn over him. She's such a sucker for that suave rich boy charm.

She pats my arm. "Why don't you two wrap up, and I'll meet you in the car?"

I'm gritting my teeth as she quickly walks out the door. She knows I won't confront her about forcing me to join Harmony's bachelorette party in front of everyone.

I shake my head as Marco chuckles.

"Your mom cracks me up."

"Glad you found that funny."

"Oh come on, Lily." He raises an eyebrow at me while grinning. It makes him look extra smug. "Look on the bright side. You might meet someone you can take with you to the wedding as a date. Maybe someone who loves art just as much as you."

His tone drips with condescension. But his little art comment also triggers something inside of me.

I look him square in the eye. "Actually, I have a date."

Marco's smile drops; his brow furrows the slightest bit. "You do?"

"Yup. And you're right. He loves art."

Memories of Calder posing in my class play out in my brain once more. I don't waver for a second in my eye contact with Marco. A muscle in the left side of his jaw bulges. A tell-tale sign that he's annoyed. I have to bite my lip to keep from grinning at just how glorious it is to watch him squirm.

"Well... that's... good for you." He clears his throat. "He's an artist then?"

"Nope. A model."

Something flashes in Marco's eyes. "I see. Can't wait to meet the lucky guy."

He tugs on his jacket sleeve before turning away. I walk out of the room, my heart thundering against my chest, exhilarated by how I've left Marco stammering. But once the weight of what I've done sinks in, I'm in a silent panic. I dart to the bathroom and splash cold water on my cheeks.

Marco thinks I'm bringing Calder to the wedding as my date. What the hell did I just do?

5

CALDER

The long pose this week in Lily's class is child's pose, so I'm kneeling on the dais with my face on the ground, arms by my ears. There's a cramp growing in my thigh and a freak-out mounting in my brain.

The situation I've gotten myself into has come into sharp focus over the past week. I dropped the underwear gig Stella had been on about in an effort to stick to my oath. The loss of a paycheck really woke me up. I have plenty of money set aside, but it's not easy to carve out a niche in this business. I'm proud of my rep, and I've worked hard to establish myself. Now, I'm essentially throwing it all in the bin on a possibility.

But it's a possibility that embodies my favorite things in life. Whisky and fine aesthetic are the greatest pursuits a man can have. To be the face of a label I grew up around would absolutely be worth making some major changes—if only I could be sure that those changes would lead to the job.

But aside from pulling out of a shoot, I've got nothing to prove I am settling down and changing my image. Saying

I've got nothing but my dick in my hand at this point would be putting it nicely. Nate has invited me to an event Saturday night, which means I'll have a grand time making excuses for my nonexistent girlfriend's absence.

"Thanks, guys. It's time to close up for the week."

Lily's announcement changes the ambient sound in the room, and I sit up and stretch out my hip. Students toss me waves and thank-yous as they leave and I cinch my robe. I wave back, glad I don't have to give another bloody speech. When the room is empty, I cross to where my clothes are stacked on the edge of her desk. Lily gives me a close-lipped smile that I return. Today's class held none of the silliness from last week, which is probably for the best but far less amusing. To be fair, I've been deep in my thoughts about this predicament, and I don't know her well enough to say she seems preoccupied, but—

"Sorry if I was a little distracted today," she says, tucking a stray strand of dark hair back into her bun. "I'm currently the meat in a weekends-from-hell sandwich."

It's an odd way to put it, but it makes perfect sense. I grimace and nod. "No worries. I'm not here to be entertained."

She frowns. "Well, yes. I-I mean, of course you're not. Just that last week was so—well, it was just more light-hearted, I guess. I just don't want to seem rude. I was raised better than that."

The bitterness in those last words arches my brows. So much venom from such a sweet mouth makes no sense. "How you were raised means nothing compared to how you're feeling now. If you're having a bad go of it, you have every right to manage it however helps you get through."

Her face is a mask of muddled emotion. Anger and frustration give way to surprise—I suppose at my blunt words—

before her expression crumbles into a tiny smile. That pink returns on her cheeks.

"Good point," she murmurs.

"Indeed."

I pull my shirt over my head as she perches on her desk. We catch eyes, and she gives an almost-imperceptible head jerk toward the blank spot beside her. I definitely might've imagined it, but when I lean on the faux wood and cross my arms, her shoulders lower.

She does a terrible job of hiding the way her eyes travel over my biceps. The look of guilt when she realizes she's busted is too much. My grin breaks out, but I resist the urge to tease her. "So. A hellish sandwich, eh? Sounds excruciating."

"You have no idea."

"But the week between, now that's not too bad, is it? Surely you've found some time to unwind and enjoy yourself."

"I guess. I have spent a lot of time at the wheel."

"Driving, knives, or bondage?"

She jolts so hard I reach out to steady her from falling off the desk. Chuckling, I make sure she's stable before letting my fingers slide slowly away from that satin skin.

"I meant pottery. Good god, do I seem like the kind to throw knives or... or... I don't know what, get sexed while I'm tied to a spinning wheel?"

Fucking bloody hell, now that is an image. And it is indeed, although nothing about this woman would indicate she'd be into such a kinky setup. Still, Ms. Lily bound and blindfolded, waiting patiently for...

"Um, what now?" I clear my throat and shake my head, but the smirk that curls her lip tells me it's my turn to be busted. "Weather? Aye, hot as hell, innit?"

That smirk explodes into a full grin before her giggles bounce around the room. I scratch the back of my head, embarrassed as hell at being so obvious but unable to resist laughing, too.

She lays one hand on my arm as she tries to control herself. “Oh, I needed that laugh,” she gasps finally. Glittery eyes turn up to me. “Thank you.”

“My pleasure.”

Her fingertips trail away slower than needed but too fast for my liking. She’s radiant from laughing, and all of a sudden I have the silliest thought in my head:

Ms. Lily Maldonado is exactly the kind of woman a man would want on his arm at a Sonce party. She’d be perfect in a black cocktail dress—but she’d also be perfect around the house in a ratty old t-shirt and wooly socks. She is exactly the kind of woman I pictured when that crazy pledge flew out of my mouth.

She’s the kind of woman who’d be worth changing an image for.

Earth to Calder. You know nothing about her.

And yet the thought is there—and is freaking me the hell out. I stand up and jerk my head to the door. “Right, well, best be going then. I’ll see you next week.”

“Did I say something wrong?” Her tone is hurt, and I instantly feel like a total shit.

“Not in the least.” I toss a casual grin to let her know all is well, but she’s not buying it.

“Oh, okay then. Of course. Have a good week.”

“Cheers.”

6

LILY

"Shots, ladies! Shots! Shots! Shots!" Brittany yells from the end of the bar.

I hold in a groan and accept the shot of tequila that one of Harmony's friends slides down to me. I can't help the grimace when I swallow. This my second shot of the whole night. So far during Harmony's bachelorette party, I've managed to keep my alcohol intake to a minimum. I only took tiny sips at the wine tasting which probably added up to a single glass. At the first bar we hit, I managed to just pound water. But now that we're at the second bar, doing group shots seems to be the direction we're headed in.

I sigh, feeling the slightest bit lightheaded. One shot of tequila plus the shot of vodka I did with all the ladies minutes ago is already hitting me fast.

I quickly ask the bartender for a giant glass of water, which I drink half of in seconds. Then I plop down on the nearest bar stool and take in the scene. For some reason, we ended up at a place called Billy's Sports Bar. There are flatscreens everywhere I look, broadcasting the same soccer game. It's eighty percent men in this place. I wonder why

Brittany, Harmony's maid of honor, decided on coming here, but then I watch as the bartender hands out a tray of cosmos to Harmony's crew. A guy sitting in a nearby booth waves over to Harmony, who blows him several kisses. A group of women in tight dresses in a mostly male establishment often means free drinks.

A shrieking noise causes me to look down the long wooden bar, where I spot Harmony hugging Brittany. A few of their other friends stand around them, all in pink mini dresses, singing along to some country song I don't recognize that's playing over the sound system.

I tug at the microscopic hem of my own pink mini dress that I haven't worn since I was probably nineteen, annoyed at how ridiculous I look and feel. I'm pushing thirty and dressed like a Barbie doll.

Just then another tray of shots is deposited at Harmony's end of the bar. I faintly hear the bartender say, "orgasms for the ladies," and then the whole group is squealing with laughter.

I roll my eyes and sigh. I don't know if I'm going to be able to survive the night. I silently curse my mom for saying I'd go, and then I silently curse myself for just nodding along with it instead of standing up for myself. *You could've refused... yeah, but did I really want another lecture on "manners"?*

Harmony stumbles over to me and yanks me into a hug while giggling. Her blue eyes are glazed over. I guess she likes to get cuddly when she's drunk.

She tugs at the sparkly tiara in her hair, which has a piece of tulle glued to it to look like a mini veil. I reach out and straighten the hot pink sash that says "bride to be" in glittery letters.

"I just have to say, Lily," Harmony slurs. "You... you're one brave girl."

"Uh, thanks."

She blinks, and her eyelids sag. She stumbles and I hold her up with both of my hands on her forearms. "I mean, to go to my bachelorette party... to go to your ex-boyfriend's wedding. You're a hero!"

"I'm not sure about that," I mutter.

Her eyes go wide. "You are! I mean, I'd be humiliated." Her head falls back in a laugh. "I would never, never go to anything for any of my exes, let alone wedding stuff. I mean, you're just really special for doing that."

She hugs me once more while I grit my teeth and absorb her insulting comments.

"And to go to my wedding without a date! Oh my gosh!! I would never do that. Not in a million years would I go to any wedding alone. Let alone my ex's!"

Again she chuckles while I bite my tongue. Instead of lashing out at her, I happily accept the shot that Brittany hands me after she walks over to us. I don't even grimace at the burn this time. Even though I told Marco that I had a date—and implied that it was Calder—that was a total lie and I shouldn't repeat it here, not even if it would save me from this humiliation.

"Three cheers for Lily! The girl who's brave enough to go to her ex-boyfriend's wedding without a date!" Harmony shouts while stepping back and raising her arm, shot in hand. Everyone gawks at us, and my face bursts into flames.

Brittany's eyes go wide as she looks at me for a split second before glancing away. A few of Harmony's other friends give me the same pitying expression. As if it's not awkward enough that I'm attending all of my ex's wedding events, now everyone knows that I'm doing it as a pathetically single woman. Great.

"I gotta go to the bathroom," I mumble. My head spins. I need a minute to myself, away from this shitshow. Or maybe I can just hide out there the rest of the evening and Harmony and her friends will get so drunk that they'll forget about me and go to the next bar.

7

CALDER

Even though the second button is already open on my dress shirt, I tug at my collar yet again. Today's Liverpool v Chelsea match is on replay on the huge screen in front of me. Billy's Sports Bar is as good a place as any to unwind while I sort through the party I just left.

Sonce is going all out to build hype for its holiday-season release. Their "family first" image is sure to be a smash hit, and they're already putting money where their mouths are on it. The party tonight was a meet-and-greet of corporate backers and industry professionals—and their children. While VIP guests schmoozed over finger foods and top-shelf booze, a small team of babysitters watched over their children as they explored a playground in the corner.

As a teen, Nate owned no clothes beyond ratty jeans and band t-shirts. Watching him work a room dressed in a Versace suit was *almost* amusing enough to distract me from the fish-out-of-water feeling that haunted me every time I heard a shriek of childish delight.

On top of that, the urge to flirt back with all the women who tried to strike up a conversation was too natural. It's just what you do at a party like that if you're in the business—except the whole point of me being there was to prove that I'm a wholesome, hearts and flowers boyfriend who embodies the Sonce attitude.

So I'd drifted around the room with a highball glass in hand, making small talk with co-ed groups of people only and checking the time a little too frequently. Nate had given me a *come on, mate* look when I said that my girlfriend was off at a hen do that she couldn't get out of, but I'd just shrugged and made some vague reference to bridesmaid obligations as if I knew a damn thing about it.

As I review the whole deal over a pint and the match, though, I have to say it didn't go terribly. Yes, a girl on my arm would've been a better look, but the hen party excuse had elicited sympathetic nods from the women in the cluster we stood in, so I suppose that's a point. And I didn't leave with a model—or three—which is definitely a shift from the usual high-end parties I attend.

I lift the glass just as Chelsea gets a corner kick. "Here's to faking it till you make it," I say to no one in particular.

"Shots, ladies! Shots! Shots! Shots!"

The age-old chant is followed by peals of laughter from the front of the bar. There's a gaggle of lasses flittering about in the main area of my favorite sports pub. Clearly, they're out for free drinks and a good time. I glance over my shoulder and am nearly blinded by the amount of hot pink these women are wearing.

A hen party. How appropriate.

I whip out my phone and text my sister.

Me: *Why TF would a hen party go to a sports bar? The match is on & they're bloody shrieking too loud for me to concentrate.*

Lucy: *Duh. Pick up guys/get free shots bought for them. See if you can take one home. I dare you to pick her up with a line about being Fabio's protege.*

A gif of Fabio follows. I've seen this one many, many times over the years. I still chuckle while I send my standard reply to such comments: a gif of someone giving the middle finger. She sends me back hearts, so I put the phone down and look around.

"Hey, Danny?"

The waiter looks up from where he's clearing a table nearby when I call to him. "Yeah, boss?"

I gesture at the bar, where the bride seems to be slow-dancing to a country song with one of her pink-clad attendees. "Buy them a round on me. Orgasms for all, got it?"

He laughs. "Done."

With a chuckle, I relax into the booth and focus properly on the match in time to catch the end. Danny brings me another pint and my bill, so I settle up and rise to hit the restroom before I tuck in another beer.

"Oomph." It's a harmonious sound uttered by me and the woman who's just collided with my back when I stepped out of the booth. I spin round as she topples sideways. She's a flash of neon pink and black-brown as her hair whips in her face and she wobbles on stiletto heels. I reach out, catching her by her bare shoulders before she crashes to the ground. She leans into my grasp to steady herself and grips my jacket blindly.

But then she speaks, and my heart fucking leaps.

"Oh, gosh, I'm so sorry, I—"

Lily.

"Thank you," she breathes as recognition dawns in those eyes.

I grin for the first time that night. "Hey."

"Hey." She's still all breathy, but there's no mistaking the delight in her expression. Alcohol is partially to blame based on the spots of pink on her cheeks, but it only makes her more lovely.

"You okay?"

She blinks hard and nods with a glance behind her. "Um, yeah. Just had to get away for a second."

"You look like you're escaping."

"Er, kind of, yeah. I'm at a bachelorette party."

"A bachelorette party?" *Did she tell me her plans for the weekend? Is that where I got that excuse for Nate?* I scan my memory of our last interaction, fairly sure she hadn't. Still, a hell of a coincidence.

"Mm-hm, a very unpleasant one."

Because she releases her grip on me and is clearly stable, I have no excuse for holding onto her any longer. Because I'm not a creep, I drop my hands and step back. And, because I am a man, I can't help the walk my gaze takes over her body in that tiny dress.

Lily isn't tall, but those heels give her legs for days. Her skirt is so short I doubt she's been able to sit down much all night. And her neckline, dear god. Her breasts swell invitingly over that pink velvet. The tiny pink straps on her shoulders serve no function other than to underscore the idea that her body is barely contained by the dress.

Bubble gum sex, that's what she is tonight. Pink velvet is hardly my thing, but goddam is my mouth watering.

She catches my appraisal and tugs at the hem of her skirt. "That's why I'm dressed like this. Bride's orders."

"Tell the bride I like her daring, but her color palette could use a bit of tweaking. Unless you fancy the pink, in which case I'm on board."

"Oh, stop it. I look like a gas station hooker, and we both know it."

My lascivious thoughts scatter. A laugh bursts from me, and she grins. I shake my head and reach for a long gulp of my beer. When I turn back, Lily's eyes snap guiltily up to my face—clearly she'd been doing her own appraisal while I wasn't looking. I quirk a brow. "Like what you see?"

She fidgets with her hem again as her gaze drifts to my shirt. "Nice suit, but I notice you're a little undone."

Her tongue darts out to wet her lips, and my brows hit my hairline. Tipsy Lily is a bit flirty, and I'm all in on it. "Suppose I am. Care to do me up a bit?"

She laughs even as she goes bright red, one hand over her mouth to hide a nervous giggle. "Oh, um, well sure."

I laugh softly, and she steps forward. Her nails aren't painted—odd, I'd expected them to match her dress—but none of that matters. She's so close I can smell her shampoo. I inhale the sweet scent while she buttons my shirt and does her best to straighten my tugged-out collar.

"Is that better?" I murmur when she's done and her hands are resting lightly on my chest.

"Yeah." She lifts her head, and I let my palms find her hips. Her pupils dilate. She startles at first but then leans into my touch.

"What were the odds I'd see you here tonight?" I ask.

"Given that the universe seems to enjoy putting me in the most awkward and ill-timed situations it can dream of? Pretty high, I'd guess."

"This doesn't feel awkward to me, Professor Lily. But if you're uncomfortable, I can leave you alone."

Her hips sway into mine, and I fight off a moan. "For the first time today, I'm not uncomfortable."

Fuck, I want to kiss her. I know she's a little drunk and should get back to her girls, but *fuck* do I want to taste those lips. "Look, I know we have a professional arrangement and all, but—"

"Lily!"

She leaps away, whirling again too fast, and grips my arm for stability even while she turns to face a fellow girl in pink. This one is wearing a dramatically concerned expression. She grips Lily's arms and shakes her head.

"Honey, Harmony didn't mean to be rude. She's just drunk and nervous about getting married, you know how it is. Well, you don't, that's kind of the point—shit, girl, I didn't mean that to sound bad either. Just, we all think it's so, *so* brave of you to come out and be part of your ex's wedding festivities. But Harmony is super glad you're here and that you're coming to the wedding, even if you don't have a date —which is *no problem*, of course. Please don't be mad at her, Lils."

Wait. What in the actual hell? I scratch my head and try to muddle out what this emphatic rambling means.

Lily sighs and gently unclasps the woman's grip from her wrists. "I get it, Brittany. I'll join you guys in a second, just going to hit the ladies' room first."

Brittany beams and hugs her tight. "Girl, you are just so the best. Okay, but hurry back or we'll come looking for you!"

She spots me over Lily's shoulder and freezes. "Oh, hey. Sorry, are we being loud? Just having some girl talk."

"You are being entirely loud, but I suspect that's all in good fun tonight, eh?"

Brittany's jaw drops. She giggles loudly. "Well, yeah, kind of. My bestie is getting married."

"So I gathered. Sent you a round of orgasms a while ago. Hope they satisfied the lucky lady."

"That was you?" she and Lily say in unison. I just laugh.

Brittany slides up and puts her hand on my arm. Lily's shoulder slump. She scuttles away to the bathroom before I can stop her. "It was a hell of an orgasm, thank you *so* much. Where are you from, stranger?"

"Brittany, my tiara won't stay on!" The bellow comes from across the bar, and so with a pout, Brittany is gone.

Lily keeps her head down when she emerges from the bathroom minutes later, but she chooses the route that brings her past my table. Not looking up or slowing down, she mutters as she approaches, "Sorry, Calder, I'll see you—"

Without thinking, I reach out and gently cuff her wrist. "Slow down, love. Have a seat for just a minute."

She freezes even as I withdraw my grasp. My hand hasn't fully retreated before she slides into the booth beside me. I grin, but the look in her eyes is anguished, and it kills my humor instantly. "You look like you'd rather be having a spinal tap than be here tonight. Care to talk it out?"

"You heard her. I'm brave and awesome for going to my ex's wedding." She twines a strand of dark hair around her finger so tightly the tip turns white, then red.

"You loved her, eh? Christ, that has to be murder, seeing her dolled up as a bride in front of you."

Her brows knit before understanding dawns. A huge grin splits her face. "Oh god no. No, no, not even. Harmony isn't my ex! God, she would *so* not be my type of woman. Marco, her fiancé—he and I broke up a year ago. Not sure *he* was my type either, but hey." She gives me the outline of the situation and explains that the only reason she's here is on her own mother's insistence.

"Well, I'm no therapist," I say at last, "but that's six degrees of fucked-up, that is. Here, have a drink." I slide her my beer, and she accepts. "Slàinte, darling."

"What did you say? What does that mean?"

"It means cheers in Gaelic."

"I thought it was pronounced gaylick, not gallick."

"Only if you're Irish," I scoff.

"I thought you were Irish." She frowns.

I gasp dramatically, hand to my heart, my expression pure horror. It makes her giggle, which is exactly what I wanted. No point in smoothing out the accent right now. "Fuck no, lass, you're talking to a proper Scotsman, thank you verra much. Born and raised in Perth, and don't you forget it."

She's helpless now, surprise in her eyes as she squints and covers her giggles. "Oh, I'm so sorry, I had no idea!"

If I've fucked up everything else in the last week, at least I got this part right. "You dinae ask, now did ya? Give me my pint back. Teach you for jumping to such conclusions, you wee beastie."

"You have to stop it," she gasps, passing the glass back and hiding her face in my shoulder. "I'm going to pee myself."

"And here you were just in the restroom." I shift back to my usual tone, take a sip, and nudge the beer her way.

She wrinkles her nose but accepts the drink. "I didn't even use it. I just hid for a few minutes."

I push a strand of hair out of her eyes. "If I didn't know any better, Professor Lily, I'd say you were too sweet for your own good."

She stares at the glass we're sharing. "It's my fatal flaw, I guess."

"You know, you're allowed to say no. It's no sin to stand up for what you want, and it's quite alright not to be nice when the situation calls for it."

She's about to speak, but Brittany's voice just behind the

booth makes us both turn.

"No, I swear, he's the one who sent the shots! Come meet him, girls, he's *so* awesome. And he's English! Hi, handsome!"

"English," I growl under my breath as a flock of women in pink, plus one in white, cluster in front of the table.

"Hey again," I say louder, tossing a wave and pushing into the corner of the booth as the ladies begin to squeeze in the opposite side. Lily is smooshed into my side by Brittany and the girl in white—Harmony, I think was the name—who both grin and wiggle their fingers at me.

"Say something in English," Brittany says, even more drunk now than she was a few minutes ago.

"Something in English," I reply, which is the funniest thing she's ever heard.

"You know what I mean."

"Shots for the ladies," I shout, snapping my fingers in the air and catching Danny's attention. "English enough for you?"

"Perfection," she squeals.

"Yeah, but Lily. Lily. Lily, listen. Listen Lily," Harmony's declaration silences the rest of the group. She turns somberly to Lily. "Going stag to a wedding is the worst," she slurs with her eyes closed. "But I can set you up with a date! I have a cousin, he's just about to get divorced and you're way cuter than he is. He'll be so happy to be your date..."

"I... I... There's no need. I already have a date."

And then her hand closes on top of mine on the table.

"Calder is my date, Harmony. That's why he bought us the shots."

Well, fuck me. I bite down on the inside of my cheek to keep from laughing my ass off as Harmony gives me another look.

"Wow. You're, like, super hot. Like, crazy hot."

"Thanks." I wink, and her eyes nearly fall out.

"Why didn't you tell me your boyfriend was here?" Harmony asks Lily.

"Oh, well, I didn't want to take the attention from your party. You're the bride. This is all about you."

Harmony scrunches her heavily-painted face like she's going to cry. Then she clutches her chest with both of her hands as her eyes glisten under the dim bar lighting.

"Oh my gosh, you're an angel, Lily. Swear to god... Oh my god! I should make Marco come out too! Brittany, call him, tell him to come buy us a round!"

Brittany whips out her phone, and I can feel the tension radiate off Lily. Her spine stiffens against my shoulder, jaw clenching as she clamps down on my hand.

I'll play along.

I use one finger to trace her jaw and swivel her head toward me. She blinks, but I touch our foreheads together. "Darling, about ready to head home? I'm not sure I can wait much longer." Looking around her, I catch Harmony's gaze. "Does the bride mind too terribly much if I abscond with one of her entourage?"

"God, I love English accents," she sighs and then waves her hand. "Not at all! You guys have a great night!"

We do a seat shuffle to let Lily and me out of the booth. As we walk away, I hear Brittany announcing Marco will be there in an hour. I smirk, shaking my head at the scene, but Lily is striding to the door so fast I have to double-time to catch up.

Outside, she groans and threads her hands into her hair. "Oh, my god, I am *so sorry*. I can't believe I said that—I just panicked and... it's nothing, just bullshit but god am I sorry — I know that was totally out of line, using you like that. I've just... had a lot to drink and I normally wouldn't say or do any of that. It's just, everyone has been giving me a hard time about not having a date to this wedding and I sure as hell don't want to be set up, so if they think I already have a boyfriend, they'll at least leave me alone until the wedding. And then I'll only have to endure the wedding awkwardly alone."

"Hush." I put my hands on her shoulders, and she stills. "You don't have to do that."

"Do what?"

"Make excuses for what you want."

"What do you mean?"

"If you want me to be your date to the wedding, then your wish is my command. But you have to have the balls to say what you want."

She scoffs a laugh. I cross my arms and wait. I can see it when curiosity creeps into her gaze. "Are you serious?"

"Do I seem like I'm kidding?"

"But I couldn't. It would be so out of bounds, not to mention an imposition on you..."

"I'll repeat myself. Just say what you want."

She fiddles with her hemline another moment, bites her lip, and then blurts, "Could you be my fake boyfriend for this nightmare wedding, Calder?"

I touch my fingers to my forehead in a little salute. "At your service, my dear."

"Seriously?" she squeaks. "You're okay with this?"

"It would be my honor to be your fake boyfriend for this wedding, Professor Lily."

She laughs and throws her hands in the air. "Okay then. Let's do this. God, how will I ever repay you?"

"I'm sure we can work something out."

In that moment, I am not thinking of Sonce at all.

8

LILY

A sharp blaring sound hits my ears. I shove a pillow over my head and groan.

"Damn it," I mutter to myself.

It's several seconds before I can even muster the energy to reach out and turn off the alarm on my phone sitting on my nightstand, and another minute before I sit up. When I do, I nearly topple back over.

I try to swallow, but the inside of my mouth is as dry as sandpaper.

What the hell was I thinking drinking so much last night?

I lean my back against my headboard as I replay the events of Harmony's bachelorette party. There was the wine tasting at the vineyard where I managed to be sensible and drink only one glass total of wine. There was the first bar we hit up, where I just had water... and then there was the second bar. The sports bar where shots rained down on us from every direction.

I sigh and groan once more. I was definitely drunk last night, but thankfully not shitfaced. Parts are a bit fuzzy, but I can remember most of what happened—the major parts at least.

I remember Brittany's and Harmony's comments about my single status and how I ran from the group just to get away from it all. I remember running into Calder by total coincidence, chatting with him, laughing with him, scooting into his booth, and practically cuddling him when Harmony, Brittany, and the other girls found us.

I most definitely remember pretending that he was my boyfriend in front of them so the "poor single Lily" comments would stop. *And* I remember how he agreed to be my fake boyfriend for Harmony and Marco's wedding. The last memory I have of him is when he walked me to the door of my duplex and made sure I locked the door after he left.

My stomach flips at just how doting he was, at how he braced me with those massive, muscled arms when I tried to balance my drunken self on those godforsaken heels as I tried to walk, how he let me sleep—and probably snore—in his car while he drove me home.

Despite the urge to down a gallon of water and eat the nearest fried thing I can find, the first thing I need to do is call Calder. I need to thank him for helping me get home safely first of all, but then we need to talk about this *proposal* I came up with last night.

I swipe my phone from the nightstand and see a text from Calder, sent a couple of hours ago.

Calder: *Morning. Hope you're not having too rough a time.*

I grin so wide, my cheeks hurt.

Me: *Thankfully it's not too bad. Just a bit dizzy. Some food and tons of water will help with that.*

Me: *Thank you again for helping me get home last night.*

Me: *And for agreeing to be my fake boyfriend*

Me: *And thank you for agreeing to be my date to the wedding*

I hit send on the last one and immediately grimace when I read the messages back over. Good god, why do I text like an insecure teenager?

Before he can reply, I send another message.

Me: *Actually, are you busy today?*

Me: *Would you want to meet for coffee?*

Me: *I could use a giant Americano right about now.*

Me: *We should probably talk about our whole arrangement too.*

I make another face at my phone screen. I need to not send multiple messages at once. Why do I even do that? It makes me sound so unsure of myself. I climb out of bed and head straight for the bathroom to relieve myself and down three glasses of water in a row.

When my phone buzzes, I walk back over to the bed and check it.

Calder: *Come on, Lily. Remember what I said last night about getting what you want? Just say so.*

I bite my lip, my tummy flipping once more.

Me: *I want to meet you for coffee at Lovely Pine Coffee Shop on Elderberry Avenue in one hour.*

Calder: *That's more like it. I'll be there.*

When I walk into Lovely Pine, I spot Calder sitting at a table for two in the back corner. I try not to stare too long at his yumminess. He's wearing a simple casual outfit of jeans and a Henley, and it looks like he hasn't shaved. My mouth waters. Thick scruff is hands-down my favorite facial hair look a guy could sport. How did he know?

He doesn't know that, you twit. He was probably exhausted from carting you home last night and didn't have time to shave.

The internal reminder I give myself sets me straight. I also remind myself why I'm here. We're here to talk logistics, nothing more.

I walk over to say hi and tell him that I'm going to order quickly before sitting down, but then I see that there are two giant cups of coffee sitting at the table already, along with a plate of pastries.

"You didn't have to get my drink." I plop into the chair and take a sip anyway, letting out a satisfied hum after I swallow.

He chuckles as I rip into a croissant. "It's really no problem."

I mumble thank you around a mouthful of buttery, flaky pastry, grinning as I chew. Calder is a totally different kind of man than I'm used to. Insanely hot, attentive, sweet, and thoughtful. I don't think I've ever had the pleasure of enjoying this exact combination of traits in a guy before.

Seconds later, when I finish the croissant, I reach for an apple tart and catch Calder's gaze on me. I try my best to hide the surprise that flashes inside of me. He's got those same hungry eyes he gave me last night, when he saw me at the sports bar wearing that barely-there dress. Now I'm a disheveled mess in yoga pants and a hoodie with my unwashed hair in a messy ponytail.

Before I can relish the feeling of his gorgeous eyes on me for too long, he blinks and sips from his coffee mug. "So. Our arrangement. What exactly did you want to talk about?"

The way he emphasizes the word "arrangement" makes me pause. He sounds both amused and confused. But then I put down the apple tart, clear my throat, and nod. "I just think we should set some ground rules."

His brow wrinkles.

"Not that I think you—or I—would do anything wrong.

It's just that I've never done anything like this. I've never... played pretend."

I wince at how weird that sounds.

"Play pretend? I like the way that sounds."

I ignore the hot flush making its way up my cheeks at the low and insanely sexy register of his voice.

"I'm serious, Calder," I say, trying to stay focused. "We have to be careful. I don't want to jeopardize anything between us when we do this."

"Between us?"

"Well, yeah, since we work together."

His eyebrows knit the slightest bit. "Right. Of course."

"It's not like we have to map out every little thing that happens between us," I say. "I just want to set some guidelines. And boundaries."

"Such as?"

"First of all, we need to get our stories straight if anyone asks us how we got together. I was thinking we could just say that we met at work since that part is actually true."

"That sounds fine to me."

"And well, as far as boundaries go..." I pause to sip my coffee. "We need to look like a convincing couple in front of people, right? So that means we'll have to hold hands, peck each other on the lips and on the cheek, hug, that sort of thing. And that's okay with me... if that's okay with you."

Calder looks like he's about to laugh. "Of course it's okay."

"No, tongue kissing though. That's way too intimate. And no PDA in the classroom. We're strictly professional coworkers there."

"Okay," he says, drawing out the word like he's doubtful.

I glance down for a second to work up the nerve to say

the next part. "And I don't mean to sound crass, but... no sex."

"Christ, Lily. That's not on my mind at all."

His baffled tone and the exasperated chuckle he lets out stings the slightest bit. Wow. Is the thought of having sex with me that outrageous to him? I take another bite of tart to hopefully hide my hurt feelings.

I guess I read way too much into all that flirty banter from last night and the way he looked at me. Calder must just be a flirty, affectionate guy as a baseline—and I can see why. He's ridiculously handsome and charming with an accent. None of Harmony's friends could take their eyes off of him. And I definitely didn't miss just how handsy Brittany got with him when she saw him last night.

It's not like he's exuding all that charm just for me... like I thought he might be.

Like I hoped he might be.

I silently scold myself for having such an inappropriate thought.

"So then we're on the same page about the no-sex rule," I say. "That's good. Really, really good."

Calder glances off to the side. "So this is just for the wedding then?"

I nearly apologize for what I'm about to ask him, but then I stop myself, Calder's words from last night imprinted in my mind.

Just say what you want.

"Well, a couple of other events are planned," I say with steadiness to my tone. "I'll need you for the rehearsal dinner the night before the wedding. And apple picking."

Calder squints at me. "Apple what?"

I wave my hand. "It's a ridiculous tradition mine and Marco's families do every fall. I've managed to get out of it a couple of times in the past, but since I skipped last year I can't miss it again. Just please keep the first Sunday in October free."

"Can do."

We share a long moment of silence as we sip and munch on pastries.

"So," I say to him. "Are there any rules you have for me?"

He shakes his head. "Nope. I think you've covered them all quite thoroughly. But I do have a favor to ask."

"Of course."

Calder draws in a deep breath. When he speaks, his words tumble out in a rushed exhale. "Can you be my fake girlfriend in exchange for me helping you out? I have a professional opportunity I'm dying for. And I don't think I can do it without you."

My chest tingles at the sincerity in his voice and the way his eyes sparkle when he talks.

"Tell me about it."

He tells me all about Sonce, his childhood friend's whisky label that just took their brand international, and how he's dying to be the spokesperson for it.

He pauses to drain the rest of the coffee. A tender expression takes over his face. "I want this job. Bad. I used to work at the Sconce distillery when I was a kid. There are so many happy memories I have attached to that place. And to think I could be part of it now would mean everything."

My chest squeezes as he speaks. It's like he's sharing part of his heart with me. I get the feeling he doesn't talk this candidly, this personally, to everyone.

"It's more than that though, isn't it?" I ask softly.

He flashes a sad smile. "It's scary how well you can read me when we haven't known each other all that long." He pauses before he starts speaking. "My work history is a bit of a problem for them."

"Seriously? Why? From what I've seen, you're a hot commodity. I'm surprised you said yes to being a model for my class honestly."

He raises an eyebrow. "'From what you've seen?' Just how much do you know about my work history, Professor Lily?"

Even though his words and his expression are playful, I'm silently scolding myself. I'm going to have to admit to him how I online stalked him now.

"Well, um, after our first class together, I looked you up online," I say while trying my best to hold eye contact with him.

"And were you satisfied with what you found?"

"Um, yeah, I mean..."

Judging by the grin on his face, Calder is enjoying my squirming.

"Okay fine, I found your Instagram. And all those romance novel covers you posed for. I had no idea I was in the presence of a ridiculously famous model."

His cheeks start to redden. He's crazy cute when he's flustered.

"Ridiculously famous isn't what I'd call it. This is a pretty niche industry, and I just managed to make a name for myself," he says while picking his nails.

I wonder if that's some nervous habit. Calder doesn't strike me as the kind of guy who gets nervous, though.

"You've done way more than that, judging by your follower count and all your endorsement deals."

The soft smile he flashes makes me think that he appreciates what I've said. I beam on the inside.

"You're an artist. Your photos aren't gratuitous. I can tell you put so much thought into them, how they're composed, the lighting, the setting, the mood. Your photos are so much more than the image—it's like they're speaking to the person looking at them. They evoke a feeling, a mood. It's not easy to do that with a picture."

When I realize I'm gesturing with my hands, I quickly put them in my lap.

"Sorry. I get a little impassioned when I talk about anything art related." I let out an embarrassed laugh.

"Don't be sorry. Thank you for saying that. Coming from an educator like you—someone who's an expert on art and all things creative—it means everything."

The conviction in Calder's tone makes me buzz from the inside out.

He sighs, the faintest hint of disappointment lingering in his face. "I just wish the higher-ups at Sonce felt the same way. I think all they see when they look at my work is a piece of arse."

I grin at him. "Then let's change their minds. What do you need me to do as your fake girlfriend?"

The corner of his mouth tugs up. "I've got a dinner coming up with the reps at Sonce next week. Just you being there with me would make a huge difference. They'll see that I'm in a stable, long term relationship with a brilliant and cultured art professor and think a bit more highly of me."

"I can do that."

"And depending on how that goes, I might need you to come to a couple of other events if that's okay?"

"More than okay."

He raises his eyebrow at me in that deliciously playful way. "Have to admit, I'm surprised you sound so eager to pose as my significant other."

"You shouldn't be. You're helping me out. It's only fair that I do the same for you."

"Right." He looks away for a second.

"But honestly, it's more than that. I know what it's like to have people doubt your integrity or your work. That's the story of my life."

"How's that?"

"My whole life, my parents put pressure on me to follow in their corporate footsteps. I could be a luxury designer like my mom or a high powered attorney like my dad. Or if those careers didn't suit me, they would have been fine with something else high profile, like medicine or finance. But wanting to be a lowly art teacher? Forget it."

The light in Calder's eyes dims just the slightest bit, like he feels for me in this moment. It makes my heart beat the tiniest bit faster.

"That's fucked up, Lily. I'm sorry."

I shrug. "It's fine. Honestly, it's the one time in my life when I didn't just roll over and do what my parents told me to. I dropped out of law school and decided to teach art, the one thing I've been passionate about my entire life. And yeah, they still make little comments here and there, but whatever." I look off to the side and stare out the giant window that serves as the storefront for the bakery. "Working in this job is the happiest I've ever been. I'll never regret choosing it over my parents' annoying expectations."

Just then Calder slides his hand across the table and takes my hand in his. "You've got some serious fire in you, Lily. You should let it out more often."

The smile he flashes sends giddiness jolting through me.

"Maybe that can be one of my qualities as your fake girlfriend—I'm bolder."

"I like the sound of that."

I stare down at his hand over mine. When he starts to lace his fingers in mine, my heart thuds. Calder looks down at our joined hands, a soft smile tugging at his lips, then his eyes cut back to me.

"Does this fall under the acceptable PDA as a fake couple?" he asks.

I bite my lip as I smile and nod. "I guess we'd better get used to touching each other."

We both chuckle. A chunk of my hair comes loose from my ponytail. Calder reaches his hand up, swiping my hair from my face in a slow, deliberate swoop. The tips of his fingers skim across the fullness of my cheek; a sheet of goosebumps flashes across my skin.

I swallow, his touch unleashing something hot and achy inside of me. It's been over a year since a guy has touched my hair, my face, my hand, my cheek. And god, it feels so, so good.

I close my eyes for a long second and let out a hum, completely and totally unplanned. And then my eyelids fly open. I need to get myself under control. This is an arrangement—it's fake. Calder knows that—and that's probably why he's not making weird noises like a creep when he touches me. And I shouldn't either. I can't let myself get carried away, no matter how good it feels.

Just then I jolt up from the table "Okay! So good talk. I guess I'll see you at the Sonce dinner next week."

"Or, you know, we'll see each other in your class. On Thursday."

"Oh. Right. That's what I—I totally meant to say that. Duh." I try to laugh it off as I sling my purse over my shoulder.

I glance down at Calder, who's looking up at me with bewilderment in his eyes. "So um, thanks for the coffee. And the pastries." My ears twitch at how pitchy my voice sounds. I grab the remaining tart and shove it in my mouth just to muffle the weird tone of my voice. "See you later!"

I give Calder an awkward wave, spin around, and leave. On the drive home, I give myself a pep talk.

"This whole setup is fake. Yes, he feels good, but..."

Even now I can still feel Calder's rough, thick fingers against my face, like a phantom touch on my skin.

"God, he feels good. So, so good..." I groan. "Damn it."

Then I shake my head and stare straight ahead. "Get it together, Lily. He can touch you without losing his shit. You can too."

But even as I say it, I can't help but wonder...

Did Calder feel any of that electricity I felt when we touched?

9

CALDER

Nate was fucking gleeful to hear I was a "yes plus one" to his dinner party. He was likely starting to doubt my girlfriend's existence. Fair enough, and yet here I am. I've somehow fallen into a perfect setup with the perfect woman.

I glance sideways at Lily. She sits with her hands folded neatly in her lap, her gaze out the windshield.

The perfect woman to act as your fake girlfriend to get you this job. To get her through this fucked up wedding season. That's what I meant. Never mind that touching her sent fucking electricity through your fingers at the cafe. Get it together, Calder. Don't lose your shit.

I shift gears and gun the engine.

Nate's place is outside of town a good ways, but I don't mind the chance to drive a bit. I gesture to the dash. "The car's wired for Bluetooth. Feel free to put on some music if you like."

She stirs in my periphery. "Really? It looks so old-fashioned. Oh, but I mean beautiful, of course," she rushes to add.

"Well, it is a classic, but I can't be playing cassettes now can I? But, thank you. I restored it myself." I stroke the red leather steering wheel.

"I know nothing about old cars-um, classic cars. What kind is it?"

"This is a 1962 Alfa Romeo Giulietta. It took a bit of work to get her how I wanted, but now she's a dream."

"You restored it? Jesus, what *aren't* you good at?"

Playing a decent family man. Keeping professional boundaries with you. Chess.

"A handful of things, I suppose. You should learn about classic cars. They're an art form in themselves. You could do a whole unit."

"I'll keep that in mind. For now, what should I play?" Lily rummages in her purse for her phone.

"Anything that pleases you."

A few minutes later, "500 Miles" blasts out of my speakers. The Proclaimers' maddeningly catchy song, infamously from Scotland, makes me groan and laugh all at once.

"Oh, fuck off." My accent comes through thick, but it probably helps eliminate any venom from the phrase.

"What? I figured that was your favorite." She giggles when I groan again. A moment later, the song stops, replaced by Bastille. I nod approvingly.

We park in the drive. On the walk to the front door, I take a quick breath and touch her spine. Her bare skin in the backless top she's wearing is warm and soft, but Lily freezes mid-stride and slides her eyes to me.

I retreat immediately. "Sorry, sorry, just getting into character."

She nods, lips pursed. "No, it's fine. You're right, I just didn't expect it."

We blow out a collective breath and eye the front door. "Right. Well, let's see how it goes."

She grabs my wrist and puts my hand back on her spine. "Let's do this."

This party is much smaller than the meet-and-greet from a couple of weeks ago, far more intimate but still a good show of twenty people or so. Couples only, no children this time. Nate and his father are there, both with their wives of course, and so are the blokes I interviewed with who felt I was the wrong fit. Added to that are a cluster of financial investors and two whisky sommeliers. I'm well aware that I'm the one person in the room with a "what's he doing here" tag on his back, but there is no fucking way I'm acknowledging it.

Nate and Eileen, his wife, greet us at the door. Nate gives me a sly grin as he glances at Lily, who's shaking hands with Eileen. "So glad you could join us," he says as he bends to kiss her cheek hello.

"Thank you for inviting me," she replies, her face a placid mask like she's done this kind of thing a million times before.

"I just love your top," Eileen gushes. "You have such a beautiful name, dear. Where are you from? Probably not around here, right?"

I've known Lily for a few weeks, but I see instantly the way her body goes rigid at the question.

"Just outside of town in Belleview actually," Lily says.

Eileen's lived in the city long enough that she clearly catches the affluent suburb name-drop. She squints at Lily. "Oh, right. So then your parents are from...?"

Inside, I'm palming my eyes at Nate's clueless wife. What a classless question. *Who asks that anymore? Just because she's not blonde and blue-eyed, we need to discuss her family origins?*

But Lily recovers fast. "My dad's from Iowa, and my

mom's from the Philippines." She cocks her chin. "I'm guessing from your accent that you're not from here either?"

Eileen blinks, but then laughs loudly. "Glasgow, but not the dodgiest bit, I swear."

Lily's posture relaxes, and my fists unclench in my pockets. I touch her back again—it's a habit I could get very used to, if I'm honest—and gesture toward the bottle of champagne on the bar. "Drink, love?"

We nod again at our hosts and head inside. "Shit, sorry about that," I murmur in her ear as we make for the beverages.

"I'm used to people assuming I must not be from around here because of the way I look. It's fine."

I hand her a flute of champagne and frown. "It's very fucking far from fine. Ignorant, presumptive questions like that. And I'm the one trying to prove my place here? Fuck's sake, Eileen, you grew up in the bloody alleys of Glasgow. Not the dodgiest bit my left nut. Her accent—"

My grumbling breaks off with Lily's giggle. She covers her mouth and shakes her head. "Shush, someone will overhear."

"Why are you laughing at me?" I'm grinning as I lay a hand on my heart.

"Because *your* accent gets so much stronger when you're annoyed. It's cute. When we first met I could hardly make it out, like you were trying to hide it."

"I was. Or, better to say, I keep it as even as I can. I guess it just comes out when I'm worked up."

"Worked up?" She quirks a brow and sips her drink. "Curious."

I return the expression. "Interpret that as you will."

"Calder Ross, is that you?" Patrick Wallace, Nate's father,

booms at me from across the room, breaking our moment of ease. "Damn, son, ye grew up right ugly, didnae ye now?"

I laugh and hurry to greet the head of the family. The corporate boys watch this reunion, which is precisely what I want—until I realize I've left Lily in the corner by the champagne. *Fuck*.

"Ah, Pat, come and meet Lily." I guide him through the group. Lily, bless her, snaps right to attention and holds out her hand. I make the introductions, and Pat chats with us for a few minutes about Lily's art class before drifting across the room.

Our private conversation is gone as the party gets into full swing. The beautiful, open grin that kicks my heart disappears from her face. Lily smiles, but it's close-lipped and far more reserved than I'm used to seeing her. She's got a knack for being in a crowd but somehow blending into the scenery, which I suppose is an ideal talent for a fake girlfriend. For me, though, it's not the Lily I've been delighted to know for the past few weeks, and I'm not sure how to interpret it. As a result, I have a gorgeous, sweeter-than-I-deserve woman on my arm that I'm hardly interacting with.

We're ushered to the dining room and sat at the long table. Dinner means a lot of talk about business, which means that Pat, Nate, and the corporate heads drive the chat. The sommeliers are in their own world, which leaves the women and me without much to do but eat and look interested.

Toward the end of the main course, I slide my arm around Lily's shoulders like a boyfriend would and put my lips to her ear. "How are you, darling?"

Dammit. Her shoulders tense again, the fork dropping from her grip. She blinks quickly and puts on that smile.

"Wonderful. Dinner is fantastic." She directs this toward Eileen. "You chose an excellent menu."

"Thank you! This is a new caterer, but I'm quite pleased too!" Eileen beams and pushes a slice of bread around her plate.

"Nicely done," I whisper to Lily.

"I know what I'm doing."

I wish I could see her smirk or give me a mischievous look, but Eileen starts saying something more about the caterer, and so I'm left wondering what the hell that comment meant. Does she think I doubted her ability to fit in here? Does she think I give a fuck about her hometown or catering knowledge? Doesn't she get that I'm just very damn lucky to have a woman like her beside me—

"Cal, what projects do you have coming up?" Nate asks, a pointed look in his eyes.

I start to tear at my left index finger. *Easy, that one's a bit sore after the last party.* If I go too long, I'll tear the skin. Disgusting I know, but I can't help it. "Oh, erm, well, I'm on a bit of hiatus right now. Am doing some work for the university as a model—that's how I met Lily, actually—but things are quiet. Got some projects I've got my eye on for the holidays, though."

"I bet you do." Nate laughs, but I can see he likes my answer. The corporate heads nod slowly, but Pat asks something about tax penalties that captures their attention again.

"Calder, where is the restroom?" Lily's voice is barely audible, but Eileen jumps in to give her directions anyway. "I'll be back. If you'll excuse me."

Her eyes are flat as she looks at me and rises. I frown, but she pats my shoulder and disappears.

When she's out of the room, Nate cocks a brow and shakes his head. "My, my, have the mighty fallen."

"What's that mean, then?"

He shrugs and leans back in his chair, idly stroking Eileen's neck until she purrs and blushes. "My school mate had the ladies lined up for a date before he had hair on his balls. Everything I've seen about the great Calder Ross tells me that his skillset only improved over time. And now, here you are, all settled down with a woman and barely laying a hand on her."

"You'd prefer I undress her at the dinner table?" There's a defensive growl in my voice for two reasons. One, I've been fantasizing about running my tongue along Lily's spine for most of the evening. A flick of a clasp, and that blousy top would flutter to her lap.

Two, he is absolutely right. I do know how to entertain a date, and I'm doing nothing of the sort with Lily.

He laughs. "While that would be interesting, I'm simply commenting on what I see. My friend seems to have settled down into a very, shall we say, staid relationship. You just don't seem like yourself with her."

"I believe I said I had made some changes. So what if things are different with her? Not every relationship has to be a tear-your-clothes-off situation."

"Fine fine, just taking the piss," he chuckles. "Good on you, settling."

"Down, you mean?"

"Absolutely."

Lily appears in her seat again a few minutes later, as the servers are clearing the plates and bringing out bottles of whisky and Glencairn glasses. The sommeliers sit up straight—clearly this is their moment, and I am all in. My tension melts as I gaze at the gorgeous amber liquid in the bottles, all three distinctly different hues, all three undoubtedly crafted to perfection.

Lily exhales a quiet sigh.

We're led through an overview of all three bottles, the varying ages, casks, etc., before the first dram is poured. "Slàinte!" echoes around the room; the light-bodied whisky explodes in caramel notes on my tongue at the first sip. We take our time on that dram, commenting on the way it opens up, the legs on it, and then move on to the second pour.

I notice that Lily's glass is missing *very* little of the original content. As the others smell and sip their new drams, I watch her lift the glass. Her lips part an infinitesimal amount, so small I'm not sure any liquid passes through at all. She sets the glass down, sips her water, and repeats this façade.

"What are you doing?" I whisper, somewhere between amused and horrified.

"Hmm? Oh, it's lovely, isn't it? Very... earthy."

"You're not drinking it, you fake."

"Here, you can have some of mine if you want, honey." She quickly hands me the glass.

I roll my eyes and finish both of our pours. "Cannae do that again and drive home, love."

"I'm just so full from the wine and champagne. But it's wonderful." Again, she's pitched her voice strategically to be overheard.

Nate's teasing in my head, I roll my eyes, cluck, and peck her cheek. "Fair enough."

We finish the tasting and wrap the meal with strawberries and whipped cream. As plates are cleared, one of the corporate fellows nods my way. "Calder, I have to say, I liked the idea you pitched earlier about expanding the target market to women. It could be a great in-road to consider."

I shrug, but inside I'm giving myself a massive high-five.

"Plenty of lasses love whisky as much as their men. If we're going for the hip millennial vibe, why cut out half the population?"

"Quite right. Definitely something to consider." His wife leans over and whispers to him behind her hand, her cheeks bright red as her eyes cut to me. He chuckles and pats her arm. "Sandy wants me to tell you that *Blazing Hearts* is her current favorite book."

My smile is for Sandy, and it's designed to be disarming and commiserative all at once. "It's such a great book, don't you think? I read my copy before it was released, and I thought the story was so compelling."

"It is," she nearly cries before reigning it in at the table.

"What, *Blazing Hearts*? I'm rereading it now," Eileen jumps in, and in a few moments every woman at the table, minus Lily, is gushing about the latest romance bestseller. Nate glances at Lily, then me, one brow arched, but I pretend not to see.

I was going to suggest we ride home with the top down, but somehow I sense the mood isn't right for a night ride in a convertible. Instead, after we say goodnight, I tuck Lily into my passenger seat and push the car to top speed, more than ready to end this decidedly mixed bag of a night.

On the one hand, I'm pretty sure it was a massive win with Sonce.

On the other, Lily looks like she's ready to tuck and roll out of this car, and I have no idea how the hell to make that better.

10

LILY

The entire car ride back to my place, all I can fixate on are the words that I overheard Nate say as I walked down the hall to the bathroom.

My friend seems to have settled down into a very, shall we say, staid relationship. You just don't seem like yourself with her... Good on you, settling.

Immediately after that, Calder's response echoes in my mind.

I believe I said I had made some changes. So what if things are different with her? Not every relationship has to be a tear-your-clothes-off situation.

I shouldn't be hurt. I shouldn't be feeling that sucker punch in the center of my chest at words I wasn't even meant to hear. I'm not really Calder's girlfriend. I should have been able to weather whatever was said.

But I can't.

"You're awfully quiet," Calder says.

I almost make up an excuse—that I'm full from dinner or exhausted from work. But I stop myself. No more hiding; I need to say exactly what's on my mind.

"Yeah, I just... I heard what Nate said to you. About how unnatural you seem with me."

He twists his head to me, then looks back at the road. "You heard that?"

"Mmm-hmm. And I heard what you said in response." I don't repeat it. He knows what he said.

Instead of waiting for him to respond, I continue.

"I mean, it makes sense," I say. "All those other women you were with, you had genuine feelings for."

Calder snorts.

I sigh and shake my head. "Well, whatever you want to call it. Feelings, urges. You know what I mean. This is just a setup."

He cuts his gaze to me again. "Lily, that's not—"

I hold up a hand. "It's okay. Really. I get it. This isn't real. So it makes sense why us being together comes off as a little unnatural. But we need to do something about it if you want to nail this opportunity with Sonce."

His frown is illuminated by headlights from an oncoming car.

"And honestly, I need us to look convincing too in front of my family and friends. Otherwise, they won't buy it either, if Nate doesn't," I finish.

My mind floats back to how easy it was to pretend like we were together at Harmony's bachelorette party. But I was drunk then. So was everyone else. People are going to be sober for the apple orchard gathering, so we can't rely on alcohol to sell us as a couple.

The idea I've been mulling around in my mind ever since overhearing Calder and Nate takes hold. It's going to be silly as hell to say out loud, but it's necessary. If this is going to work, if we're going to come off like an actual couple, we need to start acting like one.

"I guess my idea of setting rules about touching each other and PDA comes off a bit... stiff."

Out of the corner of my eye, I catch Calder pursing his lips like he's trying not to laugh.

"Maybe not the greatest word choice," I say softly. "We need to come off more natural. Believable."

"And how do we do that?"

I take a breath and turn to face him. "We practice."

My hands shake as I unlock the door to my duplex. I flip on the light as Calder walks in behind me and shuts the door. I hold in my breath as I survey the living space. Not terrible. An empty water glass sits on my coffee table and there are a couple of sweaters strewn over the couch, but it's not at all messy thankfully.

"Make yourself at home," I say, gesturing to the plushy couch against the far wall as I head to the kitchen. "You want something to drink?" I holler as I turn on the faucet and fill a glass with water.

Calder says something I can't understand, so I walk back out into the living room.

"Sorry, what did you—" I stop dead in my tracks when I see what he's holding.

His eyes go wide at the hot pink strapless bra in his hand, but then he reels in his expression when he looks at me. "This was between your couch cushions when I sat down."

I walk over and swipe it out of his hand, then hold it behind my back. "Sorry about that." My mind flashes back to the night that I came home drunk from Harmony's bachelorette party. I started undressing the minute I shut the door behind me. No wonder I couldn't find that bra these past few days.

I suspect my face is as pink as the bra as I stand in front of Calder.

"I um, I mean, do you want something to drink?" I ask him.

"I think I had enough alcohol for one night. How about water?"

I scurry back to the kitchen, toss my bra on the floor, and then return to the living room with two glasses of water.

"I think water is a good idea," I say, setting the glasses down on the coffee table and taking a seat on the other end of the couch.

I fix my gaze on Calder, who's sitting with a relaxed posture. His eyes read the tiniest bit nervous though. It's a comfort, knowing I'm not the only one currently pissing myself with nerves. I down half the water in my glass while he takes a more reasonable sip. When I look back at him, he's studying the clay sculpture sitting on the bookcase against the wall. I glance at the self-portrait bust I completed years ago. The earthy red-brown mass of clay depicts a head leaning back. Endless squiggly etches adorn the back of the head to look like hair. Two hands grip the sides of the neck. The face consists of two open eyes, a button nose, and a small, full rosebud mouth.

"That's mesmerizing," he says.

"Oh. Thanks."

He turns to me. "You sculpted that?"

I nod. "A while ago. My take on a self-portrait."

He opens his mouth but says nothing, like he's shocked. Then he looks once more at the sculpture, then at me. "Lily, why didn't you tell me you were a sculptor in addition to a teacher? That's so..."

"Typical?" I let out a chuckle.

He turns back to me, frowning at what I've said. "No. Brilliant. Talented. Impressive."

I bite my lip and stare at the ground as I absorb the wonder in his eyes and how sincere he sounds. "I don't talk much about my art."

The pain of Marco selling all of the pieces I made and gave to him as gifts flashes through me. I swallow and will it away.

"You should, Lily. You're bloody talented."

"Thank you," I say quietly.

"Did you do those too?" He points to an abstract gold sculpture the size of a dinner plate that sits on the bottom shelf of the bookcase, then to a large decorative, earth-toned vase near my front door.

"Yup," I say, taking another sip of water.

"Christ," he mutters, his eyes fixed on the vase. "How long did it take you to make that?"

"A few weeks. I have a pottery wheel in my garage. I'll show you next time when we don't have other things to do."

He looks at me and smiles. "Ah, yes, the wheel. Believe we discussed that a few weeks ago." His teasing drops as I blush, his voice gentler as he says, "You'd better show me. I want to know all about the artistic genius of Lily Maldonado."

I roll my eyes and laugh.

But he places his hand on my arm. "I'm serious. You're brilliant. Honestly, brilliant isn't even a good enough word. I'm surprised you didn't mention you were an artist before. I thought you only taught."

"I didn't think to bring it up. Not a lot of people who run in my circle are interested in my creative interests."

"That's royally fucked up, Lily."

I shrug and point to the bust he first noticed. "I sculpted that the week after I dropped out of law school. My parents were so pissed at me. They didn't speak to me for a month. That was how I felt at that moment."

"Angry? Frustrated?"

"Free."

A sweet smile tugs at his mouth. "I love that."

There's a giddiness inside of me that I haven't felt in a while. Yeah, I talk about art all day at school. And yes, I'm lucky enough to have colleagues and friends who I can share my work with. But it would mean the world if the people I love—my parents—cared too. If they acknowledged me as the artist I strive to be instead of only seeing me as a disappointment with a barely tolerable career.

It's been forever since someone expressed a genuine interest in the pieces I created.

"Thanks for being so kind," I say to Calder.

He squeezes my hand and then lets go. "Don't thank me. I'm just stating the obvious. You're a talented artist. Beyond incredible. It's weird to me that everyone around you isn't constantly saying that to you. They all must be dense."

I let out a laugh. "Just wait till you meet everyone when we go apple picking."

"You still haven't explained what that is."

"Promise I will, but first we should probably work on our... issue... from earlier this evening."

He blinks, and the amusement in his face disappears. He takes a drink of water and sets the glass back on the table. "Tell me then. What do you think we need to practice?"

"Kissing."

Calder's brow lifts the slightest bit. I'm caught off guard too at how quickly I said it. But it's the truth. Our PDA this evening was unconvincing, as evidenced by the comments that Nate made.

"I don't mean to sound so forward about all this."

"Don't apologize," he says with a smile. "What man wouldn't want to spend an evening kissing you?"

As my heart flips in my chest, a grin splits my face. Calder slides over to my side of the couch. When he pivots to face me, I do the same. I hold my breath as he leans his face close to mine and cups my cheek in his hand.

"No sense fucking about," he whispers.

And then he presses his mouth to mine. At first, contact is slow and soft, almost tentative. But a second later, I sink into the rhythm. I move my lips against his, unable to help myself as I let out a soft moan. Those lips. Oh my fucking god, those lips. How can they be so soft and so firm at the same time?

The scratch of his thick stubble against my smooth cheeks shoots fire inside of me. That little bit of roughness is absolute perfection. I've always, always loved the feel of rough stubble against my face. Yeah, it's scratchy and even hurts a bit, but it's a good hurt. Like a delicious reminder of all the gruff masculine deliciousness that's mine for the taking.

I hum again, relishing the hard feel once more. Then he hums too. I smile against his mouth and run my tongue along his bottom lip.

At that moment, I expect Calder to capture my tongue in his mouth and go to town. That's what every other guy I've kissed seems to want to do—get hot and heavy as soon as possible.

But not Calder.

Instead, he slowly runs his tongue along my bottom lip too, then parts my mouth open.

And then the teasing begins.

My breath turns ragged as he softly flicks my tongue with his. My mouth waters. He tastes faintly of whisky and strawberries from dessert. His hold on my face turns firm as he amps things up. It's gentle lap after gentle lap that sends electricity to every particle of my body.

When I start to feel dizzy, I steady myself by running my fingers through his hair. I hum even louder at how good it feels to touch even more of him.

This teasing act goes on for minutes until we're both panting and grabbing at each other. It's like we're animals in a frenzied heat.

I pull away when I run out of breath and rest my hands on his shoulders to steady myself. His hands fall to my waist, then he slowly, softly runs his palms along my back. Yet another sheet of goosebumps covers my skin at the tantalizing touch. Our chests heave in tandem as we gaze at each other. When my vision finally focuses, I notice that his eyes are cloudy—hopefully with lust. Mine definitely are.

"That was..."

Calder frowns and clears his throat. "Hopefully okay?"

I cup my hand over my mouth, my head still spinning. Holy fucking hell. No one, not anyone, has ever kissed me like that. Even though I've been kissed multiple times by multiple men, no kiss has ever been that phenomenal.

Calder starts to say something, but I cannot compute. His slow, teasing kisses have short-circuited my brain. He's moving his mouth, but my hearing has gone fuzzy. All because of that kiss.

Holy crap, Calder has one hell of a mouth... and one hell of a tongue. And in this moment, all I know is that I need more of both on me.

When I try to refocus on what he's saying, I've only caught the tail end of it.

"—or if you think it should be slower or faster or—"

I slice a hand through the air, cutting him off while I shake my head.

He frowns, seemingly confused. "Oh sorry. It's just that you didn't say anything for a while. I thought that maybe you didn't like it, or you wanted me to change something, or..."

He drifts off when I push him against the couch. Then his eyes go wide as I straddle him. I know this is way more than kissing at this point. But I don't care. My body is vibrating, in desperate need of more.

"Whoa." He chuckles. "Alright then."

"I just... I don't want to stop. That kiss was amazing and I...I..." I stammer as I struggle to catch my breath.

His grin fades into a neutral line on his face. He doesn't lose any of the amusement in his expression though. It's still dancing in his jewel-toned eyes. And even without the smile, the line of his mouth reads knowing, flitting on the edge of smug. It makes me lose all the oxygen in my body once more.

When he swallows, I'm hypnotized. All can do is gaze at the glorious thickness of his stubbled neck.

"I want...I need..."

"Lily," he growls softly. "Just say so."

"I want to kiss you some more."

My mouth is on his before he can even take a breath. And as good as all that teasing was, I don't have the patience for it this time. This time, I want as much of Calder as I can possibly have.

I tug at his hair as our tongues get filthier and filthier. He seems to be on board with the more hurried rhythm I'm employing as he moans into my mouth, clearly enjoying himself. We're out of air just as quickly as last time. But this time, I get the added perk of having more of his body on me.

Just the feel of his hard mass writhing against mine sends jolts of pleasure inside of me. Between my legs it starts to throb.

I grin against his mouth for the zillionth time as I delight in all the blissful physical sensations I'm experiencing. The arousal inside of me. The sound of Calder's panting and moaning and soft grunting. The taste of this mouth and tongue. The firm feel of his body underneath me. I shudder in pleasure. His thighs are hard as steel. So is his chest. And his arms. And his back.

I run my hands all over his torso, pressing and grabbing at all that dense, chiseled flesh.

I probably shouldn't be so shocked at what I'm feeling. I've seen him buck naked in my classroom several times already. I'm very, very familiar with all that cut muscle that adorns his flawless physique. I've spent hours upon hours staring at him and quietly ogling him...but to touch him is a whole different ball game.

I break our kiss and inhale the musky scent of his cologne. "Your thighs. Your whole body."

His hands, which are resting on my hips, give me a gentle squeeze as he smirks up at me. "I'm delighted you're a fan. I'm definitely a fan of your insanely hot body."

I start to blush, but then he hooks his finger under my chin and tilts me to look at him. "Don't you even think about denying that compliment. Accept it because it's true. You're gorgeous, Lily."

The feather-like kiss he presses to my mouth sets me on fire just as much as those more desperate, more tongue-heavy kisses. Probably because of the sweetness in his words and the conviction in his eyes as he spoke them to me.

Soon we're tugging at each other's clothes, in full defiance of the no sex rule I set just days ago. But right now, I don't give a flying fuck about the rules. It's been ages since I've had sex and, given how orgasmic making out with Calder is, I'm guessing that getting naked with him would be more of the same—maybe even better. My clit is throbbing, aching to find out just how much better. I'm on the verge of ripping his dress shirt open when his phone rings.

"Leave it," I say against his mouth.

He grunts his agreement as the ringing finally stops. But then it starts back up again. When his phone blares on for the third time, we finally break apart.

"I should probably answer that," Calder says, a frown marring his expression. He runs a hand through his hair, which is a tousled mess due to me.

I lean back and nod, taking the moment to catch my breath.

The way he says Nate's name as he answers sounds like a harsh bark. But the longer he stays on the call listening to whatever Nate's saying, the more his expression eases. And then the smiles.

"Yeah, that would be fucking grand, mate. Thanks."

He hangs up and looks at me. "Good news. The dinner left a positive impression on the Sonce execs. It sounds like they're buying me as a wholesome and responsible bloke."

"That's great, Calder." I smile, thrilled for him.

"They want me to get on the phone so they can introduce me to the Sonce brand reps in Scotland."

"Right now?"

"Yeah." He swallows. "Nothing's set in stone, but things

are looking good. It sounds like I'm actually in the running to be the face of the brand now."

I beam. "That's freaking awesome!"

The wide grin he flashes makes my chest ache. I can tell just how much this opportunity means to him and just how close he is to getting it.

"Nate said there are a couple more events to attend before I seal the deal. Some hoity-toity whisky tasting and a holiday launch party."

I hug him in congratulations. The deep rumble of his laughter vibrates against my body. It feels like heaven.

"I couldn't have done it without you, Lily," he says softly into my ear as he holds me tight. I grin so wide my mouth aches.

"I guess we did a better job of pretending than I thought we did," he says.

The way he chuckles jolts me. It almost sounds like relief. My smile drops. "Oh yeah. That's, um, great."

I quickly slide off his lap and sit next to him on the couch. "I guess we don't need to practice anymore. You nailed it." I tug my top back down.

A different kind of heat flashes across my skin. The kind of warmth that hits when I'm embarrassed.

There's a pause as Calder clears his throat. I stand up from the couch and force a smile at him. "As much fun as that was, you should probably leave to take that call, right?"

Calder stammers for a second, but then shakes his head. "Yeah, I should."

I back up to give him enough room to stand and then walk back toward the front door and open it for him.

"Thank you for helping me tonight, Lily."

I nod once, that tight smile still on my face. "No problem. See you in class. And remember, we um need to be professional there."

I lock the door after I shut it behind him. For a second I stand there, my head spinning in a million dizzying circles. And then I lean my back against the door and slide all the way down until my ass hits the hardwood, wondering how the hell I'm going to fake it through apple picking, a rehearsal dinner, a wedding, and more Sconce events if this is how badly I lose my shit after just one kiss with Calder.

11

CALDER

I press my forehead against her front door and take a long, slow breath. Goddamn, pretending just got a *lot* more fun.

Sure, I'll remember to be a professional. I'll be a professional and pose for the students. I'll be a professional and call her Professor Lily.

And I'll be a professional and wank it long and hard before I go into that classroom because thinking about that sweet, hot mouth is enough to change the class's focal point if I'm not careful.

My eyes open slowly, and I realize my hand is on the doorknob, itching to turn it. Before I do anything desperate, I stumble backwards and spin for my car. On the drive home, a question sinks deeper and deeper into my brain.

If this is pretending, then what the hell is the real thing?

12

LILY

"Okay, everyone. That's it for today. Thank you." I dismiss the students and try my hardest not to look at Calder as he slips his robe back on.

It is not easy.

Because I've tried not to look at him this entire class and failed miserably. Ever since our crazy hot makeout session on my couch this past weekend, he's all I could think about. And now that he's been standing just a few feet in front of me for the past hour wearing nothing at all, I know just how weak my resolve is.

Because I definitely snuck a peek at his muscles as they twitched and bulged while he held his various poses today.

I shake my head, trying to will away the endless images of his flawless, naked form. No more ogling. We need to talk about what happened Saturday night, and I need to apologize for how handsy and hot I got with him. My family's apple picking excursion is happening this weekend, and I need to be on the same page with Calder to make sure that we sell ourselves as a couple—while also keeping ourselves in check.

Once the last student is gone, I shut the door behind them and turn to face Calder.

"How'd I do today?" he asks, tightening the belt on his robe.

"Excellent. The students love you."

He flashes a slight smile, then glances down at the ground. I wonder if he had a hard time getting through the week like I did. I wonder if he thought about that kiss as often as I did, if he relived the heat between us, the taste, the feel, the heart-pounding arousal that I close my eyes and imagine every time I'm in the shower or lying in bed.

I quell the thought in my mind. Probably not. He was probably too focused on working with the Sonce execs to think about me much. He didn't even text me the past few days. And even though I thought about texting him more times than I care to admit, I didn't. If he wasn't going to reach out, I didn't want to come off like I was desperate for his attention—especially after I threw myself at him Saturday night.

But now there's no excuse. It's time to set everything straight.

"I owe you an apology."

Calder looks up at me, his eyebrows wrinkled together. "For what?"

"For mauling you the other night. On my couch." I swallow and try not to burst into flames of embarrassment.

His mouth hooks up into that adorable smirk I can never get enough of. "No need to be sorry about that."

I fold my hands in front of me. "I let myself get carried away. We had an agreement not to let things get too heated, and I crossed those boundaries."

"Lily, you didn't cross any boundaries. I was more than

happy to go along with it too. If you couldn't tell, I was enjoying myself quite a bit."

"I... appreciate you saying that."

He lifts an eyebrow, probably amused at my awkward wording.

"But this weekend we're supposed to go apple picking at Sawyer Farms with my family and their friends, remember? And I just want to make sure that we stick to the plan. Let's keep things PG, okay? Hand holding, kisses on the cheek, that sort of thing."

He steps toward me. "So I can't kiss you on the lips?"

Inside my chest, my heart is doing somersaults. "Sure you can. Just no tongue."

He crinkles his lips, then grins before stepping closer to me once more. We're so close that if I lean forward slightly, I could show him exactly how I want him to kiss me.

"So... something like this?" He hovers his lips right over mine, and I stop breathing. I should tell him to stop, that this violates our agreed-upon rule to never do anything physical in the classroom.

But I don't. Instead, I stay right there as the wet heat of his soft breath coats my lips.

"No... classroom... stuff," I stammer through the arousal swirling through me.

"Relax, Lily. I know your rules," he whispers. "I'm not kissing you, am I?"

I shake my head slightly.

The corner of his mouth twitches up into a playful half-smile. I want to lick his lips, but not here.

"I'm just making sure we're on the same page about what kind of kiss—what kind of peck—is acceptable in front of your family," he says softly. "I'd obviously press my lips against yours when we're there this weekend. But not right now, of course."

Just then he leans away and takes a step back. I deflate on the inside, even though I know it's for the best. I can't lose my inhibitions here, not in my classroom.

"Um, yeah," I say through a huff of air. "Just like that is perfectly fine."

"Good to know," he says. He turns around and grabs his bag of clothes, then heads over to the back corner of the room where the room divider is and changes into his street clothes. I take a minute to collect myself and quietly deep-breathe my way to a regular heartbeat.

When he walks out with his clothes on, I breathe a sigh of relief. It's a lot easier to talk about serious things when he's dressed.

"Nice try pulling that sneaky move a minute ago," I say.

"I didn't technically kiss you," he says with a lift of his eyebrow.

I roll my eyes and smile. "Fine. You got off on a technicality. But this weekend, no pushing boundaries. We need to be a cute couple who doesn't cross the line. Promise me you'll be on your best behavior?"

I stick out my hand for him to shake.

He clasps his hand around mine. "I promise."

13

CALDER

Sunday is custom-made for an autumn day outdoors, bright and blue with just a bit of chill in the air. Lily emerges from her house with two travel mugs in her hands and grins when she sees I've got the top down. I accept her offer of coffee gratefully and hit the road.

It's about an hour and a half drive out of town to this farm. Once I'm cruising down the highway, I sneak a glance at my "girlfriend" to see if she seems tense. No lie, it has the potential to be a very long day—Lily warned me we'd not be back until well after dinner—but she's snuggled in the seat, cradling her coffee and smiling at the passing countryside. Her dark hair whips behind her, making her the picture of relaxation. She catches my glance and smiles a little brighter, so I let go of any concern about how this will play out and instead daydream about Sonce. It's my new favorite pastime.

When we pull onto the country lane, she turns in her seat. I feel her gaze as I avoid a muddy hole in the gravel road. "You look like an ad for some kind of rugged outdoors store. Model-slash-lumberjack chic."

I chuckle and glance at my plaid shirt. "This is the clan Ross hunting tartan, thank you very much."

"Oh, sorry, I meant it as a compliment. Not—"

I reach across the console and lightly grasp her fingers. My thumb runs along her palm, and she stops spluttering. "Stop apologizing all the time, love. To be fair, Oak and Thistle did have it custom made for me, so you're not at all wrong."

"Wow, how nice of them." She giggles at the name-drop of the high-end men's fashion store.

"I thought so. Wore it on a photo shoot for a novel—in an apple orchard, actually. That's quite literally my only experience with farms of any sort."

"I have to assume it wasn't buttoned then?"

"Not in the least. Why? Would you like your boyfriend to show up with his shirt open, maybe hanging off one shoulder? Because we can make that happen. Here, take the wheel and I'll—"

"Calder, stop." Her musical laugh rings in my ears and fuels my grin as I park in an open field parking lot. A couple walking past turns at the noise. I can tell they recognize Lily, but she's too busy laughing to notice.

She grabs my wrist to stop my undressing process. "You're so silly. One button open is the proper vibe for this event."

"Just let me know if you change your mind. I am at your service today, Professor Lily."

"Lucky me." The soft murmur of her voice makes me cock a brow. Lily flushes a light pink, but she doesn't blink. Her tongue darts out to wet her lips, and my cock stirs.

Keep it PG. Best behavior. Right.

"Shall we apple pick?" I ask.

She blinks and nods, the intense look in her eyes dissipating. Shame, really. There was something singularly sexy about this sweet creature worked up, whimpering in my lap as she clawed at my clothes like she—

PG, Cal. Fake boyfriend. Play your role.

I wait till Lily opens her door and steps out of the car before giving myself a quick adjustment and rising to join her. We walk across the field and follow the signs that say, "To the orchard!" A little dirt path is leading us toward a barn, but I notice a paved driveway snaking toward a large house off to the right.

Lily gestures to the house, then the barn. "Normally this place is packed from dawn until dusk every weekend in the fall. Today is the day the Sawyers close for a private event for friends and family. To give you an overview, there will be about forty people total, children included. The major players you have to remember are Marilyn and Edward Maldonado—my parents. Then there's Marco and Harmony. Harmony's best friend is—"

"Brittany."

"Oh, right. Of course you'd remember that."

I hear the subtext and roll my eyes. "Hell yes I do. Harmony was so drunk she said everyone's names at least six times in a row, including as she shouted across the pub."

Lily laughs softly. "Yeah, it was a lot. So there are going to be a ton of others, but those are the big ones. We'll have lunch, pick apples, and spend the afternoon drinking cider, etc. Dinner, then hayrides and music, but we can probably make an excuse and get out as soon as dinner is over."

"Whatever your pleasure."

"Really going to need you to stop making comments like that," she says between clenched teeth, but I just laugh and take her hand as we approach the cluster of people by the barn.

They're chatting and laughing, glasses of club soda and white wine in hand as cater waiters buzz in and out of the building. Most of the men are dressed in khaki with cable knit jumpers tied around their necks. The ladies sport jeans, skirts, and a variety of plaid and wool tops. Lily's wine-colored skirt and pale blue chambray top are a touch casual, but her knee-high boots ensure she fits right in.

Her grip on my hand tightens when an older couple turns toward us. Their wide eyes make it clear these are her parents, but I don't need the hint. Lily is a perfect split of the two of them. She has her mother's complexion and eye color and her father's face shape.

"*Anakko!*" Her mother's cry causes a few people to look our way. She thrusts her glass into her husband's hand and steps forward to place her palms on Lily's cheeks. Air kisses follow, and then she looks her daughter over. "I'm so happy you made it. And you brought a friend!"

Lily steps closer to me, so I put my hand on the small of her back. "I said I was, remember? Mom, this is Calder Ross. Calder, meet Marilyn and Edward."

"A pleasure." I kiss Mrs. Maldonado's knuckles when she offers her hand, and then reach to shake with her dad.

Marilyn's gaze appraises me from top to bottom before perfectly-drawn-on eyebrows arch. "My, my. Good to meet you, Calder. Yes, Lily, you said you were bringing someone, but I didn't know if that was for sure or not."

Wow. Way to accuse your daughter of lying without actually saying it.

Lily flinches. A long blink and deep breath later, she pastes on a smile. "I wouldn't just make a boyfriend up, Mom. Come on."

"Oh, don't be so dramatic. I didn't say you made him up! I just wasn't sure if he would be available today."

Smooth, lady.

Her eyes flick over me again as her smile turns warmer. "But we are just so very happy to have you with us. Do you like picking apples, Calder?"

"Have very limited experience in it, to tell the truth."

Beside me, Lily coughs to hide a laugh. A bell rings, and the crowd begins to drift into the barn. Long tables are decorated in gingham, with a buffet of sandwiches and picnic foods in the corner. We fill our plates and find our seats. As lunch progresses, the Maldonados interrogate me about being a model, about Scotland, and about how Lily and I met. I give them the stories we sorted out via text yesterday while my arm remains draped around Lily's shoulders. We're doing much better with the couple vibe today, I'm pretty sure, but Lily is quiet yet again.

As Edward is telling me about his years in corporate law, a flurry at the door catches everyone's attention. Two people, a dark-haired bloke and a blonde I instantly recognize as Harmony, appear and, I swear, the room applauds. They laugh and wave at everyone as they hurry to the two empty chairs a few seats away from us. I take a deep breath and put my gaze on my plate. Everyone else in the room is staring at the flushed and smiling couple, but I give not one fuck. Lily's shoulders stiffen under my arm, so I give her a reassuring squeeze.

"Sorry we're late, everyone," the guy who must be Marco says.

"Yeah, we, um… slept late this morning." Harmony giggles, and a chorus of indulgent laughter ensues.

"Those two." Marilyn chuckles, trying to catch my eye.

I arch a brow and shrug. I will not wink and nod about the fact that they practically smell of sex, especially not with Lily frozen in her seat.

Take your cue, mate. I turn to her and narrow my eyes playfully. "I'm glad you put on a double alarm this morning so we didn't have to make a scene, too. I know I was hard to drag out of bed, but much better than showing up late, hmm?"

Relief floods her eyes, but she nods and smiles. "You were so grumpy, I didn't know if you'd forgive me."

"Oh, don't you worry. I'll forgive you good and proper next weekend."

I wink, but Lily cringes. Across the table, her mom murmurs an, "oh, my!"

Too far. "Breakfast in bed it'll be," I amend, and Lily bites her lips to keep from laughing.

She leans forward and dusts a kiss on my lips. "Sounds great."

When I glance back at the Maldonados, they're both beaming at us. I take it as a win, especially since the rest of the table is laser-focused on Marco and Harmony.

"Oh, my god, Lily *hi*!" Harmony waves suddenly, drawing her fiancé's attention toward us as well. "You brought your boyfriend! Hi again—sorry, I don't remember your name. I'm Harmony."

"Yes, I remember. It's Calder."

She eyes me and shakes her head once. "Damn," she breathes before addressing Lily again. "I'm so happy you came today! I was hoping to see you. Will you be able to come to the pregame party the night before the rehearsal dinner? Both of you, of course."

"Thursday night? Um, we'll see. I teach class that day, so maybe not."

Harmony pouts. "Try to, okay?"

"Sure."

Marco has been eyeing me the whole time. "Hey, sorry bro, what was your name?"

"Calder. Yours?" *Bro.*

"Marco Woodruff."

"Cheers."

"He's English," Harmony explains to her fiancé.

"Scottish, actually," Lily jumps in. She lays a hand on my arm. "There's a difference."

"My bad!" Harmony giggles.

"No worries." I shrug.

A waiter brings the couple a pair of plates, and Lily and I sink back in our chairs. We trade a glance that I *think* is a shared "ugh," but she may be thinking something entirely different. Ugh best sums up my thoughts, but I'm certain that has a lot to do with finally having a face to her ex's name. The prick is too oily and smug for Lily. That much I could tell just by looking at him. He's all about the image, calling me bro and wearing those designer sunglasses on his head. No way does creative, funny Lily belong with a wanker who—

"Apple time. Come on." Lily tugs my sleeve and crashes me out of my mental tirade.

She rises, but I just turn in my chair and face her. I need to see her smile, so I quirk a brow and reach for my shirt buttons. "Apple picking? Right, I know how to do this part. Just let me—"

Harmony, Marco, and the rest of the table turn and stare when Lily bursts out laughing. Can't blame them—it really is a fucking musical sound. She claps a hand over her mouth and then drags me out of the seat. I happily let her make a scene as I obediently follow her out of the barn.

"That was a brilliant show," she says once I'm holding a basket and we're wandering in the orchard, away from anyone's earshot. "I mean, you almost made me blush so hard my face melted with that 'I'll forgive you' part, but otherwise well done. Good recovery, too, by the way."

I indulge in a brief fantasy of rolling across my bed with Lily as the morning sun streams in the windows, then file it away for later and grin. "Our farce coupledom is definitely stronger today, innit? Sorry about that line, I'll be more careful about the PG rating for the rest, I swear. I tend to forget since my family has practically made bawdy jokes an art form."

Her smile stops showing her teeth, but Lily nods quickly. She swallows hard and drifts toward a tree. "We're really in the act today, I'd say. So, do you have a big family?"

Her question is meant to distract me, I can tell. It doesn't work, but I oblige the chit chat and tell her a bit about Mum, Dad, and Lucy. She's curious and envious that I have a sister. I laugh and make it sound far more like a burden than being a brother actually is, and by then Lily's shoulders are lowered and her real smile has returned.

Several hours of the afternoon pass in the orchard. We interact with people here and there, but a lot of the time we're on our own, filling a basket and just talking. Art dominates our chat; I'm fascinated by what she knows and what she's studied. I ask a lot of questions about her creative process. She talks freely, lighting up the more she describes sculpting and teaching. By the time we're headed out of the orchard with an overflowing basket, I'm grinning as she describes her first art class. The model fell asleep halfway through the hour, and she had a room full of students and no clue what to do.

But then, up ahead of us, is a too-familiar pair. Marco has the apple basket on one arm while he checks his phone. Harmony is talking, but I don't get the impression from their body language that she's expecting him to really listen. They both look up as we approach.

Lily cuts off her story. "Hey, guys," she murmurs.

"Hey, how are you guys? Lily, I meant to say, I love your boots, and that skirt is too cute!" Harmony flashes a wide smile that seems to be completely genuine, then keeps gushing over Lily's clothes, the beautiful weather, the apples, etc.

But it's Marco I have my eye on. He too eyes Lily's clothes, and the way he does it makes me clench my fist. I'm a guy; I know the difference between a curious glance and a leery appraisal. He's quick and artfully subtle, clearly well-practiced, but the way he looks at her is anything but neutral.

Marco puts his arm around Harmony and gives her shoulder a little squeeze. She instantly stops talking as he fixes a little smile on his face. "Get a good haul?" he asks.

I hold up the basket and nod. We fall into step with them as we head back to the barn.

"Lily says you're a model, is that right? Would I know any of your work?" Marco's question to me is, again, well-practiced. His tone is casual, but the undercurrent of challenge is there, no doubt.

"You might, if you shop high end. Or if you wear Max Weller underwear."

"I do both, actually," he says before I'm done speaking.

"Or if you read romance novels."

All three of us look at Lily. She blinks but then smirks. "Cal's been on the cover of practically every bestseller for the past three years."

"OMG, for real? Like what?" Harmony's eyes are huge.

She literally just said omg. I rattle off a few titles that pop into my head. Her jaw unhinges.

"I have, like, every one of those books in my house. Oh my *god*, I have to go look at them as soon as I get home! That's *you*?"

Marco clearly isn't enjoying this conversation. He drops his arm from her shoulders and eyes me again. "Lily said you were into art. I was going to ask if you've ever gone to an auction or own any—"

"Auction? Sure. I'm particular to Ansel Adams-style photography, the stark black and white aesthetic. But then again, art is everywhere, right? Cars are a special medium for me. I like the art deco Italian models from the post-war era."

He quirks a brow. The bloke is transparent as glass; he wants to pin me as a sham, and he can't. He has two choices: keep up the dick measuring contest, or let it go.

"We'll have to talk about cars sometime, then. I'm always curious about good investments."

"No shit." Only I hear Lily's breathed reply, but it's so icy that I jolt toward her.

"You alright, love?" I bend down and peck her cheek. Marco turns away and leads Harmony on toward the barn.

She shrugs. "Fine."

Well, that's a clear lie. I set my jaw and let her guide us back to the party, several paces behind the other couple.

On our walk, the sound of a car engine revving captures my attention. I turn around and see a Mini Cooper speed into the parking lot and slide into an open slot. A petite woman with curly black hair and thick-rimmed glasses, wearing what looks like a knit blanket as a shirt, pops out. She trots over in our direction, talking loudly on the phone.

Out of the corner of my eye, I see Lily perk up. She rushes over to the noisy, tiny lady. "Auntie Mayla!" she squeals.

The woman frowns with her phone still at her ear, but when she spots Lily, she beams. "Never mind, call me later with this nonsense. I just saw my favorite niece and I need to hug her."

"*Nakkong*!" She shoves the phone in the giant purse she's carrying in the crook of her elbow and holds her arms wide, pulling Lily into an embrace. It's a few seconds before they part. I hang back. This is a sweet moment, and I don't want to interrupt.

"I didn't know you were coming," Lily says, grinning wide.

"My mahjong game got canceled, so I thought I'd stop by and say hello. Your mom's going to be so mad." Her head falls back as she laughs, which makes me chuckle.

As she and Lily chat, I notice that she's got the same physical features as Lily's mom, minus the pinched expression. With her comfy style and loud laugh, she's a more relaxed version of uptight Marilyn. I like her instantly.

Lily turns and starts to introduce me, but before she can, Marylin marches over.

"*Manang* Mayla. What are you doing here?"

Even though her tone is pleasant, I can tell by her pursed lips and crossed arms she's not happy to see her. Mayla pulls her into a hug. Marilyn keeps her arms straight at her sides, almost like she's resisting the embrace. I bite my lip to stifle a laugh.

Marilyn pulls away and starts to grumble something about having to change the seating arrangement for dinner to accommodate Mayla's unexpected appearance, but Mayla waves a hand in the air.

"For god's sake, this isn't the royal wedding. It's dinner in a barn." She pats Marilyn on the arm and then walks toward said barn. A group of people waves at her. "Where's the hard cider?" Mayla hollers.

Lily turns to me. "That's my mom's older sister, Mayla. She's the exact opposite of her in every way. Fun-loving. Outspoken. Nonjudgmental. While Mom is all about status and image and high-end everything, Auntie Mayla lives happily and modestly so she can travel all over the world after she retired from working as a nurse practitioner. Promise I'll introduce you to her later," she says.

"Can't wait."

Dinner is a more formal affair. The barn has been lit with fairy lights, the gingham replaced by white linen tablecloths. We're served a plated dinner. Meanwhile, the side dish is Marilyn's ideas for Lily's outfit for the wedding.

I glance around and spot Marco staring in Lily's direction. She looks up, her cheeks flushing and her jaw clenching when she notices his eyes on her. He quickly looks away, pointing out something on Harmony's plate and stabbing it with his fork. I turn back to Lily and notice that she's slumped in her chair.

Whatever happened in that little moment with Marco just now and earlier in the orchard has sucked Lily back into that stiff shell of hers. She nods along to her mom's ramblings and picks at her food. When the meal is over and we're all being herded to the bonfire outside for hard cider and live music, I fall back and grasp her wrist.

"We'll join you in just a sec," I say with a gracious smile to her parents, and then lead Lily around the corner to an isolated side of the barn.

She twists out of my grasp. "What's up?"

"That's my question. Thought we were putting on a 'brilliant show'. You've gone silent on me."

She toys with her hair. "We are. It's going great. Everyone is buying us as a couple somehow."

"Somehow?" I cock my head. "What's that mean?"

She shrugs and looks away. "I just mean it's going good."

"That's not what you mean, and it's not what you're acting like. What's wrong?" I try to hook her chin to make her look at me, but she flinches away.

"Nothing."

I cross my arms. She fidgets with her hair again.

"Well, nothing. Nothing, just—come on, let's go see the fire and get out of here. Everyone's waiting."

"You're making excuses again."

"Yep, let's go."

I'm not about to restrain a woman in the dark behind a barn, so I let her lead us to the crowd and hand me a cider. We glare at each other, having a silent conversation that we simply don't know each other well enough to understand. She's not happy, and I'm not sure why.

Just then I hear a cackle in the distance, then the squeal of tires. I squint and see Mayla's Mini Cooper peel out of the parking lot.

Lily chuckles. The lightness and joy of that sound makes my chest ache. "I guess I'll have to introduce you to my aunt some other time," she says with a sad smile.

"Thank god she left," Marilyn mutters as she walks up to us. She gently grabs both of our arms. "Oh, but here we go!" She nods just outside of the flames, where three buggies wait. They're hitched to tractors with drivers sitting atop. The buggy is wooden, three-walled sides and an open back with a bed of hay and a blanket waiting ready. "You kids should go first. Harmony and Marco are already heading over. Take your cider and have fun!"

"We should head home, Mom," Lily tries, but Marilyn

rolls her eyes and shoos us toward the empty cart. "Sorry," she whispers to me as we go.

"We've talked about you not apologizing so much," I say lightly as I help her into the hay. I hop in and settle as the tractor rumbles to life and trundles us away from the barn. I've no idea where we're headed—through the orchard would be a logical guess—but it doesn't matter much. As soon as the bonfire fades, it's just us and the full moon and the wind in the trees.

Lily breaks the silence. "I didn't mean to get weird. I'm glad this façade is going well. It's almost hard to believe everyone is buying it so easily, I guess was my point. After the blowup with Marco, and over a year of being the single girl who ran off to be a teacher, I'm surprised that everyone would act like me dating someone like you is entirely plausible. And I'm super proud we're selling the sham, but that doesn't mean it's easy."

Her words knit my brows. "Someone like me? A—what did Nate say?—twenty-first century Fabio? Yeah, plausible is a bit of a stretch, but not the way I'm hearing you say it. You deserve the best, Professor Lily. I'm not him. I'm just a self-centered bloke who got lucky enough to make a career out of something I love. Don't put me on a pedestal. It's not warranted."

She rubs her eyes. "Shut up, you're fantastic and you know it."

I laugh. "Well, yeah, I know *I* think so, but that's a requirement for a job like mine. Self-doubt doesn't sell. But I'm also very damn sure that that attitude comes with a price. Superficial is my MO because I'm too busy working all the time to pay much mind to others. It's a bit lonely if I'm honest, but we all make sacrifices. Besides, I can't say it's not fun."

She's listening attentively now, sipping at her cider, eyes narrowed in thought. "Superficial?"

I nod.

"I guess that's why it's easy for you to fake this relationship."

I slide my gaze toward her, trying to decide if I hear the subtext I think I do. "I'm fucking awful with discerning tones, Lily. Hence why your rules are easy to follow. They're clear, no games or guessing. But I think I hear a hint of disappointment in your voice."

"No, no not at all, I just... I just... Really, really have a hard time following your rule about saying what I want," she finishes with a sigh. "Sorry. Again."

I shake my head. "Shush with all that. And anyway, you're wrong. Well, you're not, but. Superficiality is why I can fake this relationship, sure. But it's *you* who's making all the rest so damn easy."

"What do you mean? I make what easy?" Her voice has gone soft in the silence of the night.

"So far, I reckon 'everything' is a good summation. You make it easy to hold a single pose for half an hour in the classroom, easy for me to look like a respectable boyfriend to an amazing lass... and very, very fucking easy to get lost thinking about the way you kissed me on your sofa that night."

Slowly, she turns to look at me again. Her chest rises and falls with a labored breath. "I want... Calder, I want..."

We're leaning closer, and I'm not sure who's responsible. "Tell me and it's yours," I breathe against her lips.

"I don't care if it's a fake or not, but... Remember I said I didn't want you to push boundaries?"

"I remember."

"Push them, Calder. Please. That's what I want."

I release my held breath in a soft chuckle and thread my fingers into her hair to hold the back of her head. "With fucking pleasure."

Her lips open for me without hesitation this time, no moment of closed-lip action like at her flat. This time, her tongue finds mine in that killer tease right off. I groan when she licks and then nibbles on my bottom lip. Her fingers tangle in my hair, and she pulls me on top of her in the hay.

"Naughty," I chuckle against her mouth.

"Hush," she hisses, so I throw the blanket over us and run my hands from her face down her body. Her spine arches, another moan rumbling low in her throat. "*Calder*."

"Lily." I flick open the buttons on her top and kiss down her chest, burying my face in her cleavage. She shudders and arches again as I lick and bite the swell of each breast above her satin bra. "More?"

"More," she pants, fisting my hair and shoving my face against her body again. "More, more, please more."

"Shh, love, you can't be too loud. The driver will hear."

Lily freezes, and I laugh and put my lips to her ear. "Such a naughty, sweet thing. We can't have him knowing that I…" I snatch a kiss. "Can't," another kiss, "stop… kissing…"

My attempt to speak gives way to a long, languid exchange that has her lapping at my mouth and running her hands from my hair down my back and then up my chest. She squirms underneath me, and *Christ* am I about to lose my fucking mind. I'm aching, straining my pants, but this isn't about me.

"Lily. Tell me what you want," I murmur between kisses.

"More."

"Yes, dear, you said so. How much?"

Her heavy eyelids struggle to open. "Um... what... what can I ask for?"

"Your wish is my command. I already told you, but you better hurry." Even as I say it, we're turning in a wide arc, headed back to the party.

"Touch me."

Her words are so soft, they're barely audible. But she says it against my lips, and I feel it from my brain to my toes. It's exactly what I want to do in this quiet little cocoon of hay. Hearing her ask for it is too fucking hot.

I flip to my side and kiss her again, coasting my hand over her bra. I dip my head and bite gently at her nipple through the fabric. She shudders and claps a hand over her mouth as I attend to the other breast, chuckling to myself at her muffled whimpers. My thumb rubs a circle on her hip bone patiently until she spreads her legs further apart and lifts her hips off the hay.

"Please, Calder. We'll be back soon..."

"Don't worry, darling. You're not going to need long, and I do like watching you respond when I—" I bite her bra again. She whines and squirms impatiently.

"Alright, alright, since you asked so nicely." I hitch her skirt up and tease my fingers along the elastic of her underwear. Her thighs are soaked, her skin is hot, and I'm gritting my teeth not to plunge in too soon. "So wet, Professor."

She palms her eyes and groans, but I laugh.

"None of that. You feel fucking amazing, Lily. In fact, I think I have to confess."

"What?" her voice is ragged; her hips are twisting, seeking my touch.

I run my finger over her underwear, teasing her clit through the fabric. "I wish we weren't in this damn wagon. I'd give just about anything to taste you right now."

"*Cald*—"

"Shh," I chuckle as I hook her panties and slip one finger, then two, inside of her.

"Cover my mouth."

My brows shoot up, but she repeats the request so I oblige. Behind my hand, Lily whimpers and moans. Around my soaked fingers, her body pulses and quivers in the same rhythm.

I tease her as long as I can, backing off whenever she tightens up too much, but too soon the orange bonfire appears as a glimmer in the distance. Lily's eyes dart to the glow and then turn, panicked, to me.

"Shush. They're still far off. It's just us right now. Relax and let go for me, love."

I work her clit with my thumb and curve my fingers against her front wall. Lily's chest heaves, her eyes fluttering closed. As her body clenches around my hand, I free her mouth and kiss her, swallowing her moans of pleasure. They are what I'll use when I relieve my own tension later. They are sweet and unleashed and as fucking beautiful as she is.

Slowly, she goes slack. Her eyes flutter open, a dopey smile curving that gorgeous mouth. "Hmm."

"I'd say so." I grin and throw the blanket off us. I'm so damn hot I've got sweat slicking my hair. We both sit up and gulp fresh air as we smooth our hair, right our clothes—

And step out of that buggy smiling but completely composed. No one has a damn clue, and something about that knowledge—plus the way she won't stop holding my hand—will keep me smirking hard for the rest of the evening.

The flavor of her mouth and the way she pulsed around my fingers will keep me just plain hard for the rest of it, too.

14

LILY

With trembling legs, I hop off the buggy, still reeling from that dynamite orgasm Calder just gave me with his hands.

He lifts an eyebrow at me, then reels in the cheeky expression of his. "So I guess we should probably say hi to—"

"No." I cut him off. "We're leaving now."

For the briefest second, his eyebrows furrow. But then that smug smirk of his takes over his face. "Now?"

"Right. Fucking. Now."

Being with Calder has unleashed something inside of me that I haven't experienced before. Yeah, today was stuffy and uncomfortable and a bit of a drag... but he made it better. Just having him here to hold my hand, whisper cute comments in my ear, and make me laugh until my stomach hurt made the day a million times better than it would have been without him. And he held his own against the insufferably pretentious comments from my parents and their friends.

Not to mention he was a champ when Marco tried to trip him up by chatting art. He didn't fall for that dick-measuring contest, nor did he go all alpha when Marco's gaze lingered a little too long on me—all things that endear him to me even more.

But more than that, it's the effect that Calder is having on me. It's something I've never experienced with any other guy before. I'm actually saying what I want. I'm actually putting myself and my wants first.

And it's got me crazy turned on.

He grins wide at my growled command. "As you wish."

With Calder's speedy driving, we make it back to my place in just under an hour.

"I didn't think it was possible to make that drive that quickly," I joke as I unlock the door. I can feel my heart thudding in my ears.

As soon as I walk inside and he shuts the door behind him, he grabs me by the waist and turns me to face him. His gemstone eyes are dilated. "If you asked me to swim from here to Bermuda, I would," he growls. "You're that amazing, Lily."

"Bedroom. Now." I grab his hand in mine and lead him upstairs.

I barely have enough time to turn on the lamp on my nightstand before Calder's hands are on me once more. With a firm grip on my hips, he pulls me against the front of his body and captures my mouth in a kiss.

"Do you have any idea how hot it gets me when you tell me what you want?"

I run my hand down his chest and palm the steely bulge in his pants. A soft, strangled sound rips from his throat.

"Judging by this, I'd say very, very hot."

He grins before kissing me again. Then he walks me back to my bed. The backs of my knees hit the edge and I fall into a sitting position. As he stands over me, I yank at his belt.

"Take off your shirt for me," I command.

But he wraps his hands around my wrists, stilling me. "Do you know how long I've wanted to do this with you?"

The sincerity in his voice catches me off guard. It sends a jolt to the center of my chest. I shake my head, and the corner of his mouth quirks up.

"Pretty much ever since I walked into your classroom, Professor Lily."

His hands fall away, and he starts unbuttoning his shirt. The tips of my fingers tingle as I loosen his belt buckle and unzip his jeans. A second later, a cascade of cotton and denim falls to the ground. He's left in these snug gray boxer briefs that perfectly highlight the very blunt—and very generous—shape between his legs. I reach for the waistband, but he gently grabs my hand to stop me.

"Now it's my turn to say what I want," he says.

"Which is?"

He pulls me up to stand with him. "I want all your clothes on the floor too."

My cheeks catch fire as he peels away my blouse and skirt. Despite my boldness, I can't help the few pings of self-consciousness that plague me. I'm not ashamed of my body at all. But Calder is a living, breathing Greco Roman statue. I've seen him without his clothes on a million times ever since he started posing for my class, but he still takes my breath away. All those hard lines, that chiseled flesh...it leaves me breathless and my mouth watering every single time.

And then there's me. Cute for sure, but definitely not a perfect physical specimen like him.

Just then he hooks my chin with his hand to look at him. I didn't even realize I was staring at the ground.

"What's going on in that brilliant and beautiful head of yours?"

I let out a soft laugh and wrap my arms around my bare torso. Other than the cotton panties I'm wearing, I'm naked.

I swallow and look him in the eye. "It's just been a while since I've been naked with anyone. It feels weird."

He squints an eye. "Bad weird?"

"Exciting weird."

He smiles. "Say what you want, Lily."

His words center me; I feel emboldened once more. I run my hands through his hair, tugging just the slightest bit. He groans. And then I trace his lips with my index finger and press a kiss to his mouth.

"I want your mouth where your hand was during the hayride," I say, my lips hovering over his, just barely touching as I speak in the softest tone I can manage.

If eyes could catch fire, that's exactly what Calder's do at that moment. His mouth curves up in a grin. "With pleasure."

He pushes me gently to sit back down on the edge of the bed. Then with his palm on my belly, he presses me to lie down. I turn my head to the side so I can watch him as he kneels between my legs. He runs his palms up and down the tops of my thighs, which are twitchy with anticipation.

Everything inside me is buzzing. My heart, my muscles, my lungs, my brain.

I close my eyes as my breathing starts to speed up. His hot breath wets the inside of my thighs. Then there's the soft press of his lips on my skin. I force a slow breath in, then out. I'm going to hyperventilate if I don't get my panting under control.

But Calder... holy shit, Calder. How he can make me this hot, this quickly, without so much as a kiss is making my head spin.

Before I can think too much, he gently kisses the inside of my thigh.

"Do you know how bloody gorgeous you are?"

His accent is thick again, which makes my stomach flip. He's losing control too—because of me.

Instead of answering, I let out a whimpering noise.

He kisses the inside of my thigh once more. "Let me show you."

A slow, long lick kicks things off. My jaw drops. Holy motherfucking shit. How can one lick feel so damn good? But before I can think too hard about it, there's another. And another. And another.

I'm clutching at the bedsheets, gasping for air. It's only been seconds, and I'm barely hanging on. Pressure builds and builds from the center of my abdomen all the way up my chest and neck. Just when I think I'm about to burst, Calder changes his rhythm to something faster. It sends tingles to the tips of my toes and fingers.

"Holy..."

I go off right when he starts to switch to a suction move. A delicious, heavenly suction move. My eyes fly open and my jaw drops.

"Yes...that...right there...fuck!"

There's a grunting noise that follows my command. Once again that tell-tale pressure forms in the center of my chest, intensifying as the seconds pass. A second later, I'm hot all over.

Calder's tongue is pure pornographic magic.

My head goes fuzzy, and that's when I break. The pleasure peaks, like a tidal wave of bliss crashing through me. I'm thrashing and shouting, tugging my hands through Calder's hair. I lose track of seconds and minutes and time in general as my climax wrings me out.

I end like a limp ragdoll on the bed, my chest heaving, my lungs on fire. I barely have enough energy to lift my head. When I do, I blink and focus on Calder, who straightens up while wiping his mouth with the back of his hand.

My vision focuses and I can't help but relish that smug look on his face.

I flash what I'm certain is a crooked smile at him since I'm practically pleasure-drunk. Then I lean up, grab his arm, and pull him to lie down next to me.

"Good then?" he asks as he wraps his arms around me and nuzzles my neck.

I shake my head. "More than good. I don't know if there's a word that exists for how good that was."

I take a minute to let my breathing even out, then I pull out of his hold and sit up. "My turn."

He starts to say that I don't have to, but I slide off the bed and kneel on the ground anyway. For a second, I rest my hands on the tops of those meaty, muscular thighs. When I pull his boxer briefs down, he stops talking instantly. Instead he hisses, his brow furrowed in concentration.

I grip him at the base of his very generous shaft, then run my hand lightly up and down. He's so hard, but his skin is so soft too. It's the best feeling.

He groans. "Lily. Love. I won't last long if you keep doing that."

A wicked smile splits my face. And then I take him into my mouth. It's been a while since I've been able to do this, and I'm loving every second of it. Everything from Calder's grunts and moans and sharp inhales to the way his thighs tense under me drives me wild. I don't normally go gaga for this act, but with a guy like Calder—who's sweet and sexy and generous and set zero expectations when we started fooling around—I can definitely get on board.

It's a few minutes before his noises turn desperate. I can feel him shift on the bed. Then he runs a hand through my hair and makes a gentle fist.

"Lily, I'm close..."

I speed up until he tenses, grunts, and spills into my mouth. I lean away slowly, flashing what I hope is a cute and sexy smile.

He props himself up on his elbows, gazing at me with a bewildered expression. Then his gaze focuses and he grins. "Come here."

A second later, I'm tucked against his side, my face nuzzled against his chest. His heart thuds gently against my ear.

"Fucking hell."

I bite my lip as I quietly squeal to myself. In my head, I'm grateful that there are still a handful of condoms in the top drawer of my nightstand. Once he's had a bit to rest, I'm giddy to get started again.

For a few minutes, we say nothing. Calder runs a hand through my hair gently over and over. I close my eyes and sigh in satisfaction. And then I look up, hoping to gauge how he's feeling.

But when I lock eyes with him, I'm taken aback. He doesn't look blissed out on orgasm like before. Instead, there's a slight frown on his face, like he's worried about something.

"Is this fake anymore, Lily?"

His blunt question catches me off guard. I stammer for a second. "What? What do you mean?"

He opens his mouth, but then closes it. His eyes dart to some random spot on the wall. "Nothing. Sorry."

I grip him by the chin and turn him to look at me. "It's not nothing, Calder," I say gently.

His eyes finally connect with mine once more. "I guess I'm just wondering what we are to each other right now."

"Oh. I..." I search my brain for the right words, but there aren't any. Because the truth is I don't know what we are.

"The boundaries were pretty clear before," he says quietly. "Fake relationship. Fake boyfriend. Fake girlfriend."

"Right," I say softly, trying to figure out what he's getting at.

When he doesn't clarify, the air in the room shifts. I need to be honest; he's being honest with me.

"I'm not sure what we are," I say finally. "But that's okay with me because I like what we're doing. And as long as we both like it, I don't see why we can't keep going with this."

I expect him to nod along, but all I get is another frown that tells me he's thinking hard about something else. I'm scrambling to figure out what would be the right thing to say, but he starts speaking before I can say a word.

"Something was bothering you earlier tonight," he says. "That's why I wanted to talk behind the barn. What was it?"

"Oh. That." I'm thrown for a loop. Of all the things he could ask me in this moment, he goes with that? I answer him anyway. "It was... Marco."

His eyes widen the slightest bit. "Did he say something to you today?"

I swoon internally at the hard, protective tone his voice takes. I smile. "No. It was just... when the two of you were chatting about work, his comment about always being curious about good investments kind of set me off."

"Why?"

I take a moment to breathe. I start to turn away from him, but Calder holds me tight. "Please don't turn away. Talk to me."

"It just reminded me of our breakup and how he hurt me."

"How did he hurt you?"

Chatting about an ex with someone new in your bed just minutes after fooling around isn't what you're supposed to do. But mine and Calder's setup isn't standard by any means. I fight past my normal urge to hide and shrink. Instead, I tell myself to be bold—be honest.

"I gifted him several pieces of my artwork while we were going out," I say. "I thought that meant something to him. I honestly thought that he appreciated the heart and sentiment I put into those pieces. I was wrong."

I can feel his chest expand underneath me as he takes a breath.

"One day he told me he had a surprise," I say. "He sold all the artwork I made for him and put the money in an online savings account. He said he did it because he was worried my art teacher job didn't pay me enough. I needed a financial safety net."

Calder's jaw tightens.

"He meant well. I know he did. But it was heartbreaking to me. And it highlighted a major incompatibility that I can't believe I didn't realize until that moment. All he cared about was money, status, bullshit that I never cared about. And what I cared about meant nothing to him. Obviously."

My eyes water, so I squeeze them shut.

"Jesus," Calder rasps. He pulls me tighter against his

chest and presses his lips to my forehead. I instantly relax and my tears dry up.

"Bloody prick. I'm sorry, Lily."

"It's okay. Really. It was a long time ago."

He tilts my chin up to look at him. "That self-centered nob doesn't deserve you."

That tension in my muscles that always takes hold whenever I recall my breakup with Marco doesn't happen this time. Instead, I smile at him. "I know."

He chuckles, and I cuddle into him again. "Tell me something about yourself," I say while breathing in his heavenly scent.

"Mmm?"

"Something breakup related. It's only fair."

A soft laugh rumbles through him. Then there's a heavy sigh. "The first girl I ever loved left me for my best mate."

I jerk my head up to look at him. "What? Holy shit. That's..."

"Bloody heartbreaking." But then he shrugs. "I was a kid. We both were. Barely twenty. I thought she was the one. But I wasn't the one for her obviously."

I hug my arms around him tightly.

"I'm well past it. But sometimes when I think about how naive I was at that age, it still stings."

I lean up to kiss him. "I'm sorry that happened to you."

"I'm sorry for what you went through too."

Another kiss on my forehead makes my eyes flutter. It coincides perfectly with the flutter in my chest—in my heart.

"And I'm sorry that I have to punch Marco in the face the next time I see him," Calder says.

I giggle and shove his chest. "You will not."

I shift so that I'm the little spoon in our cuddle. I yawn as

Calder's arms snake around me. He nuzzles my hair and inhales.

"I can't make any promises, love."

I drift off with a smile on my face.

I open my eyes to sunlight streaming in through the window. When I roll over, I expect to feel Calder's warm body next to me, but there's nothing. Just a cold, empty space in the middle of my bed.

I look around and see that he's standing in the middle of the bedroom, buttoning up his shirt.

"Morning," he says, his mouth in a straight line. He quickly looks away.

"Morning." I sit up, careful to keep the sheet wrapped around me. The way Calder is avoiding my gaze lands like a kick to the shin.

"Headed somewhere?" I ask.

He nods, frowning at his phone. "Got a list of things to do today." He clears his throat.

I almost scoff. This is one awkward morning after. I would laugh out loud if it didn't hurt so much that Calder clearly can't get away from me fast enough.

I look away and roll my eyes at the window. "Okay then. Have a great day."

"Right. See you in class." He walks out of the bedroom without a glance in my direction. A few seconds later, I hear the front door close.

When it does, I tug both hands in my hair and groan, wondering what the hell happened between last night and this morning to make Calder run away from me like that.

15

CALDER

I woke up this morning with the scent of Lily's sweet fragrance in my nose and a stone in my stomach. Her peaceful slumber and the way my arms looked wrapped round her were all a little too perfect—a little too real. *"As long as we both like it, I don't see why we can't keep going."*

Right, Professor. Message received: keep it meaningless and breezy, as per protocol. I haven't been in a committed relationship with anyone since Carmen—*Why the fuck did you tell her about Carmen while we're at it?*—and it's worked just fine. It's let me focus on my career and, frankly, leave my options open whenever I please. No one to answer to, no one to think about or worry how she's doing. No one to tell me it's not working out, that I need to focus more on our relationship if I want to keep her happy, that she's been spending an awful lot of time studying with Liam and her girlfriends think it'd be best if...

Easier this way. Quite right. Let's just keep going then, Lily. This convenient coupling will last until we've both got what we want, so what's not to like?

"Cal! Jesus, your form is shit today. You want to blow out a knee?"

I jolt back to the moment. Dan shakes his head and hurries to spot the barbell I've got on my shoulders as I straighten out of a squat.

"Sorry," I mutter.

"Focus, bro. I'm here to help, but this is amateur stuff. You feel okay?" My trainer narrows his eyes, assessing me all over.

"Yeah, swear I do. Not a lot of sleep last night but feel fine otherwise."

He grumbles at that. "Hit the pool for twenty minutes, and try not to drown, alright?"

"Got it."

Rhythmically slicing through the water gives me just the thing to focus on. By the time I'm in the shower, last night has lost a lot of its luster in my mind. A fun hookup is never a bad thing, but it's not something to brood over afterward, either. Must've been the whole day together thing that made that one feel like it meant more. Just a trick of the moonlight, sure. That's it. She was a great date, and I'm happy if we do it again. No worries.

But then I check my phone.

Lily: *Hi. Sorry to bother you.*

Lily: *You left your belt here.*

Me: *Oh, thanks. I can get it from you Thursday if that's cool.*

Her next message comes half an hour later, once I'm already back at my place.

Lily: *k*

I groan and flip the phone facedown on the coffee table. "Can we not do the drama, please? A fake relationship shouldn't come with a ball and chain," I mutter at the phone.

But as I make a protein shake, I have to admit that the ball and chain are entirely self-made. Lily didn't ask for me to think on her today. She didn't ask for me to care about her, to want to punch that smarmy Marco in the teeth for disregarding her talent, to want to snuggle her and make her giggle just to take her mind off the kind-but-judgey brood that she grew up among. She didn't ask me to walk into her classroom and immediately start having foolish thoughts about how charming and gracious she was, and she certainly didn't encourage me to have the outrageous fantasy of her on my arm at a Sonce party. Yes, it's come true, but that's an arrangement to benefit us both. Whatever magic that first glimpse of her has captured in my head, she didn't request any of it.

Even last night. She asked for my hands, she asked for me to come inside, and she asked for me to go down on her. Done. Simple. Happy to.

So stop brooding on the lass, you jackass.

I reach for my phone, about to scroll through contacts until I can find someone to grab a drink with. A few hours of flirting will do me good.

But as I open my texts and see hers at the top, I know damn well that a few hours of flirting aren't what I'm going to do with my night. It'd be like having a 16-year-old single malt and then chasing it with a shot of well whisky. Nothing wrong with the standard pour at all, but you can't go trying to follow one with the other. And right now, Ms. Lily Maldonado is the flavor still very much on my tongue. Trying to substitute anyone else would be rude to the girl and useless for me.

"Fucking great," I groan. I crash to the sofa, debating porn or binge-watching *The Wire.*

Porn wins.

"Love serving thirty, you bastard," Nate calls across the net on Wednesday morning.

I smirk and shrug one shoulder as I anticipate his serve. Is it my fault I basically get paid to work out? The volley begins, and we find an easy rhythm.

"Good to have someone to play with at least." Nate likes to chat as we play. I've learned this after only two sets. "Eileen is allergic to exercise, and dad's got the bum knee."

"After Sonce launches, you'll be hiring a trainer to play against you whenever you please." I zing a backhand just over the net, too low for him to get to.

He laughs and curses as he slaps it back anyway. "They bloody well better let me win if I'm paying them. Your serve. What about Lily?" he continues as I walk to the line. "Does she play? Maybe Eileen would try a doubles match if she—"

Jesus, mate, when did you become such a chatty Cathy?

"Nah. She's all about yoga." I bounce the ball and roll my eyes. I have no idea if this is true, but you'd never know from my tone.

"Ah, right. All these Americans love that shit."

"They do indeed. Now, shut up and let me ace you."

As we play through a match, I promise Nate three times that Lily and I are counting the days to the next Sonce party, which is two weekends from now. Bless him, he's so keyed up about everything that he can barely focus on tennis, but I didn't come to play competitively. I came to see my friend—and keep up my responsible image. If I can't go to parties, post to Instagram, or take on the high-visibility jobs I used to, I might as well pour a little more of my soul into this goal.

The good news is that my agent, Stella, has finally gotten on board with my insistence to back off the playboy image.

She resisted a long time, saying that it was hard to change tracks in this business—as if I'm not acutely aware of this fact. After the women's reaction at the Sonce dinner party, I decided it was fine to keep the novel cover gigs as part of my new image. Everything else has to shift, though. After pulling some major strings and working her magic, Stella has come through with some new opportunities—maybe. Hopefully.

The first one is the next day. Thursday morning I'm up before dawn and headed to a casting call at Oak & Thistle's headquarters, sporting the same shirt I'd worn to apple pick. Hopefully the fact that they gifted me this shirt after I modeled their new line of boxer-briefs last year will sell them on the notion that, yes, I would make a fantastic editorial model as well.

There's no flexing abs or bringing my lucky green robe this time. I'm not a pool boy or an athlete or anything but Calder Ross. I go into the meeting buttoned-up, sporting dress jeans and designer hiking boots that aren't meant to see a trail. With my tartan print and accent, I'm the picture of fall casual. I practically reek of apple cider spiked with whisky.

Oak & Thistle wants to know why I'd want to be a face in their catalogue when I can be the billboard for their underwear. I shrug and hold the line I've got going with Sonce: I'm changing my image, settling down, madly in love, and wanting it to show in my work.

They buy it, the whole bloody package.

They buy it so grandly that they keep me there for some test shots until I'm running half an hour late for Lily's class. As soon as I can breezily shake hands and promise to sign the contracts once they send them to Stella, I sprint out of the building and into my car.

A barked command to the Bluetooth fills the speakers with a phone ringtone until—

"Hello?"

"Hey, Prof-uh, hey it's me." I stumble on my words. For some reason, using her nickname makes my stomach clench, so I skirt it. "I'm running late."

She laughs softly. "You said that on the first day, and you were only a few minutes behind me."

I wince. "Aye, but this is a bit different. I may miss half the class."

A brief silence, and then, "Oh. Okay. Thanks for the warning."

"I'll get there fast as I can," I vow.

"Okay."

When I run into the classroom, I'm only 20 minutes late. The students are all working on a still life of an apple which is sat on the dais. They all cheer when I appear, but Lily doesn't smile.

"Sorry, guys, I'm the worst."

They blow that off, but Lily says, "We're already working on this, so if you're busy today—"

"Nonsense. Thrilled to add to the task. But let's improvise, shall we?"

I unbutton my shirt and hand it to her. Her cheeks flush when she recognizes the plaid, but she turns quickly and sets it on her desk while I go to the pedestal, kneel, and sink my teeth into the apple.

Just as quickly, I yank the thing out of my mouth and laugh. "Hell, this is going to be a challenge. I promise to be as still as I can, just be sure to catch any drool that runs down my chin, right?"

The class laughs before going quiet again. Papers rip and flutter to the floor as they begin their new images.

Thank *god* this is only 20 minutes. By the end of it, my knees ache, drool and apple juice drizzle down my neck, and I'm considering it more than fair penance paid for running late. The students applaud and thank me even more energetically today while I grab a paper towel and clean up.

Lily hasn't said much, but the longer the quiet held the more I felt good about that. We *do* need to be professional here. This place has rules, and if I'm following hers about how we're meant to 'keep going' as we like, then we should follow these, too.

I hustle to fetch my shirt with long strides so I can beat her to the desk. She startles as I begin to button up, so I flash a casual smile. "So sorry again. Got caught up this morning, you know how it goes."

A shadow crosses her face, but she blinks rapidly and shrugs. Her attention goes to her backpack. A second later, she proffers my belt and says, "I don't, but whatever. If you're going to struggle to finish the term—"

"Not at all." My tone softens but is completely firm. I take the belt. "I love doing this and I swear it's a priority. This morning was a fluke is all. Didn't expect to be so tied up."

"Ropes or leather cuffs?" Her brow quirks sarcastically, but her voice doesn't sell the joke.

I laugh and shake my head. "Nope, plaid and tweeds, actually. Oak and Thistle are hiring me as a fashion model."

The light I'm used to seeing in her eyes flickers. Her lips curve slightly. "That's great, Calder. Why didn't you just tell me?"

"Why would I?"

Shit.

Everything about her sort of... deflates. Her expression

shutters even though she is clearly trying to hide it. "I-I don't know, just... you said you were running late, but—I just meant..."

"No, sorry, that came out shit. I only meant I didn't know I got the job till this morning and it didn't really matter, now did it? I was late. Excuses don't change it, so I didn't see a need to bother."

She bites her lip and nods. "I see your point."

She doesn't, because there is no way in hell I'm telling her flat out that if we're a fake relationship I've got to fight the impulse to share things with her. There's no way it sounds rational or cool or breezy to tell her how bloody excited I am about this opportunity, how well it could pair with Sonce even if it is a small gig to start. My jobs, my life, are not necessary to share with her or anyone, really.

And that. Fucking. Sucks.

Sometimes.

I flash another easy smile. "Quite right. Well, I best be off. Whisky next weekend, no events this coming one though, right?" Nod. "Expect you'll be glad for a bit of time to catch up with yourself. Unless you wanted me to come over?"

It sounds cheap, but hey. A bit of fun is never a bad idea, right?

"No, thank you. I'll see you next Thursday, I guess."

I swallow hard to keep the grin going. "Enjoy yourself, love. See you soon."

With every step out the door, I want to turn around and jog back to that desk, sit on it, and pull her between my legs to kiss her until all the chatter in my head shut the fuck up, just like it did in her bed last weekend.

But I don't. I go with it, just like I said I fucking would.

16

LILY

I release my foot from the pedal of the potter's wheel in my garage and focus on the clay pot I'm shaping. That's as good as it's gonna get.

I sigh, then grab a wire and press gently on the pedal once more so that the wet clay spins slowly. Holding the wire taut, I drag it smoothly through the base of the pot, separating it from the wheel. Then I set it aside so it can dry.

I hop up from my stool and wash up in the garage sink, my brain still a distracted mess. There's no use in trying to pretend anymore. I've done that for the past few days. I need to at least acknowledge the reason for my state of mind: Calder.

Once I'm mostly clean, I walk back into the house and into the kitchen and pour myself a glass of wine.

All this week, ever since Calder ran screaming from my apartment the morning after we fooled around, he's all I've been able to think about. The sad part is that I'm clearly not on his mind. That was more than obvious given the way that he barely looked at me after last week's class.

I guzzle the wine, my cheeks heating with embarrassment as I recall how hopeful I was when I saw him that day in class. I figured after I spent the last handful of days giving him space and not texting him, we'd at least go back to our fun and casual norm in the classroom. But that didn't happen.

I blink and recall how he waltzed in late and his entirely too casual attitude.

I let out a breath, wishing that pain at the center of my chest would dissipate. I have no right to feel this hurt. Calder and I aren't anything to each other. In fact, we're less than nothing. Our setup is totally fake, and I shouldn't be this upset by something that wasn't even real.

Those orgasms he gave you sure as hell felt real.

I roll my eyes at my internal commentary as I pour myself another glass. My phone buzzes on the counter. It's Morgan.

I smile when I hear her let out a relieved sigh on the other end of the line after she says hello.

"God, I miss you," she says.

"I miss you too. How are you holding up?"

"Good overall. It's tough being a caregiver, but I wouldn't want anyone else taking care of my grandma, you know?"

"Of course. Is she handling physical therapy okay?"

"So far so good, thankfully. A hip and knee replacement are hell to recover from at her age, but she's giving it all she's got. I want to have her energy and stamina when I'm eighty-two years old."

I chuckle. "God, it feels good to laugh."

"What's up? Everything okay?"

"Not really." I hesitate before saying more. Morgan knows nothing of what I've been up to with Calder. She's been so busy with caring for her grandma that I didn't want to bog her down with my petty problems.

"Lily, what's wrong?"

"It's so ridiculous."

"You always say that whenever something is bothering you, and it never is," she says. "Besides, I'm your friend. You're supposed to whine to me about whatever's happening in your life, big and small."

I take a breath. "Okay. So you know Calder?"

"Yeah..."

"We've sort of had a thing going."

She gasps and squeals. I shush her, then give her a rundown of everything that's happened so far, from our agreement to fake date for the wedding and his work events to what happened at apple picking to ending up in bed together—and to the cold shoulder he's been giving me since then.

"Damn. What a jerk."

"He honestly didn't seem like the type," I say, annoyed at how hurt I sound.

"They never do," Morgan says dismissively. "I mean, I only know him casually through work. It's not like we're even friends. But he always seemed like a genuine guy. God, I can't believe he would use you like that."

"We were using each other, Morgan."

"Yeah, but you weren't a dick to him. You communicated with him and you didn't ice him out, like what he did to you. What a coward."

I sigh and rub my forehead. "I just...this was probably one of the least intelligent things I've ever done, getting involved with someone I work with. Now I'm going to have to see him during class and all the work and wedding events we have lined up."

"Lily, come on. Don't tell me you're going to go through all that and not even confront him about how he's acting."

I bite my tongue to keep from admitting that yes, that's exactly what I was planning to do.

"You owe it to yourself to tell him exactly how you feel—how *he* made you feel. Honestly, I wouldn't even want to go to whatever work crap he has lined up when he's acted like you don't even exist."

"I can't just leave him hanging, Morgan. I promised him I would go."

"And he promised to be a decent human being to you, but he didn't hold up his end of the bargain, did he?"

I let out a weak laugh. "He never promised that."

"He didn't need to. Being a quality person is an unspoken expectation."

There's a quiet moment before Morgan starts up again.

"Promise me that you will stand up for yourself, Lily. Promise me that you'll tell him off for being a jerk to you."

Confrontation is my least favorite thing in the world. It's why I've almost always gone along with what my parents expected of me my whole life. But even a pushover like me has limits. That's why I dropped out of law school. That's why I broke up with Marco. And that's why I'm definitely confronting Calder the next time I see him.

"I promise," I say, the conviction clear in my voice.

"That's my girl," Morgan says, the smile in her voice just as evident.

When we hang up, I down the rest of my wine, and then take a hot shower. When I check my phone before bed, my eyes go wide. A text from Calder.

Calder: *Hey. Just a reminder that the Sonce people invited us to that whisky tasting this weekend. Pick you up at six?*

I clench my jaw at how casual his tone is. Like he's completely forgotten that he's barely spoken to me ever since sharing my bed.

But I made a promise to him. I'll attend the whisky tasting. But not before I set him straight. I quickly text my reply.

Me: *I'll be ready.*

"You look really pretty," Calder says from the driver's seat of his car while staring straight ahead at the road.

"Thanks." I tug at the hem of the little black dress I opted to wear tonight, then readjust the belt of my trench coat. "You look nice too."

Nice is an understatement. In that light blue dress shirt unbuttoned at the top, sans tie, and that charcoal gray suit, Calder looks downright delicious. But that's not the point. I mimic his stance of staring straight ahead at the road and take a slow, silent breath. No sense putting it off.

I twist my head to him. "We should talk about—"

My phone ringing cuts me off. When I see it's Auntie Mayla calling, I answer it.

"Hi, Auntie Mayla. How are you?"

"Good, *nakkong*. How are you?"

"Fine, just headed to dinner."

"Oh, sorry to interrupt."

"I always have time for you," I say with a smile.

"I just wanted to apologize for leaving the orchard without saying good-bye to you. Your mom and I got into a bit of a tiff, and I had to get out of there before I said anything I'd regret."

I let out a chuckle. "It's really fine. Mom was being ridiculous with all her passive-aggressive comments to you."

She lets out a boom of a laugh. "I swear, Lily, you and I are soul mates. How did you ever come from your mom?"

Still smiling, I shake my head, but then she quickly

scolds herself. "I shouldn't say that. *Ading* Marilyn and I may be as different as night and day, but we're still sisters. And she's still your mom. I'm sorry."

I soften at the regret in her tone. "It's okay, Auntie. You two are sisters, and that's a complicated bond."

"You're telling me."

"But I know you love her. And just because you're related to someone doesn't mean that you're going to automatically get along. But you always make things right with each other when you fight. That's what matters."

"You're so wise." She clears her throat. "Now that that's settled, tell me: how are things going with that very handsome boy of yours? I'm cursing myself for rushing off before I could meet him properly."

"Oh um..." I glance off to my side and observe Calder as he concentrates on the road. There's a far-off look in his eyes, like his brain is somewhere else other than this car. I wonder if he even realizes I'm on the phone.

"They're uh..."

"I see," she says in her trademark knowing tone. "Well, I'm no relationship expert. My two divorces show that pretty clearly."

I let out a sympathetic laugh.

"But whatever is going on between you two, I hope you work it out. From what I could see, you seemed to be pretty smitten with each other."

"We were. At least I was."

"Don't let him take you for granted, *anak*. I don't care how handsome or charming he is. You're a catch. He'd be lucky to call you his."

With that, she says good-bye and we hang up. Calder pulls into the driveway of yet another opulent home.

"How's your aunt?" he asks.

I turn to him, but he's still gazing straight ahead, even though we're parked now. "Fine."

When he climbs out of the car and walks over to my door and opens it, I'm crestfallen. I guess there's no time for us to talk, which means we're due for a very uncomfortable evening of pretending.

He offers me his arm and leads me to the front door. But then something inside of me takes hold. I stop walking and tug him to a halt.

He turns to me, frowning. "Everything alright?"

"Nope."

Then I tug him by the arm to the far side of the building where hopefully no one can see us or hear us. With my hand on his chest, I push him up against the wall.

Judging by the lift of his brow, he's shocked at what I've done. But I don't care.

"What the hell has been up with you?" I ask.

"Lily, what are you—"

"Don't pretend like you don't know."

I step forward, eliminating the space between us, and huff out a breath. The crisp fall air turns it to mist, which fades into the air.

"I told you what I wanted, Calder. That night after the hayride, I did exactly what you've been asking me to do this whole time we've known each other. And this is how you treat me?"

I shake my head and glance away for a second, trying to keep my composure. My heart is beating so fast at the frustration and anger that's been building up within me for the past two weeks.

"Look, I didn't expect you to go all lovey-dovey on me, but the way that you left the morning after we were together stung," I say. "It was like you couldn't get out of there fast enough. And then you ignored me. You don't even call or text. And then we had the most awkward conversation we've ever had after class last Thursday."

He starts to speak, but I reach up and cover his mouth with my hand. Instantly I'm jolted back to the moment during the hayride when Calder had me on my back, his hand between my legs playing me like guitar, his other hand pressed over my mouth, muffling my sounds of pleasure.

Tingles shoot across my body at just the memory. I swallow and drop my hand back to my side.

"I'm not a fucking doormat, Calder. You don't get to just ignore me and then use me whenever it's convenient for you. I deserve to be treated better than that."

Despite the low tone of my voice to keep anyone from overhearing us, there's no denying my conviction. I stare at him, refusing to blink. "And if that's all that you're willing to give me, then I sure as hell deserve better than you."

17

CALDER

My eyes are about to fall out. My jaw is clenched against a flood of angry replies. But my heart is pounding because *holy fuck* is pissed-off Lily hot.

Fury flashes in her dark eyes. That pursed-lip look that usually means she's trying not to laugh is sour now, and the baser parts of me want to kiss her mouth until it's soft and yielding to mine.

But I'm a bit more evolved than all that.

I narrow my eyes and cross my arms, careful to unclench my jaw just enough. Leaning down so we're nearly nose-to-nose, I grit out, "You deserve to have exactly what you want, *Professor*, and if you've gone ahead and decided you're too good for someone like me, well. You won't be the first one to think so, nor the last I'd bet. But let's get clear about one thing: I wasn't the one doing the using."

An angry growl gurgles in her throat. "You asshole, are you seriously trying to shame me for doing exactly what you told me to? Do you think I'm in the habit of dragging guys back to my place and telling them to go down on me?"

Her cheeks flush deeper, maybe with rage, but I'm very

sure that hearing that mini recap of our night is the thing that's got heat creeping up my neck. Still, I hold my ground.

"Watch the name-calling, love. It's a slippery slope into saying things you regret. And, not in the least. It was one of the hottest fucking things I've ever seen, the way you said exactly what you wanted all bloody night." My voice gets raspier with every word. Just the memory of bold Lily telling me what to do to her...

I clear my throat and continue. "But you set the rules to keep this a good time as long as it pleases us, and so I honored that just as I did every other one of your wishes. And now you're calling me an asshole."

Her breath tickles my cheek, but she's silent for several long moments while we stare each other down. Finally, she mutters, "I didn't say anything about ignoring me."

"And I haven't. I offered to come over last weekend. You said no."

She stamps her foot, her brows pinched again. "Does that sound anything like me? 'Yeah, babe, how's 9 pm sound?' Please, Calder. You've met me. In what universe does that track with who I am?"

My lips curve despite attempts to keep a neutral expression. "Lily on the hayride would've said something of the sort, and not just the time to show up. Hayride Lily would've told me what color underwear to have on and likely what props to bring, too."

She yelps and pushes my shoulder. "Oh, stop that! You're teasing me, and you're the one who told me to say what I..." She palms her eyes and takes a deep breath. "That's my point. I thought we were having fun, but since that night things have been different. And don't pretend like they haven't."

Her sad frustration softens me. "No, I'll not pretend

that."

She lowers her hand and stares up at me again. "Thank you. So, what the hell happened?"

"You named the rules. 'As long as we like it, we keep going.' I've never been in a fake relationship, but I've certainly had that kind of setup before. I know those rules: give her her space and look after yourself."

That frown deepens. "That wasn't what I meant."

My heart thuds a different rhythm as I cock my head. I refuse to label it as hope. "Then what did you mean?"

"Just that, I don't know. The boundaries I'd set had, ha, kind of been lost to the wind, and I didn't really want to try and make up new ones. Making rules hadn't worked so far with you. You just kept coming in and... and... and making me break them."

"*Making* you?"

"Inspiring me to, I guess," she grumbles. We trade a look that melts into a guilty smile on her part and a chuckle on mine. "Shut up, this whole thing has been crazy for me."

"You think this is the norm in my world?"

She shrugs. "I really don't know. I guess partly because we don't know what the hell this is."

I know it's a huge mistake to say the next words that fall from my mouth, but I can't help it. "Exactly my point. I don't either. That's not the way I handle relationships. But," I reach out and caress her cheek, "I cannae stop thinking on ye, lass."

Letting the accent slip out was the right move. The last of her ire falls away, and Lily steps closer to me, her palms resting on my chest. She breathes a laugh. "Damn, that accent is kryptonite."

I hold her hips to bring her closer. "That was my strategy."

She giggles. "Jerk. You play dirty."

"Professor Lily, you have *no* idea how dirty I'd be with you," I murmur before my lips find hers.

Before I let myself get swept away, I pull back and meet her gaze. "I'm sorry I hurt you. It wasn't my intention at all. I just… I don't know what we're doing here, and I'll not lie: it unnerves the hell out of me."

She lays her hand on the back of my head to bring me closer. "This is what we're doing. One more kiss, then this party. After that, we'll figure out the next step together. Okay?"

"Your wish is my command."

"That's what I like to hear."

When we disentangle moments later, I'm surging with more confidence than I've felt since I had my face buried between her legs two weeks ago. I straighten my collar while she swipes on a new layer of lipstick and then, with her arm threaded through mine, we stroll to the front door.

"By the way," Lily mutters just before the door opens, "I don't drink whisky, but I'm good at faking it."

I just laugh.

The first hour or so is finger foods and chat. Lily and I are becoming pros at this part. We float around the room together, saying hello to whoever we meet. *God*, parties are different with a date on my arm. I flash back to the first Sonce event, the one I'd gone to solo, the one where my fake girlfriend was only a vague idea. Not flirting with the single women had taken a lot of effort. It's my MO at parties, and it's gotten my foot in the door for a good lot of business connections in the past.

But with Lily beside me, I don't think about circulating or making sure to dole out attention equally. With Lily beside me in that smoldering hot black dress, I can barely *see* any other women in the room.

The first chance I get, I bend to her ear and let her know it. "You're stunning tonight, my dear."

She leans into me as I whisper, a smile lighting up her face. "Stop that," she says, but the look in her eyes says something quite different.

I dust a kiss on her lips and straighten up—just in time to catch eyes with Nate and one of the marketing execs. They both give me a smile and a nod, then turn away to speak to someone else. Lily and I trade a look of silent agreement that that was a good sign.

Small tables are set up around the great room, and a while later we're invited to find our designated one. *Calder Ross & Lily Maldonado* are scrawled on a placard on a two-top in the corner. Lily picks up the cardstock and purses her lips at me.

"So fancy," she whispers.

"Keep it as a souvenir."

"You read my mind." She drops it in her purse and slides into the chair I pull out for her.

Two lines of Glencairn glasses sit on the table, filled with whiskies of varying color. Lily's brows furrow as she gazes at her four pours, but I take her hand and squeeze. "This is where I teach you about whisky."

"I told you, I don't like it."

"Only because you don't know how to drink it."

"I do though. With sour mix."

I recoil, hand on my heart. "Shut that yankee mouth right now," I hiss, getting her giggling. "And open your mind. Let me show you what you're missing."

"If I hate it, do I have to finish it?"

"Not at all."

"Fine. Teach me."

I gesture to the glass on the far left. "We start here. Look." The descriptions are printed on a menu, so I show her the first pour's profile. "If you swirl it in the glass, you can watch it run back down. Those are the legs. Now, take a tiny sip but don't swallow. Just kind of chew it, let the taste coat your mouth."

She obliges, the line of concentration between her brows utterly adorable.

"Now, swallow. It'll burn—the first sip of the day always does. But it won't after that."

She cringes as she swallows but then says, "Caramel and vanilla. That's what I tasted."

"Brilliant. Moving on."

We work through the next two slowly. With each sip, Lily looks more practiced. She decides she likes the second one best. But when we get to the last glass, she lifts it to her nose and immediately slams it back down on the table.

"Oh god. It's one of those that smells like a fireplace. No. No, I'm drawing a line."

"Take it easy. It's the peat. Peat comes from the bogs; they toast the grain over a peat fire to make it so smoky."

"Hmm, interesting. I didn't know that. I'm still not drinking it."

I laugh again. "Give me a chance. Open your hand."

She does, so I take a dropper from the vial of water and pull a little of the whisky into it. I squeeze a single drop on her open palm. "Close your eyes and taste it from your hand. Tell me what it makes you think of."

With her eyes closed, Lily obliges. Again, that furrowed

brow as she says, “When I was a little girl, my mom would make banana s'mores."

I squint at her. "What on earth are banana s'mores?"

Lily flashes that flustered smile that makes my dick throb. "You've heard of regular s'mores, right?"

I nod.

"Banana s'mores are when you leave a banana in its peel but cut it lengthwise. Then you stuff it with chocolate chips, mini marshmallows, and graham cracker bits. You wrap it in foil and set it on an open fire for a couple of minutes."

Her eyes sparkle as she speaks. I don't think she's ever talked about her mom with such fondness, such joy. She looks so pure and happy in this moment. This time it's my heart that's throbbing. “Sounds messy,” I say.

“Incredibly so, yeah. But so much fun, too. Anyway, we would sit outside on summer nights and eat them around a bonfire.” She sniffs her palm and frowns. “I don’t know why I just thought of that. It didn’t taste like this at all, but that’s what I thought of.”

I nod. “That’s the idea. Now, have a sip from the glass. Tell me what you think.”

She sips, lips puckering. “I-hmm. I think it’s not nearly as awful as I imagined. But I don’t really want to drink more of it.”

“Fair enough. Finish your favorite, if you like.”

And so we sit there and talk about whisky while the waiters offer us another pour of our choice. By the time her glass is empty, Lily’s eyes are bright. Her cheeks are flushed. I’m certain I’m the same, given how warm my face is. More than that, I can’t stop smiling.

“Okay, so I guess I drink whisky now,” she says as we finish up. “Sonce whisky, at least. Hey, speaking of that, what does Sonce even mean? I thought at first it was supposed to be sconce, but then wondered why you'd name a whisky after a wall fixture."

She claps her hand over her mouth as I bark a laugh, which has to be turned into a fake coughing fit to avoid drawing attention. I chuckle into my fist for another long moment before I'm able to say, "Ah, good point, although I'm sure with enough of the 'water of life' in you, you could come up with a good reason to use a wall fixture as the name of a drink. But, no. Sonce is derived from Gaelic. It's a catch-all for good luck, good health, prosperity to ye, all that."

"That's definitely more clever than sconce."

"Indeed."

Lily studies the now-empty glass again. "So now I drink Sonce whisky. Who knew?"

"I could tell you had it in you. Keep talking like that and they'll bypass me and make your beautiful face their icon."

She blushes. "Yeah, right."

I reach across the table and lace my fingers in hers. "Don't play the 'you-don't-know-you're-beautiful' game."

"*You're* the model. I'm just me."

"I am the model, which means I know beauty when I see it. Objectively, darling, you're a stunner."

She bites her lips, then blurts, "Harmony used to tease me in elementary school about how I looked. I know we were just kids, but she... well. Never mind, except to say I always just think I make the best of what I have. But beautiful?" She shrugs to finish the thought.

My eyes narrow. "Harmony? As in the future wife of what's-his-name? She seemed to be working hard to be kind to you. I thought—"

Lily waves a hand. "Yeah, I know. I don't get it, but hey. We all grew up, I guess. It's fine."

"Sound a wee bit more like you're fibbing, and your nose will start to grow." I huff out a breath and drain my whisky. "Fuck it, and fuck whatever she told you. I want to hear you say you're beautiful."

"*You're* beautiful." Lily's eyes go wide as she claps a hand over her mouth. "Damn whisky," she mumbles.

I roll my eyes and shake my head. "Try again. You're beautiful. Say it."

"You're beautiful." This time, she laughs and reaches for the half-full first pour.

I swipe it from her in time. "No, Professor. Don't be daft —and don't hide behind the liquor. It *is* a bit of truth serum, maybe, so I'll take the compliment, but that doesn't change our focus."

"Ugh, I hate moments like this, when guys try to be cute and pay compliments. Fine. I'm beautiful. Happy?"

Her eye-rolls and petulant tone make me smirk, but I shake my head, too. "Not on this point, but we'll get there."

She eyes the whisky. "I really did like this. I'm full of surprises these days, aren't I?"

"It seems so."

"No, it is so. Since when do I drink straight whisky and tell hot guys to—shh, damn, people are around, Lily. Watch your tongue, young lady." She claps a hand over her mouth, but her eyes are still smiling.

I cock a brow and lean closer. "Once we leave, I'd love to hear the end of that thought."

Her eyes glow a little brighter. "Okay. Hmm, but in the meantime, I was thinking that I wish I could do something like this with you. Introduce you to something I'm good at. Oh, like art!"

Her glazed-over eyes shine bright. I'm godawful at even drawing stick figures, so I know without a doubt I'd be a terrible student, even with a brilliant teacher like Lily. But I'll say anything to keep that glorious smile on her beautiful face.

"Sounds like a fair trade to me. Maybe next weekend?"

"If you're good, maybe."

"I'd love to know what being good means in that brain of yours, Lily."

She looks down, then up again. Her pupils are dilated. "When you flirt with me, Calder, I—"

"Shh. People." I nod as the waiter heads our way to clear the table.

"People," she whispers. "Let's get out of here."

We say a quick goodnight. In the car, I lift Lily's knuckles to my lips. She watches as I dust another kiss on her hand.

"Professor Lily, it is not the whisky talking when I say that I want you to come home with me tonight."

Before she can do more than open her mouth, a rap on my window makes us both jump. Nate is grinning down at us.

"After-party on the beach. You all interested?"

"Of course."

I turn to Lily, who's just spoken for us, and then look back at Nate to say, "Well then, I suppose that's a yes. We'll follow you."

He disappears, and Lily shrugs. "I want to go to your place, but this is a good chance to be seen."

"Must you be so right so often?" I sigh, and she laughs.

We drive to the beach and park. I take one glance at Lily in that sleeveless black dress and jog around to my trunk to fetch the blanket I keep there. Lily rubs it between her fingers when I open her door, humming appreciatively.

"Scottish wool, love. We do this right—along with, you know, everything else."

She laughs and takes my hand. "Do you miss it?"

"What?" I ask as I lead her to the dark path out to the beach.

Her hand clamps tight on mine in the darkness. "Scotland."

"Nah. Well, it's home, if you know what I mean. But I'm not sorry I left. I knew what I wanted to do, and I'm doing it. No sense in homesickness if that's the case, eh?"

"Makes sense. I—shit!" She stumbles on a loose plank and lurches forward, but I pull on her hand and have my arms around her in a heartbeat.

Lily's shoulder lands on my chest as I steady her and turn her to face me. She's gripping my arms tight, and I don't give her a chance to even look up at me before bending to capture her lips with mine. Her tension disappears, her body melts into me, and I'm rocked by this insane need to touch her.

'As long as we both like it'... I don't know what in the bloody hell you want from me, Lily, but I want to be it to you.

The thought opens my eyes even while I continue to kiss her. Why is she so compelling? What is it about this woman that's had me operating from a whole different set of rules since day one? She needs a fake boyfriend; I need a clean image to get this gig. Why can't that be enough?

I have no idea, but I'm beyond sure it isn't.

"Calder," she murmurs. Her fingers tangle in my hair, and I pull her tighter.

In the distance, an orange blaze drags us both out of the moment. Cheering follows, and she and I pull apart and catch our breath as we gaze at the growing bonfire.

"Right. People," she mutters, and I chuckle.

We walk gingerly toward the party and are greeted by Eileen with beers for both of us. I help Lily settle on a wooden bench and wrap us in the blanket. She snuggles against me, but her hand slides to my inner thigh.

"Watch it, Professor," I hiss in her ear.

She squeezes, and I have to fight off a moan. "But I want to."

Fuck. "Then you shouldn't have brought us here."

Her musical laugh has the dual effect of arousing me further *and* making me laugh. "I regret my choices. But come on, this is awesome, right?"

I kiss the top of her head and breathe deeply the sweet scent of her shampoo. "Darling, I daresay every moment spent with you is awesome."

"Oh, hush. The bachelorette party wasn't awesome."

"Ah, but if not for that hot pink dress and the call for 'shots, shots, shots,' we might not be here right now."

"True. Hmm. I have a higher opinion of that pink dress suddenly."

"You're a fool. That pink dress is a godsend."

She laughs and smacks my leg.

That's the night. The conversation fluctuates between the whole group, led primarily by Nate's and my stories from our teen years which entertain everyone, and one-on-one chats between all the couples.

I learn about Lily's childhood. I learn about art school. We talk about art, museums, favorite pieces. I learn her favorite color. I learn about her childhood cat's name. She laughs herself silly as I recount the first time I was well and truly drunk. She laughs even harder as Nate and I trade insults, our accents stronger and stronger until half the group has no idea what in the hell we're saying. And when I translate the back-and-forth, my girl giggles until she's got her face buried in my shoulder, helpless with mirth as I hug her close and admit to myself that there has never been a lass I liked nearly as much as her.

It's not a night of moans and sweat and tangled sheets. But it is one I'll never forget.

18

LILY

I hazard another glance at Calder as he sits on the floor in the middle of the classroom. His left leg is bent up and his left elbow rests on his knee. His right leg rests flat on the ground, along with his right hand. The sound of charcoal dragging slowly across sheets of paper is the only sound that fills this space. Just then he darts his eyes to me, and his mouth twitches up.

My face heats instantly as I bite my lip to keep from grinning. I quickly force myself to look away at a random sheet of paper on my desk. Almost busted.

Because if anyone saw that goofy grin aching to break free on my face, they'd know something's up between us.

Ever since the whisky tasting and the beach bonfire after-party with Calder this weekend, I've been smiling nonstop.

As I continue to stare at the piece of paper, my mind floats back to my favorite parts of that night: how he taught me to properly drink whisky, how he and I cuddled together on the beach, me kneading his thick, muscled thigh to the point of him having to bite back a groan, how he made me laugh until my sides ached… how I kissed him until we were breathless…

It was the perfect night, even the part when I was so tired from all that alcohol and staying up into the wee hours of the morning, that Calder had to carry me half asleep back to his car. I fell asleep on the way home and had to be carried to my place. As much as I wanted to ravage him, I wasn't in any shape to do so.

Instead, I stripped myself and Calder down to our undies, pulled him into bed, then cuddled into each other until we both fell asleep. Not as hot as the first night we shared in my bed, but still completely and utterly satisfying.

A few days later, and I'm aching to have him back in my bed as soon as humanly possible. That's exactly why my heart is thudding in my chest, why my mouth is watering as I gaze at him. I don't think I can take another day without him.

I blink, and then it's the end of class. The usual routine commences, with Calder robing up while I answer students' questions as they filter out. When the last student leaves, I shut the door and turn to face Calder.

"You need to watch it." I aim my best serious look at him, but the sly grin on his face tells me I'm not convincing at all.

"Do I, Professor?" he asks while slowly sauntering up to me, his hand on the belt of his robe.

He stops when we're just inches apart, seeming to remember the boundaries we've both agreed to abide by within the walls of the classroom.

"If you keep shooting those sexy smiles at me, I'm going to lunge at you like a crazed animal."

He wags an eyebrow at me. "Why do you think I keep doing it?"

I shove his shoulder as I chuckle and turn around to pack up my bag. "So do you have plans tonight?"

When I look at him, Calder's gazing at me with a hopeful expression on his face. "I was keeping my night open. For you." He clears his throat. "No plans, then?"

I shake my head, finally letting that goofy grin of mine loose.

"Good. I have a surprise for you."

An hour later, I'm at Calder's downtown condo. When I walk in the door, I'm not surprised at what I see. Typical single guy pad with a dark leather sectional, flatscreen TV, sleek coffee table, and minimal decor.

When I turn to glance at his kitchen is when I see something I don't expect at all. On the slate counter are bananas, a box of graham crackers, a bag of mini marshmallows, and a stack of chocolate bars.

My mouth opens the slightest bit as I take in the surprise he's set up for me.

"I can't believe you remembered," I say softly.

He winks when he smiles, but instead of making him look sly like that move normally does, he looks the slightest bit shy. Like he was nervous to see my reaction. It's the sweetest thing in the world.

"How could I forget? You were so happy when you told me the other night how much you loved this dessert."

I remember how in my tipsy state I gushed to Calder about my favorite childhood memory of making banana s'mores with my mom. I'm warm from the inside out at just how thoughtful his gesture is.

I walk the few steps over to him, slink my arms around

his neck, and press a slow kiss to his mouth. "This was the sweetest surprise ever. Thank you."

"My absolute pleasure, love."

My breath catches at the nickname he uses. He's called me "love" countless times before, but not like this—not when he's pulled a super sweet, super romantic gesture that's straight from the heart.

I swallow, my nerves buzzing. But he flashes that sly grin once more, and once more I'm giddy. I forget all about the implications of that nickname.

"Now. Show me how you make these banana s'mores. I'm breaking my strict model diet to try them."

We settle into two lounge chairs on his balcony, that plushy plaid blanket over us. I breathe in, relishing the cool crispness of autumn. We're stuffed with banana s'mores, gazing at the city twenty stories below us.

I tuck the blanket under my thighs. "So. Was that worth possibly losing your six-pack for?"

Calder grins and leans over to kiss my cheek. "Absolutely."

When he laces his fingers in mine, I let out a soft, satisfied hum. The twilight sky shines periwinkle blue. Muffled traffic sounds echo below us.

I lean over and rest my head on Calder's shoulder. "Thank you for that. It's been forever since I've eaten banana s'mores."

"You don't make them with your mom anymore?"

I shake my head. "It's been years. Not since I was in grade school."

"Why? I don't mean to pry, but it's clear how happy that

dessert makes you. I'd think your mum would want to see you that happy all the time."

"Yeah, well, it became pretty clear early on that my happiness wasn't what my mom or dad was concerned with."

Calder shifts, and I lift my head to look at him.

"What do you mean by that?" he asks.

I sigh. "I just mean that when I was a kid, life was a lot simpler. And fun. I wasn't old enough for my parents to put serious pressure on me to go to the same college they went to or pursue the same careers. When I was a kid, they let me be a kid. Carefree, happy, uncomplicated, obsessed with dessert."

I pause to swallow and take in the darkening sky in front of us.

"I remember the day that my mom came up with that recipe for banana s'mores. I was in kindergarten. I came home from school so proud of myself that I made two new friends. I remember the smile on my mom's face and how she said, 'well, we need to do something special to celebrate that, *anak*.' And then she pulled out all the ingredients for s'mores from the pantry, grabbed a few bananas from the counter, and led me out to the backyard where our firepit was. And she whipped those up. I remember my dad came out and ate with us too to celebrate me making new friends. They said they were so proud of me."

I glance down at the ground, my smile from thinking of that memory fading slowly. Calder squeezes my hand gently.

"But when I got older, things changed. They cared less about that sort of thing and more about the kind of adult I'd grow into—they wanted to make sure I was the right kind of adult, like them. And so celebrating making new friends went straight out the window. So did caring about my interest in art. They were fine with it when I was a kiddo, but once I hit high school, the focus changed completely. They wanted me to earn high grades and get to the top of my class. And when that shift happened, everything between us changed."

Calder squeezes my hand once more, and it's more comforting than anything he could say.

"I'm never this candid when it comes to talking about my family," I say while gazing straight ahead at the sky. "You must bring it out in me."

When I twist my head to look at him, his gaze falls to the ground. He taps his socked feet lightly against the concrete floor. "I didn't mean to bring up something sad. I'm sorry."

I tug lightly at his arm. He looks up at me. "I'm not. I'm happy to talk about these moments. They're happy memories I have with my family. It's been a while since I've had any. Thank you for reminding me that they're still there."

A sad smile tugs at his mouth. "I'm sorry your parents don't realize what a bloody brilliant daughter they have. My family would be ecstatic to call you theirs."

I chuckle. "Really? But you're amazingly successful."

A flustered smile takes over his face, and he rubs the back of his neck. "Aye, they're proud of me for sure. I'm lucky in that respect. Hell, my sister, Lucy, loves it—gives her a lifetime of Fabio jokes to take the piss with. And no matter what I do, my parents support me one hundred percent. As long as I'm happy and financially on my own feet, they're content.

"But I was a bit of a hellraiser growing up. I never broke the law or anything like that. But I would stay out all night sometimes, drink too much with my mates, skip school, that sort of thing. They would have killed to have you, a budding and brilliant artist, as part of their brood instead of a hellion like me."

I let out a soft laugh, then lean my head on his shoulder once more.

"If only we knew each other when we were teenagers. I'd have been spending my nights painting and sketching and sculpting with you. You would have kept me out of trouble," he says through a chuckle. "I'd give anything to have a talent like yours."

"You have loads of talent, Calder."

"I don't know about that. I'm good at what I'm good at, I suppose. Sometimes it feels like what I'm most talented at is flexing my abs, though."

I sit up straighter and turn to him. "You don't have to put it so crudely. You're incredibly gifted. Posing, connecting with the camera, connecting with the artists who are sketching you in class, connecting with the people who are looking at your photos or covers, coming up with all those creative concepts on your Instagram posts, all of that requires skill and technique. That doesn't just happen."

He blinks, his face blank like he's trying to take in what I've said.

"You connect with people like I've never seen before. In-person and through your social media presence. It's more than just the gorgeous color of your eyes or your flawless body or your smile. You make people truly feel something when they look at an image of you. No matter what the medium, you can get anyone to fall in love with you. That's talent, Calder."

It takes a second before I realize what I've said. When I do, my eyes widen the slightest bit. But Calder just stares at me and swallows. I hope he didn't read too much into what

I've said. Because that would sound like I'm falling in love with him... and I'm absolutely not.

My breathing quickens just at the thought. I quickly reach for my glass of water and take a gulp.

"Thank you for the kind words," he finally says. "That's... exactly what I try to do on every job I take. To hear it summed up like that from you is... an honor indeed."

When I see the easy look on his face, that knot inside my chest loosens.

"I still maintain that you're the superior talent," he says, tucking a loose chunk of my hair behind my ear. "You look at a lump of clay or a blank page, and from it springs something entirely new and original. That kind of skill blows my mind."

I shiver slightly at the way his fingertips skim that sensitive patch of skin behind my ear, right above my neck. "It's a lot easier than you think. Here, I'll show you."

I pop up, walk back inside his condo, and grab a couple of small notepads from his kitchen island and two pencils from his desk. I return to the balcony and sit back down next to Calder, but he's preoccupied with his phone.

"Sorry, just a sec," he mutters while typing. A second later, he looks up and quirks a smile. "Getting a bollocking from my mum and sis all at once for forgetting to call lately."

"Oh. Do you want to call them now? I could go for a walk or something." I loved how his face lit up the other night when he talked about his family, especially his little sister. The big-brother vibe makes him even more adorable, if that's possible.

The look he gives me is answer enough, but the soft growl in his voice gives me chills when he says, "I want you nowhere but right here, Professor. And I want to talk to you and only you today."

I wet my lips. "Sounds good to me."

He blinks, and that intense stare dissipates. "So, what were you going to show me?"

"Here." I hand him a notebook and a pencil. "I'll teach you how to draw."

Calder frowns for a moment, then shakes his head. "You don't understand. Even my stick figures are atrocious. I've never, ever been good at drawing or anything artistic."

I burst out laughing, then settle myself back down. "Okay, try this. Draw a circle."

Calder's tongue sticks out of the corner of his mouth. His concentration face is rugged and adorable.

"Now, outline the circle again a few times. Now try to shade the bottom of it a little bit."

Calder follows my instructions as I tell him to darken the bottom curve of the ball until the bottom third of the ball is grayed out.

He squints at it for a long second at the image, then makes a "not bad" face.

"Nicely done. Okay, try a bit of cross-hatching."

With my pencil, I demonstrate how to draw a series of small crossed lines in the shaded curve of the ball. He mimics my movements perfectly. It gives a shadowy depth to the ball that makes it look almost three dimensional.

"Shade just underneath the ball. Just a little bit."

Calder nods and perfectly shades it. I tell him to draw a line behind the ball.

"This will give even more depth. Just wait."

A minute later after he's done shading, he wrings out his hand and leans back while fixating on the picture.

"Bloody hell. That's not bad at all."

"See?" I clap my hands. "Told you that you could be an artist."

Calder pivots those killer blue-green eyes to me, and suddenly I'm breathless. Those gemstone eyes of his are a mesmerizing mix of hunger and tenderness. Rosy cheeks flank his soft smile. "Thank you, Lily."

And then he grabs me by the back of the neck and kisses me until I can't breathe. We go at it so hard that the blanket, both sketch pads, and pencils fall to the ground. When Calder finally releases me, I lean my forehead against his and gasp for air, my insides buzzing at the crazy sexy kiss he just planted on me.

Both of our chests heave as we attempt to steady our breathing. Sitting up, I plant my palms against his chest and look him straight in the eye.

"Show me your bedroom."

19

CALDER

I leap to my feet so fast the chair topples over behind me, but who fucking cares? My fingers lace with hers, my eyes unable to move from the dark, lusty stare she's got pinned on me. I walk backwards to the sliding patio door and push it open, but before I go in I pull her close and kiss her again.

She moans, her lush mouth opening immediately as her tongue tangles with mine. That tongue is such a fucking tease, and I'm fairly sure she's not even aware of it. I force myself to keep some shred of control and answer with a gentle lap. If I give in to exactly what *I* want, I'll be tasting banana and chocolate from her mouth until she can't breathe.

But then Lily growls and bites down on my lower lip.

"Fuck, woman, what are you doing to me?" I groan and lift her off her feet. She squeals but doesn't break the kiss as I stumble through the door and down the hall to my bedroom.

"Bite me again," I beg when I'm standing in the middle of the room, in no rush to put her down.

She nibbles and sucks my lower lip into her mouth before her teeth sink in, another exquisite tease that rockets pleasure through my body. Blood surges to my dick; I've been walking around hard for this woman for weeks now. The memory of her kneeling in front of me, sucking me off, has gotten me off plenty, but this is different. I know tonight there will be no stopping. Fake relationship or not, there is nothing fake about the way she's kissing me.

I pull back and set her on her feet. Lily's eyes are still closed. She tilts her face, lips parted for another kiss, but I shush her and put a finger to her lips. She whines and opens her eyes, the question clear as day: *why did we stop*?

"I just want to hear you say yes."

"Yes."

I laugh softly and stroke her cheek. "No, love. I mean I want to know we're on the same page here. Lily, I... well. I suppose I want to hear what you want."

She blinks several times and takes a deep breath. "Not this time. I want to hear what you want first."

"I want you on my bed right now. I want to take my time removing every piece of clothing you have on. I want to taste your skin and suck on your body until you come all over my face. I want your hands all over me, and, when we both can't take it anymore, I want my cock inside you, Lily Maldonado. No interruptions, no second-guessing. But," I cross my arms and step back, "I don't want a damn thing you don't."

Her eyes have gone round, cheeks a luminous pink. She wets her lips several times and then nods frantically. "That. I want that. All of that. What you said. Now. Yes."

My chuckle ends quickly when she steps forward and yanks my shirt off. Soft, wet kisses trail across my chest. She bites my nipples gently, and I hiss. "All of it," she repeats softly.

Okay then.

We fall to the bed, unable to stop touching each other. Part of my brain wants to remind me that this is a "fake" relationship, but goddamn she makes me feel so much that I simply do not care. She is so sweet and hot all at once that my heart is thudding with anticipation.

I discard her shirt so my hands have better access to her silky skin. Touching her is addictive. Kissing her is a drug.

"What is it about you?" I slur as I unclasp her bra and trail kisses from her neck down. My tongue circles one nipple, then the other, and she arches her back with a moan.

"Nothing. You're the one making me crazy." She tugs on my hair, her head tipped back in pure pleasure.

"Mm-mm, it's *you*, Professor Lily. I've never known a woman who was so sublimely sweet, and yet so... fucking... *hot*." I close my lips on her breast and suck hard, pinching the other at the same time.

She howls and bucks her hips. My scalp tingles where she tugs even harder, and that blanks all the questions and words in my head. I close my eyes and suck on her body until she's writhing and I'm at risk of losing tufts of hair.

"Calder, Calder, please I need—"

"Say no more." I had promised to take my time, but fuck that. I strip her jeans as fast as I can, panties too, and throw myself on my stomach between her legs.

The first lick makes her groan. My tongue on her clit makes her scream. When I laugh at her wild abandon, she covers her face with a pillow and shudders.

I pull back an inch. "Oh, no you don't. I want to hear every sound you make, or I'll stop and make you touch yourself while I watch instead."

She gets still and then peeks out from behind the pillow. "Would you really?"

My hips flex against the bed at the thought. "I'd fucking love to see that show, no lie. But, hmm, not sure there's much that could pull me away from you right now, love."

The pillow tumbles to the floor as I run my tongue over her pussy again. I gently bend her knee and encourage her to open wider for me. She hums and rests her foot on my back while she trails her fingertips over her breasts.

"God, I'm so sensitive," she murmurs.

"Mm-hmm," I hum so she'll shiver.

I tease her, switching between licks and sucks, then bring my fingers in to keep her on the edge. She shudders and tenses up, but every time she does I back off or kiss her thigh until she's groaning in frustration.

"Dammit, Calder," she shouts at the ceiling when I get her closer than ever. Her beautiful face scrunches up. "Stop teasing."

"But that's the fun part."

Her fingers reach between her legs, bumping my face out of the way. I emit something between a growl and a laugh as I catch that wrist and pin it to the bed. "How dare you interrupt me, Professor."

"I *need* to—"

"Shush."

I dive back for more of her, licking back to front before closing my lips around her clit. She tenses again, soft murmurs of "Mmhmm, yeah, that, please" slipping from her as she tenses up yet again.

"Please don't stop this time," she whimpers.

"Mm-mm."

Her body pulses. She's soaking wet, her juices running down my chin. Her whimpered pleas get louder and louder until the moment I tap my tongue against her and shove two fingers deep inside.

"*Calder!*"

My name bounces off the walls as her orgasm crashes down on her, wave after wave that I ride with her. My eyes want to close as I absorb her pleasure, but there is nothing like watching my girl come, and so I barely let myself blink.

At last she goes slack, chest rising and falling with shaky breaths. I lick my lips and grin, then kiss my way back up her body.

Lily opens one eye when I hover over her. Her dark eyebrow arches. "For a fake boyfriend, you give one hell of a real orgasm."

I grin, but that term punches my gut. "Nah, I think you were faking that part, too."

She laughs. "Yeah, that was totally an act."

"No doubt about it." I dip my head and kiss her so she can taste herself on my tongue. She kisses me back, then pulls away again with a shy smile.

"How'd I get so lucky to get a fake boyfriend like you?"

Before I can reply, she touches my lips and blushes. "The real question," she adds softly, "is how the hell can this *really* be this good?"

"Why shouldn't it be?" My throat is tight. I realize vaguely that I'm holding back words, but exactly what they are I'm not sure.

"Because my life doesn't work this way. I don't wind up in bed with hot models who are also insanely sweet and funny. I don't have relationships, real or fake, with guys who make me feel like the most important person in the world no matter what we're doing. It's just not my life, Calder."

"Well." I swallow hard and quirk my lips. "Unless I'm very much mistaken, your life still doesn't work that way.

You are not, in fact, in bed with *models*, nor are you in relationships with *guys*. There is only me—again, unless I've seriously miscalculated."

She rolls her eyes and dissolves into that musical laughter that I can't resist. "Oh my god, you're as picky as my grandmother when I'd ask if I could have a cookie. 'I don't know, *can* you eat a cookie, Lily?'"

Her high-pitched grandma voice is too much, and I bury my face in her neck and laugh. She wraps her arms around my neck. Her nails on my back start as a gentle caress, but the longer I have her pressed against my mattress, the more my body registers details of her soft curves under me. My laughter dies as I begin to nibble on her earlobe, and that changes her gentle scratches to something a little more primal.

"Calder?" she murmurs in a lazy, teasing tone. "Can I touch you?"

"Lily, you not only can, but you also may," I growl into her ear, loving how she laughs as she slips her hand into my jeans. "Fucking hell," I groan when her hand closes around me.

"You're telling me," she breathes, and we trade a glassy-eyed look. "Take them off, Calder, I want you now."

"Your wish, darling, is as ever my command."

I roll off the bed and drop my jeans, reaching for a condom in the nightstand drawer. Lily sits up and helps me roll it on, her eyes not leaving mine. Then, she lays back and lets her legs fall open as she motions for me to come to her. I crawl between her legs and hover over her. My mouth is dust, and I've no idea why.

That is a bloody lie. I know exactly why.

My eyelids droop as I stare at her. "Professor Lily, I think you should know. Whatever our arrangement is, there will be no faking from me from here out. Got me?"

She lifts her head and captures me with her kiss as she pulls my body down to her. "Thank you," she murmurs in my ear as I thrust inside her.

20

LILY

The moment Calder's inside me, my jaw drops. I don't howl like I did before. This time, I'm gasping. When I inhale, I take all of the air in the room with me.

"Holy...holy...holy..." I can barely say that four-letter word as Calder slowly thrusts into me.

I knew he'd be a lot to take. For weeks I've been eyeing his very impressive length during class. But I didn't anticipate just how intense he would feel—and I feel him everywhere, from my fingertips to my toes, from the top of my head to my chest. Every single time he slides into me, I'm shaking with pleasure.

"Holy fuck," I finally say, my fingers digging into his shoulders. "That feels...you feel..."

"You feel fucking incredible." Calder's voice is a low rasp.

My eyes roll back when he hits a particularly deep spot. "So... do... you..."

He emits a rough chuckle that makes me grin. I focus my gaze back on Calder. With his arms braced on either side of me, he lowers his face so that his nose just barely touches mine. When he starts to slow down a bit, I grip his deliciously firm ass, pressing him into me harder.

"No, don't stop. Please," I whine.

Again he chuckles. But this time there's a shy edge in his eyes. "Sorry, love. If I go too fast, this'll all end way too soon. And I don't want to leave you disappointed."

My chest squeezes at what his words imply—that he's enjoying being with me so much that he has to pace himself, otherwise he'll come too soon. It sends a hot flush all over my body.

I run my hands up his back, relishing the hard feel of all that muscle under his smooth skin. "I'll take that as a compliment then."

"You should. You're unbelievable, Lily."

It's another few moments of that slow, shallow thrusting. Then Calder swallows and leans up, hooking my legs over his shoulders. My head falls back with the deeper angle that he's positioned us in. He starts up that slow rhythm once more, and my head goes cloudy and dizzy. Even when I try to blink, I'm seeing stars.

"Yeah. Just like that," I say through ragged breaths.

I feel Calder's stubble against my calf, then he presses a soft kiss to my leg. The combination of sensations—that super soft, super sweet kiss and the desperate way he's taking me—sends all my senses into overdrive. This guy. This guy is beyond incredible in bed. I've never had anyone physically satisfying me like this. But more than that, he knows how to be sweet, and that makes all of this a million times more intense. More meaningful.

Pressure builds inside of me, starting from my clit and slowly moving up my core. It's only been two handfuls of minutes since Calder's been inside of me, and already I'm nearing the edge. As incredible as this feels, I can't let this be the end. I want more. So much more.

I reach up and pull Calder down to kiss me. "I want to be on top. Of you. Now."

He grins against my mouth. "Gladly."

In an impressively smooth move, he flips us over. I steady myself with my palms pressed flat against his chest. And then I take a breath, close my eyes, and slowly ride him. That delicious pressure still courses through me, but it's a more controlled intensity.

When I glance down at Calder, his eyebrows are furrowed, like he's concentrating.

"You good?" I rasp.

He nods. "I just need you to get yours first before I get mine."

Smiling, I bite my lip and slowly start to speed up. Then I slip a hand between my legs and rub small circles against my clit.

Calder's eyes go wide. A strangled sound rips from his throat. His reaction to me touching myself gives me a newfound confidence.

"Fucking hell," he mutters, gripping the fleshy parts of my hips with a force that tells me he loves what he sees.

"You said you wanted to watch."

I speed up both my riding rhythm and my hand. My heart thunders against my chest as that glorious heat between my legs gets hotter. It amps up the pressure inside of me to an unbearable peak. My legs start to quiver. It won't be much longer.

As my gasps get higher and more desperate, I try to speak.

"I'm so close, Calder. So, so close."

With his hands still on my hips, he moves me up and down over his cock, keeping the rhythm I've set.

Seconds later, all the heat and pressure inside of me comes to a head. I explode all over him.

My head falls back and I'm shouting once more. I'm surprised the volume of my voice doesn't shatter his bedroom window. I'm thrashing like I've lost all control over my body. I try to plant my legs firmly against his bed to keep myself in place, but it's no use. I have zero control over them as orgasm ravages my body. Thankfully Calder's still got me by the waist. He holds me up as I convulse, landing like a rag doll on his chest. It's a second later that I feel him tense and grunt underneath me. Then he lets out a growly breath and wraps his arms around me, hugging me tight against his chest.

He heaves a long, hot sigh that condenses on my forehead. "Fucking..."

"Hell?"

I glance up at him right as he bursts into laughter. Then he kisses my forehead. "Yes. Exactly that."

After a minute of catching our breath, he eases me off of him, then sits up and removes the condom. He throws it in a nearby wastebasket before lying down and pulling me back into him.

I'm spooned against him, his arms wrapped snugly around my waist. After a few minutes, the sweat coating my body turns cold and I start to shiver. Before I can even move, Calder shifts behind me. "You cold, love?"

"A little, yeah." There's a pressure in the center of my chest once more at hearing him call me that. And this time, I know exactly what it means.

He pulls his comforter over us and nuzzles the back of

my neck. "That was incredible. *You* are incredible," he whispers in my ear.

I close my eyes and smile, every cell in my body buzzing. Because in this moment I know beyond a shadow of a doubt that I won't be able to fake a single thing with Calder ever again after what we've done.

Because I'm falling in love with him.

I hum and twist my head to kiss his bicep, which is pressed against my shoulder.

"So are you."

~

In the morning, I wake up to an empty bed. It's a few seconds of blinking and rubbing my eyes before I take in the scene: Me alone in bed. Again.

Inside I start to deflate. Did he really leave me again?

But then I hear footsteps outside his closed bedroom door. It swings open to reveal Calder wearing nothing but flannel pajama pants that hang deliciously low on his hips, the perfect frame for that flawless Adonis belt. In his hands is a tray with a plate of waffles and a small bowl of fruit.

I grin so wide my cheeks ache.

"I thought you might be hungry," he says.

When I nod excitedly and pat the spot next to me in bed, he laughs. He walks over, sits on the edge of the bed, and sets the tray in my lap. I swipe a waffle from the plate and grin at the generous smear of chocolate on them.

"All I had were frozen waffles, chocolate hazelnut spread, and some raspberries," he says. "Sorry it's not more impressive."

I've already devoured half of the waffle when I turn to

him and give him a light smack on the shoulder. "Don't even apologize," I say while chewing. "This is the greatest breakfast ever."

He leans over and kisses me, licking the chocolate on my lips. I giggle.

I hold up the waffle to him. "Want a bite?"

He shakes his head. "I wish I could stay and have a little breakfast of my own." He eyes the lower half of my body, which is still tucked under the duvet, then looks back at me and wiggles his eyebrows. I roll my eyes while chucking.

"But I have to run soon. I've got a shoot scheduled for this morning."

"Oh, for Sonce?"

He shakes his head. "Book cover. Then a call with my agent."

"One of these days I want to go to one of your shoots. I'm dying to see you styled like a hunky romance hero."

He grins. "I'd love that." When I finish chewing, he leans over to kiss me, then stands up and darts around his bedroom to get dressed.

I'm halfway through the raspberries when those tell-tale nerves hit the pit of my stomach. If he's leaving, does that mean I should leave too? I really don't want to. I'd rather lounge around in his bed and wait for him to come back, then maybe we could have a second round of mind-blowing sex… then a third and a fourth…

I shake my head, snapping myself out of the fantasy. I clear my throat and start to scan the room for my clothes right as Calder walks back over to me. He's replaced his flannel pajama pants with worn dark jeans. A casual button-up hangs over his shoulders.

"I don't know how long this shoot will be, but you

should stay. If you want. It would be nice to spend the day together... if you don't have anything else going on." He fumbles with the buttons of his shirt. There's a shyness in his eyes that's the cutest thing I've ever seen. It settles the nerves in my stomach instantly.

I grin up at him. "I'd love to stay."

The most beautiful smile spreads across his face as he leans down and gives me a slow kiss. He cups my cheek with his hand. When he pulls away, he's still holding my face. I close my eyes and let out the softest moan. God, he feels so, so good. And, god, I could get used to seeing him like this every day.

"Make yourself at home," he says.

I thank him, and he walks out. A second later, I hear his front door close. And then I fall back into bed, my chest tight and my heart pounding, fully aware of just how deeply I'm falling for Calder...and scared to death that he may not feel the same.

Two hours later, I'm in a pair of Calder's boxers, his hoodie, and a pair of warm wooly socks I found in the top drawer of his dresser, sitting on his balcony with a notepad. I glance up at the cityscape in front of me, then back at my sketch. It's a pencil drawing of the dozen skyscrapers that mark the horizon. I sip from my mug of tea I brewed. This is one of the more relaxing days off I've had in a long time.

My phone rings, and when I see it's Morgan I quickly answer.

"Hey, you. How's it going?"

"Pretty great, actually."

I can hear the smile in her voice. She gushes about how

her grandma is smashing physical therapy. She's strong enough that she can even go for multiple leisurely walks every week.

"Oh my gosh, that's great!"

"Her doctor says she's making a quicker than expected recovery," Morgan says. "He even gave her the okay for her cataract surgery next month. We thought she'd have to wait until after January. But it looks like it'll be happening before Christmas."

I grin while gazing ahead at the city skyline. "Does that mean you'll be back sooner than expected?"

"Maybe. Hopefully. I love my grandma and will stay with her as long as she needs me of course. But I miss you. I miss the city."

"I miss you too."

"So tell me. Did you read lover boy the riot act like I hope you did?"

I bite my lip as my gaze falls to my feet. "Yeah..."

"And?"

"And it went well. Like, really, really well. I told him exactly what I wanted and what I wasn't going to put up with... and he apologized. And got on board with everything I wanted."

"That's my girl." There's a clapping noise in the background.

"I think... I think it turned him on to see me like that. Like, all demanding."

"Oh damn. Tell me all about it."

My face heats as my smile grows even wider. Then I give Morgan a run-down of everything that's happened between Calder and me since we got back on track at the whisky tasting. The entire time I gush over Calder, from his sense of humor to his thoughtfulness to his dynamite skill and stamina in the bedroom.

When I finish, I wait for Morgan to say something. But there's just silence on the phone.

"Are you there?" I ask.

"Oh my god. You love him!"

I let out the most awkward and embarrassed scoff-chuckle. Then I clear my throat. "Um, well..."

"You love him, Lily!"

I hunch over in the lounge chair and cover my face with my free hand. "Okay, so I think I'm falling for him, but I'm not completely in love with him."

She makes a "pssh" sound. "You can tell yourself that, but I know better. You are completely in love with him, even if you refuse to admit it. You never gush over guys like you just did. You've never once spoken about any guy before like this. Not even douche canoe Marco."

I let the words soak in for a second. "Okay, so let's say for the sake of argument that I'm in love with Calder. Should I tell him?"

"Duh."

"But like...when?"

"When it feels right."

I roll my eyes. "That's not helpful at all. I don't even know if he feels the same way."

"Okay, that's fair. It's scary as fuck to tell someone you love them when you don't know if they love you. But people don't often fall in love at the same time. That's fine if you don't want to run out and tell him this minute. But ask yourself this: do you want something serious with Calder? Can you envision a future with him?"

I know the answer before I even say it.

"Yes."

"Then you should tell him at some point. Because yeah, it'll hurt like hell if you tell him you love him and he doesn't say it back. But you know what'll hurt more? Never knowing if he loves you because you held your feelings back."

I let out a breath. "Why do you always have to be right about everything? You're like my own personal life coach, pointing out the hard stuff I need to do, even though I don't want to do it."

"It's called being a best friend."

Just then I hear keys in the front door.

"Gotta go. Call you later, okay?"

When I hang up my phone, I stand up and see Calder walking through the kitchen to the balcony.

"I thought you said you'd be gone all day," I say.

He drops his backpack on the floor, then reaches his arm out to grab me by the waist and pull me against him.

"The shoot wrapped early."

"Wow. I'm impressed. I assumed photoshoots were all-day affairs."

"They usually are. Guess I was just in the zone today."

He trails soft kisses along my neck.

I close my eyes and hum. "Or maybe you just missed me and wanted to come back as soon as possible?"

"Definitely that," he growls softly against my skin.

And then he kisses me in that slow, teasing way that has my clit pulsing in an instant. I run my hands through his hair as he runs his hands all over me.

"How did the call with your agent go?" I gasp for air.

"I rescheduled it."

"Why?"

He slides a hand up my sweater and circles my nipple with this thumb. I pant at just how good it feels. "Because I'd rather be here making you come over and over on my tongue and my cock."

I grin at him before pulling him back to my mouth.

"Fuck, Lily," he growls. "Do you know how hot it is to come home and see you in my clothes?"

"How hot is it?" I say between kisses.

"So hot that I want to rip them off of you."

I break our kiss and walk toward his bedroom, stopping in the doorway. "What are you waiting for?"

A wicked grin spreads across Calder's face. He runs over to me and scoops me up in his arms. I squeal, remembering how he pulled this same move last night. When he drops me on the bed, I can't help but fall into a fit of giggles. A second later he's on top of me, caging me with his arms. The wild look in his eye sends my pulse racing. I'm grinning, giddy with anticipation.

When I reach for his shirt to take it off, he grabs my wrists and gently pins them against the bed as he trails light kisses along the side of my neck. Then he peels his sweater off me, then his boxers, then his socks. Soon I'm naked underneath him, pulsing and writhing.

He kisses down my stomach to the spot where I want him most. "I could do this forever with you," he says against my skin.

My chest tightens and my heart soars. "Me too."

He stops just before pressing his face between my legs to glance up at me. "I'm done faking it with you, Lily. I want us... I want this to be real."

For a minute, I just stare at him, wondering if I've heard him correctly.

"I want that too."

"Then it's settled," he says before kissing the inside of

my thigh. "We're no longer in a fake relationship. We're the real thing."

My head falls back as I savor the sensation of his lips on my body for the millionth time. "Yes. God, yes."

"You're my lass, Lily."

"And you're my... lad?"

We both laugh. But then Calder reins in his expression to something more serious, more heartfelt. "I've been dying to hear you say that."

And then he puts his mouth to my throbbing clit, and I howl, my head spinning and my heart bursting that Calder Ross is officially my boyfriend.

One week later, Calder and I have fallen into a routine that consists of going to work, then heading to each other's places to screw each other's brains out.

I've never, ever been happier. I have a perma-grin on my face at all times. When I'm brushing my teeth, when I'm teaching class, when I'm driving. I guess consistent and frequent orgasms will have that effect on a person.

I'm even smiling right now as I shampoo my hair in Calder's shower. Out of the corner of my eye, I see the door swing open. There's Calder, naked and grinning.

"Mind if I join you?" he says as he walks toward me.

"You never have to ask."

I step back and make room for him under the showerhead. Water cascades down his body in glistening sheets that highlight how cut he is.

I lick my lips as I gaze at him. "You're like a super sexy human waterfall."

He laughs, then pulls me into him and kisses me. Our

tongues tangle, teasing each other until we're breathless. I'm clawing at his body with desperate hands; he does the same. Soon his hand slips down between my legs. I inhale sharply as he starts to work his fingers on me.

I run my hands through his hair, tugging harder the more intense it gets. The fire inside of me burns hotter and hotter as he swirls faster and faster. Soon I'm shouting, my pitchy cries bouncing against the bathroom walls. I have to clutch his shoulders to keep myself steady because my legs are jelly from the orgasm ripping through me. With his free arm braced against my back, he holds me up.

When I start to come down, I slow-blink while giggling. Then I glance up at that smug smile on his face. "Your turn."

I wrap my hand around his steely thickness and slide up and down. I start slow, my eyes glued to his face. That glazed-over look in his eyes appears, and I can't help but grin. I love knowing that I can make Calder feel this good. His jaw muscle bulges when he bites down. Then he grunts and squeezes my waist with both hands.

I speed up, excited by just how much he's trying to hold on—and curious as to how quickly I can get him to lose his composure.

As it turns out, it only takes a few minutes of me making out with Calder while working his cock with my hands to get him to the end. With a growl, he spills into the shower. I rinse my hands off while dotting his neck with kisses and soft scrapes.

He flashes that satisfied grin that always tugs at his lips after orgasms. "Fuck me, that was good."

"You took the words right out of my mouth."

He washes up while I rinse off. When I'm dried off and dressed, my phone blares from the coffee table. I sigh when I see it's my mom.

"Hey, Mom. How are you?"

"Fine, fine. Why didn't you come Thursday night?"

"What?"

"To the dinner for Harmony and Marco."

"Um..."

Mom says something about a celebratory rustic Italian dinner arranged by Harmony's parents to kick off the pre-wedding festivities. It takes a second for my memory to catch up. That's the dinner Harmony mentioned at the apple orchard last month.

"Oh. That." I hold back a sigh. "Sorry I missed it, but I was teaching."

The truth is that yes, I did teach class, but I had the whole evening free and instead of going out and doing anything, Calder and I spent it at my apartment, having sex on my couch, then against my kitchen counter, then again in my bedroom.

"To be honest, Lily, your dad and I were very embarrassed that you just decided not to show up," Mom says. "How do you think that makes us look? For our daughter to no-show at an important pre-wedding event for a family friend?"

"Mom, please don't guilt-trip me. I told Harmony when she invited me that I wasn't sure I could come."

I roll my eyes just as Calder walks out of the bathroom, a towel wrapped around his waist.

"Everything alright?" he whispers.

I shrug and mouth the word "mom." He nods in understanding.

Just then I hear Auntie Mayla in the background.

"Oh for god's sake, Marylin. Lily isn't contractually obligated to go to anything. She's an adult. If she didn't feel like going to her ex's rustic Italian whatever, she doesn't have to go. Would you give the poor girl a break?"

I smile at Auntie Mayla's defense of me.

There's another minute of bickering between them while I listen.

"I certainly don't expect you to understand the importance of wedding events given your history," Mom says.

I cringe at mom's dig at Auntie Mayla's two divorces. But then I hear Auntie Mayla's laugh echoing in the background.

"You're right. I don't. Because I know better than most what a waste all that wedding nonsense is." She laughs once more. "You made the right choice by not going!" she hollers in the background.

I hold back a laugh. "It sounds like you and auntie are in the middle of an important conversation. I'd better let you go."

Mom sighs. "Fine. But for goodness sake, please show up for the rehearsal dinner this weekend. We're counting on you."

"I'll be there. With Calder." Just saying his name out loud makes me giddy.

We hang up and I turn around to see Calder with his naked back to me. He's wearing these snug silky boxer briefs. I'm about to pounce on him when I realize he's on the phone.

"Mate, are you serious? Fuck me, that's good news."

It's another few seconds of Calder excitedly talking before he hangs up and spins around to me, the biggest grin I've ever seen on his face.

"What is it?" I ask.

"Nate just called to tell me that Sonce made a final decision for their brand spokesman. They chose me."

I jump up and down while squealing. Then I run up to hug him and he scoops me up. Wrapping my legs around his waist, I cup his stubbled face with my hands and press a long kiss to his mouth.

"Oh my god, that's amazing, Calder! Congratulations!"

He pulls me into another kiss before setting me down on the ground. He runs his hands through his messy damp hair, a look of disbelief and joy on his face.

"I can't believe I got the job."

"You did it," I say softly while beaming at him. My chest squeezes at just how proud I am of Calder, at how I get to witness in person him achieving his dream.

His gaze focuses and he looks at me. "I couldn't have done it without you."

He pulls me into a tight hug, then kisses me.

"You did the hard work," I say. "I just helped."

He shakes his head. "No way this would have happened without you. Thank you, Lily."

He presses a light kiss to my mouth before cuddling me against his bare chest once more. I close my eyes and hum. My heart feels like it's swelling in my chest. Seeing Calder succeed—seeing him so happy—is a whole new level of bliss.

His phone buzzes with a text. When he looks at it, his eyes go wide and his face goes pale.

I grab his arm. "What is it? Calder, what's wrong?"

He swallows. "Nate says the Sonce brand execs want me to make a speech at their big holiday party in two weeks."

"That's amazing." I hold back the squealing and clapping I'm aching to do because right now, Calder looks like he's going to be sick.

"I hate public speaking. It makes me want to vomit. I get so bloody nervous and can't think straight." Calder shakes his head and runs a hand through his hair. He flashes a sheepish smile. "Weird, isn't it? I can stand in front of a class full of people completely naked with no problem. But I can't speak in front of a crowd with my clothes on if my life depended on it."

There's a frightened look in those blue-green eyes of his. It makes me want to hold him forever.

I grab him by both hands and look him straight in the eye. "That's not weird at all. That makes total sense. You're perfectly comfortable being a model because you've done it for years, but public speaking is out of your comfort zone."

He nods. "That's exactly it."

I cup my hand against his cheek. He closes his eyes and lets out a soft moan, like my touch is the comfort he craves.

"It's okay. I'll be there with you the whole time. And you can practice in front of me as many times as it takes for you to feel comfortable."

When he smiles, all the worry disappears from his face. "You'd do that for me?"

"Of course I would."

He rests his hands on my cheeks and stares at me with affection in his eyes. "Thank you. You offering that, you even wanting to be there for me, that means everything." He pulls me into a hug and for the longest moment, all we do is stand and hold each other.

When we pull apart, I head to the kitchen and grab a bottle of Sonce whisky from his cupboard. "We should celebrate. With a proper drink."

His hands fall to his hips as he grins. "God, I love..."

I glance up at him.

"... that you suggested that." He rubs a hand over his face, clears his throat, and walks into the kitchen.

He stands behind me as I pour two glasses and wraps his

arms around my waist. Then he kisses the back of my neck through my hair as he nuzzles me. And even though my stomach is flipping at just how tantalizing it is to have Calder's mouth on my body again and again, there's also a warmth that consumes it. A whole new kind of comfort.

That's when I know. I'm not falling anymore. I'm completely, head over heels in love with Calder.

21

CALDER

"Ladies and gentlemen, if I could just say a few words—erm, no. Ladies and gentlemen, sorry to interrupt, but I wanted to say... I wanted to say... Sonce is fucking delicious and you should all get pissed on it and make Nate the richest bastard this side of the guy who owns Amazon. What's his name?"

Lily rolls her eyes at me as she applies her lipstick. I flip the blue silk tie over itself and cinch a Windsor knot, then bump my hip against hers to get some room at the vanity.

"Come on, you're much further along than that," she says with a pop of her lips.

I laugh and comb my hair. "Aye, but I'm also too busy thinking about how to be your perfect arm candy for this evening to focus much."

She laughs. "You're always the perfect arm candy."

"I love it when you objectify me, love."

Her arms wrap round my neck, so I dust a light kiss on her, careful not to muss her makeup. We both turn to look in the bathroom mirror and smile. "Look at us," she says.

"Quite a team," I agree. My hands are on her waist, itching to sneak underneath the tiny blue dress she has on.

The contrast of her pale dress and dark skin with my dark suit and fair complexion are, in my estimation, a perfect balance all around.

But then, I admitted to myself at least a week ago that I'm bloody smitten with this lass. Hell, the L-word had nearly snuck out of my mouth, and I'm not sure she's ready for all that.

You are, though. You damn well know you love her. There's no one like her, has never been, and will likely never be. If that's not love, then what is?

The first time I had a thought like that, it dropped my stomach to the floor. But over this past week of sex, snuggles, and riding high on being named Sonce's rep, the thought has just become part of it all. Yes, I love this brilliant, beautiful woman. So what? Life is short, she is beautiful, and what reason do I have to deny it? Just because I don't want to scare the hell out of her by saying so too soon doesn't mean it's not real.

I kiss the tip of her nose and look at us in the mirror again. *No more faking. This is the real thing.*

"Right, so. Ready for finger foods and a side of my family?" she asks, rolling her eyes.

"I'm mostly ready to whisper naughty things in your ear whenever you start looking too tense."

She blushes. "Don't you dare."

"Oh, I think we both know I damn well will."

"God, I—"

Lily bites her lips into a line so fast that my heart jolts. Clearly she's holding back a thought. "You what, Professor?" I tease gently.

"I, uh, I was just going to say that I *so* don't want to go to this."

Not the words I wanted, but I can work with them. "No?

Then we'll stay right here in this hotel room and do all the naughty things I was going to whisper until the other guests have to call about the noise." I plop on the bed and pat the spot next to me. "Your wish, as ever, is my command."

She steps into her heels and shakes her head. "While I've gotten much better at saying what I want lately, I'm not quite to the point where I'm prepared to completely blow people off when I've made a commitment. Ready?"

"Hmm? Sorry, what? I was just sitting here thinking of all the things you've said you want lately. Got a bit distracted, you understand. And I definitely had stopped listening after the word 'blow.'"

Her giggles ring through the room as the door shuts behind us.

Harmony and Marco have invited so many people to their rehearsal dinner, I have to wonder how it's not easier to just call this the wedding and have done with it. We step into a good-sized ballroom. Lily whispers to me that the next day will be twice as big at least—their guest list is rumored at around 500. It is an *event*. Suddenly the 100-or-so in the room make a bit more sense.

"Hi, you two!" Harmony squeals when she sees us and drags Marco our way.

I put my hand on Lily's lower back as they approach, loving the way she leans into me. While Harmony showers air kisses on my girl, I do not miss the way Marco's eyes walk over her a few leisurely times.

My jaw clenches.

He glances at me and sneers. A jerk of his head is meant to be a nod, so I give it right back. "Hey, man. What was your name again?" he says, and from the slur in his voice, I can tell he's already drunk.

"Calder. His name is *Calder*." Lily beats me to a reply.

Her hand wraps protectively around my bicep, and I want to laugh and tell her it doesn't mean shit to me what this arsehole says.

"Right, sure. Lily, thanks for coming. You look fantastic."

Harmony blinks but doesn't let her smile slip. She puts her arm around Marco and hurries to agree with him, even though she's complimented Lily's dress three times already.

Lily's brows knit in a what-the-fuck look. "Um, well, we're going to grab a drink."

"Try the caviar, it's divine," Harmony chirps.

Lily flashes her a smile. "Will do."

I guide her toward the bar, and she glances up at me. "Was he wasted or what?"

"Definitely," I mutter.

We don't make it halfway across the room before her mother intercepts us. Her penciled eyebrows draw together, lips pursed in a way that looks so much like Lily's pout—but then again nothing like it at the same time. Marilyn Maldonado would be as much of a stunner as her daughter if she hadn't spent most of her life disapproving of the world.

"Really, dear, isn't that dress a bit... revealing?"

Lily freezes, and then tugs at the hem of her dress. "I mean, it's just a dress."

"Looked terrible on me, you see. Didn't go with my coloring at all," I jump in, not giving a damn if she finds it funny but willing to do anything to keep her scowl away from Lily.

Lily's lips twitch while Marilyn gives me a sardonic eye-roll. "Hello again, Calder. Thank you for coming."

I kiss her knuckles, which seems to appease her a bit more. We're joined by a woman I vaguely remember from the apple picking, but Lily lights up and flies to hug her.

"Hi, Auntie Mayla," she murmurs.

Lily turns to me and introduces us. Mayla's eyes are on me as we shake hands. She arches a brow and winks, and I grin at the silent message: *Take care of my niece.*

Yes, ma'am. Will do. I nod my reply.

"*Anak*, this dress is stunning. Where did you get it?" Mayla threads her arm into Lily's and guides her to the bar, leaving Marilyn and me to follow behind.

We order while Lily and Mayla chat/gush about some department store I've never heard of. Mayla raises her glass at Lily. "Flaunt it while you've got it, I say."

I don't miss the glare Marylin shoots her sister, but Mayla simply shrugs while sipping her champagne. I chuckle behind my own whisky. I think I really like Mayla.

For the next hour, we mix and mingle enough to appease her parents. We also stand off to the sidelines a good bit so I can whisper whatever pops into my head into her ear. The way she blushes and hides in my sleeve to giggle is, beyond all doubt, the best part of the night for me. The pretense and phoniness of this family and their friends is strange to me. The Rosses are noisy and fond of sharp digs and over-sharing when they get a little booze in them, but my family is authentic. This group is anything but, and I cannot fathom how they can call this enjoyable.

But nothing is stranger than the way that prick Marco keeps appearing in our line of vision. If I'm imagining it or not, it sure as hell seems like he finds a reason to walk by and look our way far more than necessary. Lily notices him a few times. Usually she tosses him a backhanded glance or outright turns away, but she definitely doesn't realize the full brunt of his shadowing us. Half the time he walks past, she's too busy laughing to notice. On those passes, the bloke scowls at me and shouts for Harmony to join him.

He strides by *again*, and I catch both of Lily's hands and gently turn her so her back is to the room. In the corner of my eye, I see him drain his glass and stride away, but I'm focused on Lily as I say, "Do you remember our first party together? How awkward we were?"

She tilts her face up to me, a smile making her glow even as she nods and wrinkles her nose. "Ugh, I felt like such an obvious sham. Like anyone would believe a quiet art teacher was your girlfriend."

"Funny, I spent the night feeling like a sham too. Quite sure no one would buy the idea that I'd actually been lucky enough to trick a classy, beautiful woman like you into falling for me."

"Classy? You mean shy," she laughs.

"I mean classy as hell—but just the right kind of bossy and filthy too," I add with a wink.

She shakes her head. "God, I can't believe myself with you sometimes. Like, when did I find this side of me? And where has it been all my life? Ugh, I wish I'd had a little of it when I was dating Marco."

"No regrets, love. Just enjoy where you are now."

"I guess so." She pokes her tongue playfully at me, so I bend down and kiss her.

"Hey, Lily?"

We both whip around to see Marco. My jaw clenches again, and I instinctively put my arm around Lily's collarbone, drawing her back to my front.

She gently picks up my wrist and laces our hands instead. "What."

It's not a question. Her voice is so flat and cold that I smirk at him.

"I was wondering if we could talk. I'm getting married tomorrow, and I just thought we could..."

Lily groans and looks at the ceiling. "Marco, go away. Isn't it enough that I'm here, making an appearance? We have less than nothing to say to each other. Just go stuff your face with caviar. I'm happy where I am."

"Lily. I'm saying I want you to—"

"You heard the lady." My voice growls when I cut him off.

Lily squeezes my hand reassuringly. "Come on, Calder. I need another champagne."

She tugs me away as I throw another glare at him.

"Easy, big boy. You're about to lose your cool," she mutters, bringing my attention back to her. "Getting a little protective, huh?"

"I don't like how he's skulking around you tonight."

"Forget him. We're nearly done here. Dessert, and then we can go upstairs and have some actual fun."

I grumble but don't argue at that.

There are a few toasts, and then pumpkin pie is served. I don't care for it, so I drink a cup of tea while we wrap up the evening.

"Excuse me, I'll be back in a minute. Restroom," Lily announces softly to the table and then leans close to my ear. "This is what I want: wait three minutes, then excuse yourself and find me in the unisex bathroom around the corner at the end of the hall. I can't wait any longer to have your hands on me."

"Yes, Professor," I breathe back before she vanishes.

I set a three-minute timer on my watch and then try to listen as her father drones on about the average cost of weddings these days. For some reason, he has an in-depth knowledge of the subject. When Mayla teases him by saying as much, he flusters.

"Well, I suppose I got rather interested in the topic a few

years ago when Lily was dating Marco. From a finance standpoint, it *is* rather interesting even now."

Fuck. I clench the teacup so hard I'm worried it'll break. Just the thought of Lily in a wedding gown next to that smarmy—

"Pardon." Screw the three minutes. I need my girl now.

I purge the ire from her parents and their rigid traditions by imagining what I'm about to do. I'll knock on the door and find her sitting on the sink, then I'll drop to my knees and shove that tiny skirt up to her waist as I kiss up her thighs. She'll moan and beg for more...

I'm lost in this image, already semi-hard as I round the corner and come to a dead halt.

At the end of the hall, just outside the restroom where I'm supposed to be feasting on that beautiful girl, stands that prick Marco with her instead. He steps forward and cages her against the wall, but there is nothing romantic about her stance. Her arms are crossed, jaw set hard as she glares up at him.

"Back the fuck up," she growls. Neither of them has noticed me. Lily shoves his chest, and at last he complies.

"Come on, Lil. It was you and me forever, baby. I'm getting married tomorrow, and *fuck*, you've gotten so sexy lately. So... bold. Don't tell me there's anything real between you and that boy toy you've been dragging around. Just, come out to my car. We'll talk, old times and all that, and... see what we want to do." He puts his hand on her shoulder and strokes her arm.

Lily leaps away, hissing. "Marco, are you out of your mind?"

I am, that's for damn sure. My vision goes red, and I stalk down the hall seeing nothing but a fucking target on his face. Goddam that asshole, it wasn't enough he smashed her heart and belittled her talent. Now he's putting his hands on her the night before his fucking wedding?

My fist connects with his nose before I realize what I've done.

Lily shrieks, and the asshole's head snaps back as he groans. He swings back at me and lands a blow to my temple that I know will equal a bruise. *Going to have to reschedule Monday's shoot with Oak & Thistle*, I think vaguely even as I grab his collars and shove him against the wall.

"Keep your fuckin' smarmy hands off my lass, you wee bawbag."

"*Calder*!"

Lily's nails dig into my arm and snap me out of it. I drop the human scrotum and turn to her, rage morphing into pure concern.

"Did he hurt you, love? Are you..."

The look on her face stops my words. A storm cloud is brewing in her eyes. That wide, sexy mouth is turned down in a horrified snarl. "What the fuck, Calder? You can't just *punch* someone, for crying out loud!"

"Erm, sorry, think I just did."

She doesn't smile, but then again I wasn't joking. I spear my hand through my hair and try again. "This cunt was putting his hands on you, Lily. What do you expect me to do?"

Her chin lifts. It's the hurt in her eyes that tells me I've fucked this up much worse than a couple of bruises.

"I expected you to trust that I can say what I want and get it."

Fuck.

22

LILY

All I see is red. I can't believe it. Calder of all people, stepping in, throwing his weight around like he knows better than me.

"Are you kidding me right now, Calder?"

He frowns like this the most confusing moment of his life.

Marco groans as he stumbles onto the floor. We both glance over for a second, and I roll my eyes before looking back at Calder. I start to walk away, but he grabs my arm to stop me.

"Don't!" I bark as I yank out of his hold.

"Lily, please. Will you just—"

I hold my hand up, cutting him off. "After all those times you encouraged me to say what I want, to stand up for myself, to put myself and my feelings first. That's exactly what I was doing just now. I don't need you to barge in like some testosterone-crazy caveman and smash in Marco's head to defend my honor. God, what decade do you think this is?"

Yeah, my piece-of-garbage ex was more than out of line.

He invaded my space and touched me multiple times without my permission. But I knew exactly what I needed to do to get rid of him. That's why I shoved him and told him off. I was doing just fine until Calder inserted himself into the situation.

Calder's face scrunches in disbelief even more. "I was just trying to protect you, Lily. Do you really expect me to just stand there and watch while your ex creeps on you?"

"Yes!" I yell. "Because I'm not a helpless, weak little flower who's too meek to do anything bold. If I needed your help, I would have asked for it." I shake my head. I'm dizzy with frustration. I take a breath to ease my pounding heart, but it doesn't help. "I know that's what everyone thinks about me, and honestly, I don't care. Because I know what I am and what I'm capable of now—and I thought you knew that too. But I was wrong."

He opens his mouth, but he doesn't speak.

"Don't. I want to be alone right now. Just leave."

I stop talking before my voice breaks and walk back toward the dinner service. Just then Harmony comes running over.

"What is all the yelling—" She cups her hands over her mouth. "Oh my god!" Her shocked voice is muffled against her hands as her gaze centers on Marco, who's rolling around on the floor while cupping his face.

Harmony runs over to him and crouches down next to him. "What... what happened?"

"I punched him." Calder's tone is humdrum, like he's reading his grocery list. He shoves his hands in his pockets and shrugs. I let out a disgusted sigh.

I'm tempted to run off and leave this mess, but I can't help but focus on Harmony as she crouches over Marco. Her eyes glisten with unshed tears as she gazes with worry at him.

I walk over to her. "Harmony," I say softly. She looks up at me, her blue eyes dazzling as a few tears fall. "Minutes ago, Marco groped me and tried to get me to leave with him." The breath I let out shudders through me. "I know... I know this isn't what you want to hear, but he's a piece of shit. You deserve way, way better."

For a second, I wait to see what she'll say. Will she lash out at me or accuse me of lying? Will she twist the scene and think that I was the one coming on to Marco? Will she refuse to believe me?

But she says nothing. All she does is stare at me with that bewildered and heartbroken look on her face.

"It's true, Harmony," Calder says from behind me. I register how much softer his tone is now. "That's why I hit him."

My head spins at the chaos of the last few minutes. I need to get the hell out of here. A handful of people from dinner who must have overheard the commotion start to filter into the hallway.

"What's going on? What was all that shouting about?" Mom asks when I stop back at the table to get my purse.

Just then Marco emerges holding a napkin to his face. I notice that Harmony isn't with him. Part of me wants to run back and check on her, but I fight the urge. Instead, I focus on my parents. The anger coursing through me from minutes earlier still has me on edge. Instead of just brushing what happened aside, like I've done so many times before in my life, I decide to tell them the truth, no matter how ugly it is.

"What happened was your golden boy Marco pulled me aside on my way to the restroom so he could grope me and proposition me to cheat on his fiancée. At his own rehearsal dinner. The night before his wedding. With his wife-to-be in the next room. So I told him off, then I told Harmony what a sack of crap she's about to marry."

Mom's jaw drops just as Dad's brow furrows.

"He's not the perfect guy you two seem to think he is. I tried to tell you that before. Hopefully now you'll finally believe me."

I yank my purse strap off my chair and walk toward the lobby of the hotel before they can say anything in return. I'm clenching my jaw so hard, I start to feel the beginnings of a tension headache. I was supposed to spend the night with Calder in our hotel room, getting up to endless naughty antics in the bed and shower and anywhere else we felt like it, but that's obviously not going to happen anymore. Not after the stunt he pulled.

My head aches as I wander over to where the elevators are. Hurried footsteps echo behind me.

"Lily!"

I turn around when I hear Auntie Mayla's voice. She pulls me into a hug.

"What a disaster tonight was," I sniffle as she squeezes me tight. "I just... I was just trying to do the right thing." I suddenly feel exhausted.

Just then she pulls away and grabs me by the shoulders to look at me. Her kind brown eyes gleam with fierceness and determination. "It's a disaster all right, but not because of anything you did. You *did* do the right thing tonight, *anak*. Now, let's get you to bed."

I babble something about how I can't stay in my room. Her eyebrows wrinkle with confusion.

"It's a long story," I mutter. "I'll explain once I can change out of this dress."

She nods once and pulls me into the elevator when it opens. "You'll stay with me tonight and tell me all about it."

I start to say that I can get my own room, but she waves a hand to cut me off.

"No, no. None of that." She squeezes my hand in hers. "I'm always happy to spend time with you, *nakkong*. And when's the last time we had a sleepover? Not since you were little. We're due for one."

Auntie Mayla's room is on the same floor as mine and Calder's, so I quickly pop in, grab my stuff, then follow her to her room. She insists that I take a hot bath to unwind. When I finish soaking and walk out of the bathroom, the table in her room is loaded with plates of desserts.

Dressed in the floral mumu she wears to sleep, she gestures to the table. "Since we missed dessert, I ordered room service for us."

I smile at the yummy offerings. I plop down into the plush armchair next to the table and dig into a slice of carrot cake. Auntie Mayla grabs a single-serving trifle and settles on one of the two queen beds in the room.

"Now," she says while digging her spoon into the dessert. "Tell me everything."

I spill everything between bites of cake—the moment Marco accosted me on the way to the women's restroom, how he drunkenly propositioned me, how good it felt to shove him and tell him off, how Calder stepped in and punched him in the nose, how I went off on him for pulling that excessively alpha move, and how after Harmony rushed in I told her exactly what her bastard husband-to-be did to me.

When I finish, I've devoured the carrot cake, a mini tiramisu, and a cannoli.

I sigh and wipe my mouth with my napkin. "I feel awful."

"About what, exactly?" Auntie Mayla says while adjusting a pillow behind her head.

"About everything. About how Harmony's heart is broken. About how her wedding weekend is ruined."

Auntie Mayla wags a finger at me. "You don't get to feel awful about any of that. It wasn't your fault, you hear me?"

"I know. I just mean it in a general sense. I know Harmony and I aren't best friends. And I'm still not over how mean she was to me as kids. But she didn't deserve for this to happen to her."

"The only person who should feel bad about that is that bastard Marco," she mutters.

I slip to the bathroom to brush my teeth and settle into the second bed. "Thank you for letting me stay with you," I say through a yawn.

"Of course," she says before yawning herself. "I know you're angry with Calder. But do you think the way you left things was the best?"

"What do you mean?"

She opens her mouth to speak, but then closes it. Then she looks away, like she's trying to carefully choose her words.

"I understand why you got upset with him. He shouldn't have hit Marco," she says. "But I can certainly understand why he reacted that way. Even the coolest heads go nuts when they see someone threaten the person they love."

My stomach flips the minute she says the word love. "I don't know about that. I'm not even sure he loves me."

Auntie Mayla's head falls back as she laughs. "Oh, *anak*. Look, I know I'm a trainwreck when it comes to relationships and marriage. But all that experience gave me a lot of insight. And I know when someone is in love. He's in love with you, just like you're in love with him."

I stare intently at the bedsheets as I fist them. Just the thought of Calder being in love with me has my heart pounding and my insides turning to mush. I'm in love with him, no doubt. I fell hard and fast... but I doubt he did. He's way too charming and too experienced to be so foolish.

"Lily."

I look up.

"Has Calder ever done this before? Does he just walk around punching people who look at him or you the wrong way?"

I nearly chuckle at how absurd that is. "No. Never. He's incredibly sweet and gentle."

She tilts her head at me. "I think what happened was a one-off for him. I think he saw Marco in your space, his hands all over you, and he saw red. No, it's not okay what he did, but I think you can work through it. You can explain to him that what he did crossed a line, and if he wants to continue being your boyfriend, he needs to not insert himself into situations that you can take control of perfectly fine on your own. You just have to talk about it."

I quietly think over what she's said.

"It's just that... my whole life, people have pushed me around, made decisions for me, belittled me because I was quiet and shy and passive. He was the one person who encouraged me to find my voice, to stand up for myself, to say what I want, to be unapologetic—to believe that I could be strong." I stop and sigh. "But tonight, when I was doing exactly that, he barged in like he knew better than me. Just like what everyone else did to me before. He was the last person in the world I thought would ever make me feel so insignificant and helpless. That's what hurts the most."

I shake my head and let out a defeated sigh.

Auntie Mayla responds with an understanding nod. "I understand how you feel. But I really don't think that's how he thinks of you. I think he just made a mistake. And we all make mistakes."

I nod in agreement.

"And I'm betting he'd do anything in his power to make this up to you, and to show you that he's worthy of you."

I squint at her. "You barely know Calder, Auntie. How can you assume this is what he's thinking?"

"All my time on this earth has given me a lot of insight." She takes off her glasses and places them on the nightstand between us before tucking herself under the bedsheets. She holds my gaze. "I can tell that you're in love with him. It's in how you look at him, the way you smile at him. I've never seen you as happy as when you're with him."

I hesitate for a second, but then I nod.

"And yes, I'll admit, I haven't known Calder long. I don't know how he acts with his friends or around other people. But I know how he looks at you—like you're the only creature in the room worth looking at. The way he dotes on you is the way a man dotes on a woman he's completely smitten with." She smiles and closes her eyes. "No question, he's in love with you."

With that, she closes her eyes. I turn off the lamp on the nightstand and lie in the darkness wondering—hoping—that what Auntie Mayla says is true.

Just then my phone buzzes on the nightstand with a text message. For the slightest moment, I wonder if it's Calder.

But then when I read the message, my stomach sinks.

Harmony: *Hey. Can we talk?*

23

CALDER

Lily strides away, her slim shoulders square. She is a woman on a mission, taking no prisoners, laying everyone in her path low. It is a beautiful sight.

Or it would be, if I hadn't just cocked up everything with my idiotic caveman move. As it is, I am one of the fools in her path, and she wants none of my attempts to explain.

Fuck, fuck, fuck.

I glance over my shoulder at an interesting tableau: Marco is on the floor, pinching the bridge of his nose. Harmony stands over him. She pulls a tissue from her tiny purse and drops it like it's nothing more than rubbish. It floats down, and Marco snatches it up.

"Baby, do you really think I—"

"Shut up. I don't know what to—"

But she breaks off as they both realize I'm within hearing range. He glowers at me, but Harmony blushes and bites her lips in a worried line. I nod at her once, but my lip curls as I regard him.

"Thanks a lot, you waste of space. Wasn't enough you stomped on her heart. Wasn't enough you had another perfectly lovely lass ready to marry you. You had to go and make me fuck up, didn't you?" I snarl at the asshole and rub my temple. "And you've fucked up my photoshoot."

"Fuck off," he snaps.

"Gladly. Easier to do when you've actually got a cock to do it with."

I roll my eyes at his spluttered attempt at a comeback and glance once more at Harmony. She looks so bloody sad it breaks my heart. I mouth, *I'm sorry*, then turn and make for the lift to our hotel room. As I'm striding down the hall, Brittany flies out of the ballroom, sprinting in her heels toward Harmony. She's such a blur of motion that our eyes don't even meet. I can hear her calling for her friend, but all I want to do is go to my room.

Lily's scent hits my nose as soon as I'm through the door, but I know she's not here. It's dark and quiet, so I turn on one light and lie back on the bed.

She'll want to cool off, maybe take a walk. Mayla will look after her until she's calm. Then she'll come back, and we can talk. I'm thinking an hour, maybe two. Oh, Professor, I didn't mean to speak for you. I'm so sorry. I haven't punched anyone since I was 18. Why the fuck did he have to put his hands on her?

I rub my eyes and groan at the ceiling. An hour, maybe two, and then we can talk. Get this worked out. That sounds reasonable. I reach for my phone.

How was it just a while ago I was setting that silly 3-minute timer? This time, I set it for two hours, a countdown to Lily's return. I open my news app and try to read to pass the time.

~

The blaring alarm jolts me awake. Disoriented as hell, I hurry to shut it off and look at the screen.

"What the fuck?"

Four hours have passed. I must've tapped refresh on the timer and didn't even remember. It's 2 am, I'm still in my suit, the light is still on...

And Lily still isn't here.

That thought sinks from my brain right down to the bottom of my stomach. She didn't come back. There will be no talking, no apology, no makeup sex, no... us?

I grab the phone in a panic, desperate to right this wrong and have her hear me, but the screen reads nothing but the time. The truth sinks in, and my hands freeze. She hasn't texted, called, *or* returned.

"I expect you to trust that I can say what I want and get it."

Her words ring in my ears, and I darken the screen and set it down. She said that she wanted to be alone. Pretending like she didn't bloody well mean it would only reinforce the idea that I don't trust her to say what she needs. Just because I want to beg an apology and do everything I can dream of to make it right doesn't mean I can override her wishes.

"Your wish is my command," I mutter to the empty room, then grab my bag, throw all my stuff in it, and let the door slam behind me.

My car growls down the empty highway as I drive at top speed back to my flat. My knuckles grip the steering wheel hard because, suddenly, it's the only fucking thing I feel like I have control of.

It's about an hour before dawn when I stumble into my living room, checking my phone for a message I know won't be there. I drop my bag on the floor with a muffled thump and look around. Somewhere in the back of my brain, the tiny wail that has been ringing since I woke up gets louder.

It's the sound of disaster, of being so damn close to having everything only to have it slip away last second. I don't know if I'm being dramatic, and that's the worst fucking part. She didn't text. She didn't come back.

She didn't need us to be okay.

I dig the heels of my hands into my eyes and shake my head. "Dammit, Lily, I thought we were real."

For a long minute, all I do is breathe in and out, forcing away the compulsion to act, to text, to deny the truth of the matter. And then, I exhale hard and spin for the kitchen to grab bananas, chocolate, grahams, and marshmallows. I trudge through the living room and snatch the blanket off the back of the couch, then throw myself onto the bed and hide under the wooly plaid while I gorge myself on the sickly sweet treats.

24

LILY

When I slide into the corner booth of the coffee shop where Harmony asked to meet me, every muscle inside my body is tense. I have to remind myself to breathe.

"Hi," I say softly.

"Hi," she says, her voice weak. "Thanks for meeting me."

"Of course."

I try not to stare at her face for too long. It looks like she didn't sleep a wink last night—or wash off her makeup. Mascara is smudged all around her eyes, her lipstick is faded, and her normally angelic complexion is red and puffy. It's the morning of her wedding, hours before she's due to say "I do". Judging by the state of her, I doubt that's going to happen.

She looks up at me, her blue eyes bloodshot, probably from crying. "I called off the wedding."

"I'm so sorry. I mean, I'm glad you're not marrying him." I bite my tongue when I realize how insensitive that sounds. "I'm sorry, Harmony. I just meant that—"

She shakes her head. The corner of her mouth lifts in a

weak smile. "It's okay, Lily. I know what you mean." She sighs and takes a long sip. I follow her lead and take a sip of my chai tea.

"I just want to say thank you."

I frown at her. "For what?"

"For telling me what Marco did. Honestly, I don't know if many people in the same situation would have been brave enough to tell someone that their future spouse is a slimy, cheating bastard the night before their wedding."

I quietly reflect on what she said. "I'd like to think most people would, actually."

She shakes her head. "Brittany wouldn't have." Harmony gazes off to the side and shakes her head. "After you walked off last night, I pulled Marco aside and broke it off. Then I punched him in the stomach."

I let out a surprised breath.

"Brittany ran after me, asking what happened. When I told her how you told me that Marco harassed you and propositioned you, she said you must have been lying. She said you made it up because you were jealous."

"What?" My voice is so shrill that a few people look over at us. I clear my throat. "Harmony, I would never, ever lie about that. I have nothing to gain by ending you and Marco! I can't believe..."

That weak smile makes an appearance on Harmony's face once more. "I know you wouldn't, Lily. You're a good person. Like, a seriously decent human being. You showed up to all my wedding events and supported me with a smile on your face. Me, the girl who was awful to you in school. And on top of that, I was going to marry your ex-boyfriend."

She lets out a joyless laugh, but it sounds so defeated that it makes my chest ache.

She gazes down into her mug, then looks back at me again. "I was so angry when Brittany said that about you. Because I knew in my heart that Marco was a piece of shit. I knew deep down that he would totally do something like that." She grips her coffee tighter. "He wasn't the most loyal guy on the planet. I don't know why I ever thought he would change."

I let her revelation float silently between us. At last, I hesitantly whisper, "Then why..." and let the unfinished question hang in the air: why the hell were you going to marry him?

"I guess I just wanted to be married so badly. I wanted to be a wife. I wanted to start a family..." She trails off as her voice breaks. It's a few seconds of sniffling and tearing up before she speaks again. "I guess that's why I put up with him for as long as I did."

I reach across the table and grab her hand in mine. "You'll get your dream, Harmony. I promise," I say firmly.

Uncertainty fills Harmony's teary eyes as she stares at me. "How can you be so sure?"

"Because you're young and hot."

She bursts out laughing, which makes me laugh too.

"But seriously, I know this sucks so bad right now. But you dodged a bullet. There are a million guys who I am positive would trip over themselves just to have a shot with you."

Even though she's smiling, she's shaking her head like she doesn't believe me.

"You really are too nice," she says softly.

"I'm really not. Not about this. Remember Billy's Sports Bar at your bachelorette party? Every guy in there couldn't take his eyes off you. You could walk back in there right now, smeared makeup and messy hair, and half of that bar would propose to you. Seriously." I give her hand a gentle squeeze before letting go.

A small smile makes an appearance on her dainty face. "Every guy but one. Tell Calder thanks for me."

I swallow, the image of Calder's fist crunching down on Marco's nose fresh in my mind once more.

"He did an excellent job breaking Marco's nose," Harmony says.

My eyes go wide. "His nose is broken?"

She shrugs. "He deserved it."

For a moment I wonder if I've been the slightest bit harsh to Calder. But then a wide smile stretches across Harmony's face, and I focus back on her. "Thanks, Lily. You've made me feel a million times better than I was feeling before you sat down."

"Sure thing."

I start to slide my arm back to my side of the table, but she grabs me by the forearm.

"I'm so, so sorry."

"For what?"

"For being such a bitch to you in school."

"Oh. Harmony, that's not—"

"Just let me get this out, okay? I've felt so guilty and embarrassed about the way I treated you. I just didn't know how to apologize. I was too ashamed that I ever said such horrible things to you in the first place. I thought that ignoring it was the best way to deal with it, to move past it. But I was wrong." She pauses to take a breath. "I should have apologized to you years ago. I just never did because I was a coward. I know this doesn't make up for how I hurt you, and I know that we'll never be best friends, but I just want to say that I'm sorry. And I want to thank you for being such a kind-hearted person. God knows I don't have enough of those in my life. You were better to me than my own friends were."

When she lets go of my arm, I rest it in my lap. For a minute, we just sit and sip our coffee in silence while I soak in Harmony's apology. Yes, she was cruel to me as a kid. Yes, I was mad about it for years. But I believe her when she says she's sorry—and I believe her reasons for why she held off on apologizing.

"I accept your apology, Harmony. Thank you," I finally say.

She flashes another weak smile in response.

"And if you ever need a friend, you can always call on me."

Her brow lifts. "Really?"

I nod. "We all screw up. We're all mean little brats at some point in our lives."

"Yeah, but I took the cake."

"I can't argue with that."

Harmony chuckles; I smile.

"But you're a better person now. I can see that. Plus, you're not marrying my ex anymore, so I like you extra for that."

Her head falls back as she laughs.

"But seriously. If you ever wanna meet up for coffee or drinks or to bash Marco, call me."

A small smile tugs at her lips. "I'd really like that."

I quietly admit to myself that I'd really like that too.

~

When I pull into my driveway after having coffee with Harmony, I'm shocked to see my parents' car parked there. I pull up next to them and get out. They do the same.

"What are you guys doing here?"

Dad fumbles with his sunglasses before shoving them in the chest pocket of his topcoat while Mom stands and folds her gloved hands in front of her. They both sport sad frowns on their faces.

"We're here to apologize to you, *anak*."

"What?"

Dad sighs and shoves his hands in his pockets, his blue eyes sad. "Honey, you were right about Marco. All these years we were wrong about him."

"Very, very wrong," Mom adds.

I cross my arms and nod, annoyed that it took Marco harassing me the night before his wedding for them to finally see him for who he really was.

"I know us saying all that doesn't magically make things better," Mom says.

"You're right. It doesn't."

The wind picks up, making the chill in the air even more bitter. I bet after seeing how upset I was last night at the hotel, Auntie Mayla called Mom to scold her and Dad and told them that they needed to make things right with me.

Dad huffs out a breath. "I fired Marco."

"Are you serious?" I gawk at him, shocked.

He clenches his jaw. "Give me more credit than that, honey. I know you and I haven't always gotten along, but do you really think I'm going to continue to employ the man who mistreated my daughter?"

I feel the slightest bit heartened at the protectiveness in his voice. When I look back at Mom, I notice her eyes are glistening with tears.

"We have a lot to make up for, Lily. I know we do. But we have to start somewhere. You're our only child—our only baby. Let us try to set things right with you. Please?"

I quietly acknowledge that she's right. I don't want to maintain these strained relations with my parents forever. And if they're willing to change for the better, I should meet them halfway.

"I'd like that," I say softly.

Mom's quivering lips stretch into a shaky smile as she walks over to me and pulls me into a tight hug. Then dad walks over and hugs us both. My eyes tear up as I enjoy the most wonderful group hug ever.

"Can we see your home art studio?" Mom asks while wiping her nose with a tissue.

"Oh. Sure."

I'm thrown off. My parents haven't once asked me about my artwork ever since I dropped out of law school and started teaching. I lead them inside the house and then to the garage, where my potter's wheel and easel are. They slowly scan the various pottery pieces and the painted canvases I have drying on the shelves in the garage.

"This is very impressive," Dad says while taking in the space.

"Oh wow." Mom turns to me. "You sure you don't want something bigger? We can help you buy a studio if you'd like. Something spacious so you can set it up just the way you want. That way you don't have to do it all in your garage."

I chuckle at her hopeful smile. I should have known she would go full-on interior designer on me.

I rest my hand on her arm. "I actually like the setup I've got. It's cozy. I work better in a smaller space like this."

I brace myself for her rebuttal, but she just smiles and nods once. "Okay. Then I like it too."

She points to a sculpture drying in the corner of the garage. It's a segment of waves crashing into each other.

"Wow. That's stunning."

My chest swells. "Thank you."

"Can I buy it?"

I frown at her. "You want it?"

Smiling, she nods. "I'd like to display that in the house."

"Sure, Mom."

"Just send me an invoice and I'll send the payment to you right away."

"How about this painting? Is it spoken for yet?" Dad points to an oil pastel landscape I finished months ago.

"You can have it, Dad."

"I think it would look good at the office. Just send me an invoice too."

I chuckle. "Will do."

They stay for a cup of tea and ask me how work is going. We've never had a conversation this long about my work, and it feels nice to have them show genuine interest in what I do.

When they get up to leave, we do another group hug and I walk them to the door.

"Thanks, you guys. That meant a lot. Really."

"No, honey. Thank *you*. For letting us into your life again when we've been so shortsighted for so long."

Mom nods along with Dad's assessment. "We're lucky to have you, *anak*."

We exchange I love you's, they leave, and I text Auntie Mayla.

Me: *Thank you for that.*

Auntie Mayla: *For what?*

Me: *For whatever you said to Mom and Dad to get them to come to my place and apologize for disapproving of my artist lifestyle for so long.*

Me: *I never thought I'd see the day when they took a genuine interest in my work.*

Me: *But it happened today because of you.*

Just then Auntie Mayla calls me. "Darling, I don't know what you're talking about. I didn't say anything to your mom or dad."

"You didn't?"

"Nope."

That means they came to this place all on their own. My heart swells at the thought.

Auntie Mayla chuckles. "They finally came to their senses, didn't they? They finally realized what a stellar kid they have? Finally!"

I smile.

"Well, since I have you on the phone, I may as well ask. Have you called Calder yet?"

My heart sinks. "Not yet."

"I guess it's only been a day. You should hear him out eventually."

I exhale and try to think of a nice way of changing the subject. After spending all of today making up with my parents and Harmony, I don't know if I have it in me for another emotionally charged conversation.

Mayla goes on when I don't reply. "*Anak*, look at it this way. You made up with Harmony and your parents. You weren't on the greatest terms with them. Did you ever think that would happen?"

"No," I admit.

"Well, you were on much better terms with Calder for

the entire time you knew him, right? Don't you think he deserves the same chance to make up with you?"

She's right. I owe him the chance to at least try to talk things out.

"Promise I'll talk to him after I get off the phone with you," I say.

I thank her, hang up, then pull up my text message chain with Calder.

Hey. Are you free anytime soon? I'd like to talk to you.

25

CALDER

My phone buzzes and jolts me awake. I'm flat on my back on top of the bedspread. The blanket I'd been sitting under is in a heap beside me. My mouth has a sticky film sealing it shut, and I can feel graham cracker crumbs on my lips. When I reach blindly for the phone, I get a banana peel instead.

Christ, mate, is this what your rock bottom looks like? With a groan, I push aside a chocolate bar wrapper and lift the phone so I can see it.

Lily: *Hey, are you free anytime soon? I'd like to talk to you.*

All I can do is blink at what I'm reading. Am I *free*? What the fuck, Lily? Like you need to schedule an appointment with someone you called your boyfriend just 24 hours ago?

Twenty-four hours. God, how short a time to change so much.

I have no interest in playing it cool by giving her time before I respond. My thumbs fly over the keyboard.

Me: *Of course. Fancy a drink? I could use one. Billy's Sports Bar? Worked well for us the first time.*

I nearly add a joke about her wearing the pink dress, but

I think I've been enough of a jerk lately, and texts are no place for humor right now. As it is, there's an eternal lag before:

Lily: *Okay. I'll be there in 2 hours.*

I'm about to darken my phone when another bubble pops up.

Lily: *But I'm not wearing that pink dress. :)*

Lily: *Sorry. I was just kidding. Probably not the time for humor, huh? Ugh. Sorry.*

Lily: *And now I'm texting too much. Great.*

My heart thuds with nothing but hope that this is a good sign.

Me: *We've talked about you saying sorry, I believe.*

Me: *Whatever you wear, I'll not be able to keep my eyes off you. Can't wait to see you, Professor.*

A thumbs up appears over that message. Good enough for now, and anyway I've got to get going. I've got just enough time to go for a run, shower, and pressure-wash the sweaters off my teeth. Perfect. I roll out of bed and go for my clothes. As I'm pulling on my trainers, I get a call.

"Ready for tomorrow night?" Nate greets me.

My stomach churns, only slightly from the carb overload. "Aye, no doubt. But, erm, Lily and I have both been a bit feverish today. If..."

He growls. "If you have to go have a bloody IV of fluid, inject bovine testosterone, sit in a sweatbox, or be so stoned on flu medicine that you're seeing fairies dancing in your whisky, of course I understand. That's how you were finishing that thought, right? Because if you, the face of our brand, aren't there for the *fucking launch party*—"

I chuckle, selling my humor pretty well despite palming my forehead at the same time. "Whoa, whoa, ease up! Just taking the piss, mate! Christ, you need a sweatbox to unwind a bit. You think anything would stand in my way of this?"

"I'll murder you in your sleep one day for giving me that heart attack, you arsehole," he groans. "Oh, and by the way —we want you in full kilt."

"I wouldn't want it any other way."

"Right. Dead by my hand, but first tomorrow. Cheers."

"Cheers."

I hang up and cinch my laces. *Lily, please don't let me down.*

Two hours later, my sheets have been changed, my body is slightly less angry at me thanks to a short run, and I'm sitting in the same booth as the night she showed up and changed absolutely everything. Then, I was pondering how the hell to fake a girlfriend and land the Sonce contract. Now, I've got the contract and am trying to figure out what the hell I can do to keep my *real* girlfriend. How do you prove to someone you trust them? How do you say sorry for being an asshole, even though the other asshole totally had it coming?

How do you do a relationship right? That's the real question, and the one I truly don't know how to answer. I've never wanted to before this. Even with Carmen, I was too young and naive to worry much about doing things right. I just figured we fancied each other, we banged each other's brains out, and so we were a good couple. Being a partner to someone was never something I thought about working for. For the first time in my life, I'm ready to work for something other than my career. I'm ready to work to be a proper partner, to give Lily what she needs and trust that she's there for me, too.

As I'm sitting there, pondering all this and barely sipping a beer, my phone blares with a WhatsApp call. I'm acutely aware that I have three missed calls from the same number over the last two weeks, and so I sigh and answer it. "Can't talk now."

"And fuck off to you too," Lucy returns promptly. "Why'd you answer if you cannae talk?"

I push my hand through my hair and twist my lips. "Didn't want you to think I'd died. I know I've been a bit MIA lately."

"Good plan, otherwise I'd be getting Mum to change the will in a heartbeat. Ah, no, Ma, I swear he didnae answer his phone. He must be dead in the gutter, trust me. Leave it all to your darling daughter, now that's a good lass." She laughs. "I don't think that's how it works, sadly."

Lucy never fails to get me chuckling. "Fair enough. So what do you want?"

"I was calling to give you my best on Sonce. Nate Wallace, now there's one of your mates I fancied back in the day."

"Did you now?"

"Oh, aye, he was a troublemaker with a smile that'd melt any mother's heart. What wasn't to love? I'd have let him deflower me in the back of my Vauxhall and not minded the hip cramps, that's for sure."

I groan and squeeze my eyes shut. "Is this congratulations or torture?"

She cackles into the phone. "Well it was meant to be a bit of both, but you've got the voice of a man who's got a load of worries on his mind. What's making you so grumpy?"

She's two years younger than me and thousands of miles away, but my sister's question is an invitation to talk that I didn't know I needed. Every way I've turned the situation over in my mind has yielded nothing but more complications, and this isn't the kind of thing you go crying to your mates about over a pint. But Lucy was always a good listener, smart enough to call out bullshit but kind enough to comfort me, too.

I pop in my headphones, set the phone on the table, and have a long pull of beer before saying, "If you must know, I'm in a bit of a... situation."

"I see. Well, you're not one to be in debt to the mob. Is it opioids? Prostitutes? Gambling?"

"Christ, woman, no, nothing like all that," I grumble.

Lucy huffs. "What do I know? They're all easy vices to fall into!"

"It's a woman, Luce. It's... relationship problems."

There's a long pause before: "Relationship? Fucking hell, I'd have been less shocked if it was whores."

I roll my eyes. "That's it, we're done. Forget I said anything. Go about your day casting spells and eating toads, you wee witch."

"Shut it and tell me all, you giant wanker."

We both laugh.

"Her name is Lily," I begin after a beat, and then spill it all in broad strokes, ending with the disaster of last night and, "She's meant to be meeting me soon, but I don't know what the hell I'm going to say to her."

"How about you're madly in love with her and you want to father all her babies, so can she please look past you being a daft oaf just this once?"

"That's the gist of it, yeah, but I need a bit of a gentler phrasing to make it easier to hear, don't you think? Ugh, I don't know how to do this. You know I'm not the guy who falls in love."

"You did, once."

"Yeah, and look where that got me. Fat lot of good the whole relationship thing is."

"You better watch that lying. It'll give you wrinkles, pretty-boy."

I smile and shake my head. "I hate when you're right."

"So what're you gonna do?"

"Tell her the truth, I guess. Messy though it might be."

Lucy squeals and claps. "That's a good lad. Can't wait to hear the happy ending. Call me soon?"

"Promise."

I pull out the earbuds and check the time. Lily's running late, no text as a heads up. With a deep inhale and exhale, I refuse to set another fucking timer. *She'll be here. We'll work it out.*

But, like last night, she's not here. And when an hour has gone and I'm still alone, the exhale isn't nearly as calm anymore. I stab her contact on my phone and put it to my ear. Voicemail. Fuck that. I dial again—twice. On the fourth try, I growl into the phone,

"I'm sat here wondering if you're hurt—or if you've stood me up. If you're not dead, can you please just fucking let me know?"

Two minutes later, I get a bloody text:

Lily: *I'm not dead.*

Me: *Why are you doing this? You've stood me up and left me waiting twice now, Professor.*

No reply.

I dial again and wait through another round of ringing to say, "If there's a grand gesture I can make, let me make it. If there's a thing I need to hear, let me hear it. But we're not done here, not yet. And while it's clear by now you're content to let me go alone tomorrow night, I don't care. I've got things to tell you, Lily Maldonado, and I'm a patient man. You know it's true—you've seen me hold a pose for an hour straight. Giving you space to get sorted I can and will respect. It would be decent of you to give me a wee bit of consideration as well, though. I want to hear from you the second you have words for me. Until then, just know I'm waiting—and I'm here for you."

When I set the phone on the table, I'm somehow calmer. Yes, tomorrow is going to look terrible. Nate will murder me twice now, but what matters most is that I'm there. If I don't think about giving a speech to hundreds of people without her lovely face to focus on, and if I don't think of what kind of excuse I need to make for her absence, then it's all alright. I've said something. It might be half of what I need to say, but it gives me a sense of control in this chaos.

I love her. I'll tell her. Will she likely tell me to fuck off? Yes. Do I care?

No. For her, it'll be worth it.

26

LILY

My hands shake as I try to grip the steering wheel of my parked car. After a few failed attempts to hold onto it, I drop my hands in my lap. Another sob shudders through me. I don't even know why I'm attempting to drive. I'm not in any condition to. I'm crying so hard I can't even see in front of me.

Calder's words that I overheard minutes ago as he sat in that booth—*our* booth—at Billy's Sports Bar echo in my head.

You know I'm not the guy who falls in love... Fat lot of good the whole relationship thing is.

I wasn't meant to hear him. He was clearly talking on the phone with someone else. But still...

I can't deny what he said. He was speaking openly and honestly about his feelings, about love, about how he feels about being in a relationship...

My head spins. That spot in my chest where my heart used to be is an empty, throbbing hole.

Calder doesn't love me. Because he's not the kind of guy who falls in love. He said so himself.

I let his admission tumble over and over in my head. It doesn't matter how long it silently plays. It kills the same every single time.

When I heard him say those words as I stood just a few feet behind him, it landed like a kick to the gut. For a second, I was frozen in shock. But then the tears came, and I wasn't just going to stand there and sob in public. I didn't want anyone to see me break down, especially not Calder.

So I spun around and walked out of the bar and straight back to my car, Calder's devastating words reverberating in my head.

Sitting in the parking lot, I blink and another downpour of tears soaks my cheeks. I was so hopeful when I drove to Billy's Sports Bar. I even smiled when he suggested meeting there in his text. It gave me the slightest glimmer of hope. Because if that night at that bar conjured up the same sweet memory for him as it did for me, then that meant that we were both sentimental mushes who were willing to do anything to fix this rift between us. We'd both say sorry, then hug, then kiss, then start a very graphic makeout in the booth that would end at either his place or mine...

I thought it meant that we would go back to what we were—two people who were crazy about each other and wanted to be together. But now, after hearing what he said, that's not going to happen.

My head throbs with a million questions.

Why did he suggest meeting at the bar that held such a sweet memory for the both of us if he's not in love with me?

Why did he agree to make things official between us if he's not the kind of guy who falls in love? If he's not a relationship guy?

Is that why he agreed to meet with me in the first place?

To tell me that he wasn't the kind of guy who falls in love? Was he going to break up with me?

I shake my head, halting the barrage of questions that I'll never get answers to. None of that even matters. What matters is that I'm in love with him, but he's not in love with me. And there's nothing that can change that.

When I manage to stop sobbing, I take a long, deep breath. Then I grip the steering wheel with both hands. They're finally steady.

I'm about to start my car when my phone rings. I glare at the screen when I see it's Calder.

"I have nothing to say to you!" I yell at my phone. My cheeks flush when I realize how ridiculous I must look to anyone who happens to walk through the parking lot and see me shouting alone in my car.

Closing my eyes, I lean my head back against the headrest as my phone blares on and on for the next few minutes. Finally, it beeps with a voicemail. I let out a sigh and listen to Calder's message.

"I'm sat here wondering if you're hurt—or if you've stood me up. If you're not dead, can you please just fucking let me know?"

I huff out a breath as my eyes go watery once more.

Me: *I'm not dead.*

He replies instantly.

Calder: *Why are you doing this? You've stood me up and left me waiting twice now, Professor.*

My thumb hovers over my phone screen. I almost do it. I almost text back and tell him that I don't have the strength to speak to him or look him in the eye right now after he's hurt me in the worst way… after overhearing him declare to that mystery person on the phone that he's not a relationship kind of guy, that he could never fall in love—not even with me.

But then my phone rings again. Calder's name flashes across the screen, and I freeze. It goes to voicemail, he leaves a message, and I hold my breath as I listen, relishing the low growl of his tone, the melody of his accent.

"If there's a grand gesture I can make, let me make it. If there's a thing I need to hear, let me hear it. But we're not done here, not yet. And while it's clear by now you're content to let me go alone tomorrow night, I don't care. I've got things to tell you, Lily Maldonado, and I'm a patient man. You know it's true—you've seen me hold a pose for an hour straight. Giving you space to get sorted I can and will respect. It would be decent of you to give me a wee bit of consideration as well, though. I want to hear from you the second you have words for me. Until then, just know I'm waiting—and I'm here for you."

I hang up and drop my phone in the passenger seat, pull out of the parking lot, and drive home in a daze of Calder's words.

Tomorrow night.

The clipped way he said that sticks with me. I can tell just how nervous and worried he is about his big speech at the Sonce holiday event. Despite how broken I am right now, I can't help but feel for him. Can I really stand him up for a third time, on a night when he needs me the most?

I pull into my driveway, turn off the car, and sit inside as I attempt to wrestle once more with all the thoughts in my brain. In the end, one thing remains true: Calder doesn't love me, but that doesn't change how I feel about him.

And when I get out of the car and walk into the house, I know exactly what I'm going to do.

27

CALDER

I wake up the next morning amid another wasteland of banana s'mores. The bloated, nauseous sugar hangover makes me wish I was the kind of man who drowned his sorrows in whisky, but whisky is a pleasure, nothing guilty about it. Junk food hasn't been a part of my life since I was in my teens.

For good bloody reason. I groan and pat my irritated stomach, then roll off the quilt and hit the shower. Two hours at the gym are required, partially for this caloric binge but also to calm my already-building nerves about tonight. That bloody speech isn't enough; now, I'm going to get to make excuses for why I'm stag again.

Throughout the day, I'm hell-bent on strategizing why I'm arriving solo and remembering what I'm going to say when I stand in front of that mic. I waffle on texting Nate a heads-up that Lily won't be coming, but ultimately decide that a last-minute family emergency is cleverer. He nearly had a stroke yesterday when I hinted at a change in plans. Likely he'll know my excuse is bullshit, but it'll be a convenient facade to get me through the evening.

The speech, though, won't stay in my head, and so I go back to the flashcards I've been carrying damn near everywhere for two weeks. Throughout the afternoon, I wander round my apartment muttering key lines. Even while I'm buckling my kilt and fastening my sporran, I've got the cards scattered on the bed in front of me.

It's when I'm standing in front of the mirror, fussing with my fly plaid and brooch, that the speech and the party take a backseat again. Once I've got the plaid on my shoulder, threaded properly through the epaulette of my jacket, I pause and regard myself in the mirror. This is a task that goes much easier with a bit of help, and, for just a moment, I admit to myself that I had totally envisioned Lily standing beside me. Her lips would've been pursed in concentration as I explained the rules for putting it on. She would've helped me pin the brooch in place and smiled when I recounted my mum helping me when I was a boy. I'd have told her that this was the most formal version of kilt dress, reserved for black-tie events—and that I fully intended to wear this exact getup if I ever got married. She would've turned pink, I'd have grinned, but the comment would've been anything but casual conversation.

I groan and rub my eyes, breaking out of this little fantasy and returning to the task at hand. "Ladies and gentlemen, good evening..."

With the cards tucked in my coat pocket, I stride out the door to the car that's waiting. Those little blue index cards are practically a security blanket by now, and I whip them out again for the ride to the party. If I focus, if I can flip through them and keep my mind on getting through the speech, then I don't have to think about the gaping hole that is the empty seat beside me.

The gaping hole that is my heart.

"Suck it up, mate. Time to look sharp," I mutter to myself as the car swings up to the venue. A quick check of my hair, my for-the-camera smile plastered on, and I'm ready.

Cocktail hour is in full swing, so I grab a highball glass and glide through all the guests, stopping anytime anyone catches eyes with me so that I can talk up the product and introduce myself. Given that I am a walking visual of Scotland, people catch eyes with me every few paces. It's good to be working, to slide into the zone and do what I'm best at. It reminds me just how much tonight means to me. To have gone from a kid running through the barrels to the face of this fantastic brand takes all my life dreams and passions and rolls them into one. The more that sinks in, the easier it is to manage the dull ache still tugging at my heart.

I'm chatting with the head of distribution about this year's rugby World Cup when Nate appears. He folds himself into the conversation, but when things dwindle he excuses us and guides me away.

"Where's your lass tonight?" he asks as soon as we're out of range. There's no eye contact; he's scanning the room, a big smile in place even as he hisses at me from the side of his mouth.

"Family thing last minute. Mum wasn't feeling well. She had to drive out this afternoon."

He chuckles and finally turns to me, but his eyes aren't angry. No one is close enough to hear us, and for a second we're just Nate and Cal. With a shake of his head, he says, "You're a horrible liar and always were. Having a spat, are you?"

I shrug. "Of course not. Family man and all that. Everything is bloody Shangri-La."

The humor in his expression disappears. "Look, jokes aside for a moment. Lily is fantastic, and from what I've seen, you two are a match. Dunno what you've done to cock it up, but make it right. You don't want to lose the one who calls you on your bullshit and turns you on just by a look in her eye, you hear me? Even when she drives you absolutely batshit crazy, that's a woman you want to keep. Not for your image—for your life, mate."

While I'm reeling from this sudden bout of gravity, Nate's gaze flickers behind me. Suddenly, he's grinning again.

"Case in point," he mutters before saying louder, "Ah, there she is, the Queen of the Isles. Hello my darling, you're looking embarrassingly hot tonight."

Eileen blushes as Nate slips an arm around her and kisses her cheek. He gives me a look, and I puff out a breath and nod.

"Was easier when you were seventeen and I could take the piss out of everything that came out of your wise-arse mouth," I mutter while Eileen waves to someone across the room.

He barks a laugh. "Yes, but a good bit less useful, eh? Come, let's mingle."

We stroll over to say hello to some VIP financial backers. The women ogle me while the men grip my hand in a firm shake. No one gives me a raised-eyebrow look to question my validity. More than one person comments on the new Oak & Thistle line.

This has worked. I've stepped into a whole new phase of my career in *exactly* the way I'd dreamed of. Part of me is giddy and elated.

If only that damn hole weren't there, sucking the shine out of everything.

"There's our man," Pat Wallace shouts across the room at me. He and his wife come over to join me. "You still look like hell, Cal, but I'm damn glad your ugly mug is the face of our brand," he chuckles.

"Wouldn't have it any other way."

"Where's that pretty gal of yours?" Pat looks around, a curious frown suddenly on his face.

Without thinking, I dig my index finger into the cuticle of my thumbnail. It's a terrible habit, I know, but I don't care. I scratch at my thumb and try to smile. "Oh, ah well—"

"Right here."

Slender, cool fingers lace with mine, interrupting me from my self-destructive mission. Her too-familiar scent hits my nose. When I turn my head and stare into those big brown eyes, I swear I'm hallucinating. My jaw unhinges, but Lily simply tips her lips up in an enigmatic smile.

She turns to Pat and Nate. "Sorry I'm late. Had a small family emergency, but it's all worked out now. How are you, gentlemen? Eileen, that dress is gorgeous."

While I stand there dumbstruck, Lily chats like everything is normal. She holds my hand easily. Her shoulder leans against mine just enough to send the message that we're together. The simple stance has scrambled my brain, and I waffle between anger, disbelief, and adoration at how stunning she looks in that crimson party dress. Her black-brown hair is pulled up, her makeup luminous but subtle.

If I didn't know her so well, I wouldn't even notice the fact that she's terribly pale underneath. If I hadn't become so damn attuned to every tiny detail about her, I wouldn't catch the way her fingers squeeze my knuckles oh-so subtly from time to time, or the way her shoulders are just a little too high to be at ease.

But I do know her that well. I want to know every damn detail about her. And so I notice every single thing. None of it adds up to an answer for why the hell she's here or what I can hope it means, but I don't need an answer right now because—

"Well, my dear lad, what's say we kick off dinner hour, hmm?" Pat claps my shoulder. It's my cue to head to the microphone and speak to the whole damn room.

Lily squeezes me hard at that one. I nearly lean in for a cheek kiss, but I'm not sure I'm allowed right now. Instead, I nod at Pat and give her one more squeeze before turning to the podium.

"Calder."

I turn around.

Lily's smile is a bit wider, but she's got sadness in her eyes. Her delicate neck constricts with a hard swallow, and suddenly those dark eyes are sparkling with unshed tears. "You've got this, *love*. Go be great."

She croaks when she uses my pet name for her on me, but her smile is unwavering in its encouragement.

I knit my brows and twist my lips. "Never greater than when I'm with you, *love*."

She winces, and I want to blow off the speech and drag her to the first place we find where we can be alone and sort all this shit out. Before I can seriously consider it, she waves her hand in a shooing gesture and then turns to take her seat at one of the large dining tables.

One thing at a time.

Tunnel vision hits me as I adjust the mic and pull the cards from my pocket. All the guests are seated, waiting for me to charm them, waiting for me to kick-off dinner.

Can't I just take off my shirt and wink for a minute and let that be that?

The thought makes me chuckle and breaks my haze. I clear my throat and begin.

"Ladies and gentlemen, good evening. Thank you for coming out to celebrate Sonce's big debut with us tonight.

"Growing up, my parents always told me school was important. I needed a good education to be successful in life. I guess that's all well and good, but if you ask me, my real education happened among the tuns and barrels at Sonce Distillery. And, to be honest with you, the true marker of success in my life is this moment right here, where I can say to you all that I'm Calder Ross, and I am honored to be the face of Sonce's debut in the USA."

The room erupts in applause so suddenly that I'm startled to silence, but it gives me a moment to sip water and take a breath. *This is going okay. Don't cock up now!*

I check my notes and go on about growing up with Nate and falling in love with whisky, then bring us to the present day, highlighting the awards Sonce has already won and talking about the plans for the future.

But when it's time to close, I set the cards down and look out over the audience, really letting myself see them for the first time so far. Not surprisingly, my gaze finds Lily almost immediately. The whole time I've been speaking, I haven't let myself look for her. Just knowing she's there has been enough. But when I catch her eyes, that sweet smile deepens, and she flashes me a thumbs-up.

My next words come from somewhere in my brain that I'm not even sure of. They just kind of tumble out when I open my mouth. "Love is a word people throw around a lot, don't you think? 'I love this song, I love this pizza, I love this book.' Nothing wrong with that, if you ask me. Why not love freely? Why should love be complicated or secret? If you love something, you want to share it. If you love some*one*, then you should bloody well tell them at every opportunity you get. Life is short. Love makes it sweeter.

"And so, as we share this meal together, I hope you talk about all the things you love best, and I challenge you to tell someone you love them, even if you said it just a few minutes ago. But for now, please raise your glasses for a love we all share: Sonce whisky! Slàinte!"

"Slàinte!" comes the reverberating cry from every voice in the room, followed by another round of thunderous applause. I tip back my dram and step away from the mic.

Waiters have already sprung into action, hustling to the tables with trays of dinner plates. The applause fades smoothly into clanking silverware and chattering voices. Still buzzing with adrenaline, I skirt through the tables toward my own.

Nate stops me by grabbing my jacket. He jumps up and claps a hug on me. "Fan-fucking-tastic, mate. You're a fucking natural. So glad you're part of this."

His smile is so broad, I'd almost not believe this was the same kid I used to smoke cigarettes and get pissed with when we were 14, dreaming about girls and trouble and talking bullshit like we knew a damn thing about the world. It's that moment that the magnitude of this hits me, and my throat tightens too. I return the hug with one of my own.

"Piss off, mate, we both know you're secretly in love with me," I say into his ear when I embrace him.

"Wanker," he laughs, giving me a shove.

I wink and blow him a kiss. Then, I turn and continue toward my table.

Lily's gaze connects with mine, and my shoulders go square. Joys and triumphs aside, I have one more mission tonight. I just dared myself to do it, so no sense waiting or doubting now.

I don't sit down, just hold out my hand, inviting her to take it. She hesitantly slips her palm across mine.

"A word, Professor, if you please." My tone is kind, but there is no bullshit or hesitation in it.

"Now? No, Calder, I'm here for you, but—"

"A word. I think you know which one, but it's time for me to man up and say it."

Every emotion I can think of flashes in her eyes. Confusion, sadness, shock, fear, hope, all one after another, but she stands up anyway. I touch the small of her back and lead her out of the room to the coat closet down the hall. It's full, but there's enough space for us to face each other.

"Lily," I say when the door shuts. "I'm so bloody angry at you for standing me up. I waited for you. Friday night, then last night. How could you disappear on me?"

Her gorgeous mouth is curved down in a frown. "I needed time, Calder. I—"

I hold up a hand to silence her. "Sorry, love, but hush. I'm not done. It wasn't a question I wanted an answer to, because the truth is it doesn't fucking matter. It doesn't change things for me. It doesn't do a damn thing but make me even more sure."

"Sure?" Her voice trembles, those eyes too bright yet again. "I know, Calder. I—"

"Hush and let me do this," I chuckle, letting my hands slip to her waist. She tenses, but she doesn't step away. "I'm sorry, darling. So very sorry for what I did, for how I acted. I swear on anything you want me to that I will *never* pull a caveman move like that again. It wasn't anything to do with thinking you didn't know what you needed. It wasn't to do with thinking you couldn't tell him to fuck off all on your own or doubting your strength."

I take a deep breath. Saying it in a speech was easy. Saying it in this tiny closet is a whole other matter. But I'm past ready to say these words to Lily Maldonado.

"It was everything to do with loving you so damn much that seeing that scumbag trying to pressure you snapped something in my brain. I know, I know, I won't let it happen again, but I'm new at this. And I-" I break off with a self-deprecating laugh and touch my forehead to hers. "I am so deeply in love with you. I just hope you can forgive me. I trust you, Lily. I hope you'll trust *me* when I say I will let you fight all your battles moving forward if you want. But I'll be much better off if we move forward together."

Her hands flutter up and rest on my chest, but all I get is wide-eyed silence for so long that I finally clear my throat. "Right, so now would be a good moment for you to say something, maybe."

28

LILY

I'm speechless. As I stand here, crammed in the coat closet with Calder, my hands pressed on his chest and my eyes locked with his, I don't know what to say.

He's said everything I've ever wanted him to... but it makes no sense anymore. Because it goes in direct opposition of what he said yesterday when I overheard him at Billy's Sports Bar.

I open my mouth and try to speak. Nothing but a stuttered noise comes out. Calder's eyes widen, then he swallows. As the seconds pass, his grip on my waist loosens.

"Lily. Love. Please. I'm dying here." A sad-sounding chuckle falls from his lips. His blue-green eyes gleam with worry. "Say something. Anything."

"Sorry, I just...."

The corner of his mouth quirks up and the slightest bit of worry melts from his face. "What did I say about saying sorry?"

I let out the smallest laugh. "Okay. I take back the sorry."

For a second we both just smile at each other. And then I swallow and say it all.

"Hearing you say that—hearing you say you love me—is... everything. It's all I wanted to hear."

Calder claps a hand to his chest and groans. "Then what's with the long silence? Are you trying to give me a heart attack? Because you're doing a bang-up job of it."

Smiling, I grab both his wrists and lower them to his sides. I raise an eyebrow at him. "Hush, and let me say this."

He flashes a smirk at how I've borrowed his phrase.

"I'm just thrown because you said you didn't love me."

That smirk drops into a frown. "What? I *never* said that."

"You did," I say gently. "At the sports bar yesterday."

My throat tightens at the memory of his words, but I swallow and press on.

"I was walking up to the booth where you were sitting, but then I heard you on the phone. I heard what you said about not being the kind of guy who falls in love... about how pointless relationships are."

His brow shoots to his hairline. "Lily, I—"

"Please." I gently squeeze his wrists. "Just let me get this out, okay?"

Pursing his lips, he starts to nod. But then he shakes his head. "No. Fuck that. I'm bloody sick and tired of letting this misunderstanding screw us up."

Now I'm the one frowning. "What misunderstanding? I heard what you said."

That gentle smile I love so much tugs at his lips. "Maybe so, but you only heard one side of the conversation."

A bulb goes off in my head. Shit. He's right.

"I was talking to my sister, getting advice from her about how to make things right with you. She could tell how wrecked I was over you. So I laid it all out for her. I told her how crazy I am about you, how I couldn't get you out of my head after that first class together, how I did a pisspoor job of faking a relationship because my feelings for you were and still are very, very real. I told her how you make me happier than I've ever been, and how I fucked it all up that night with Marco and didn't know how to fix it. I needed her help to make this right with you because as a man who hasn't really been in love in my life, I had no idea what I was doing. I was going out of my mind without you."

My heart pounds and my mouth parts open as I try to breathe. It all makes sense now.

"So yes, Professor. You're half right. I *was* never the kind of guy to fall in love or to ever want to be in a relationship. Until I met you."

A long pause hangs in the air between us.

Calder clears his throat. "So—"

I grab him by the lapels of his jacket and pull his mouth to mine. And then I kiss him until my mouth aches. When we break, our chests are heaving. We're sucking all the air out of this closet.

"Bloody hell," he says with a laugh while wiping his mouth with the back of his hand.

"Okay," I say through a sigh, my hands still on his chest. "I'm done with all these misunderstandings, so I'm going to say everything I need to say right now." I take a breath. "First of all, I'm so, so sorry I stood you up yesterday. You're right. I shouldn't have made that judgment based on only hearing your end of the conversation. Second, I won't do that ever again—I won't ever jump to conclusions and run away. I promise I will stay and work things out with you. Even if that means we fight like crazy... because I'd rather fight with you than lose you."

I take a breath. "And third, I'm sorry for how I iced you out when you punched Marco. Yes, I needed time to process what happened, but I shouldn't have cut off communication with you like that. I'll never be okay with violence, but...I understand why you reacted that way. You were reacting out of protectiveness for me."

He nods and tucks a chunk of my hair behind my ear.

"And even though I can take care of myself, I like that you feel protective of me."

The look in his eyes softens even more. "You've got my whole heart, love. I can't help it."

"No more cold-cocking douchebags, okay?"

He smirks. "Okay."

"And fourth."

"There's a fourth?" he chuckles.

"It's a good one, I promise."

A smile lingers on his lips.

"Fourth is this: I am completely in love with you, Calder Ross. And I've been in love with you since the first time you rocked my world in your bed."

His eyes widen, and that sexy smirk of his reappears.

"That probably sounds... creepy."

"It does not," he says, his voice soft. "It's bloody hot, Professor."

He cups my cheek with his hand. I close my eyes and hum. It feels so, so good to have his hands on me like this again. Then he pulls me to his mouth. Once again we're a breathless tangle of tongues and gasps.

We stop and rest our foreheads against each other.

"Fifth," he growls. "No more faking for us. Ever again. Everything we do from this point on will be real and true. I can't exist any other way with you."

"I can't fake anything with you, Calder. Not when I love you this much."

I fight the cringe inside of me. I don't think I've ever sounded so cheesy.

But Calder slips his hands around my waist and pulls me tight against him. When he looks at me, I'm breathless. His whole heart is in his gemstone eyes. Instantly, that cringe feeling disappears. He feels the same way about me. My heart pounds a new rhythm as we stand here, together, in this moment, two people completely and utterly in love.

"Neither can I, love."

29

EPILOGUE

10 MONTHS LATER

CALDER

I'm a Highlander. It's a very noble thing, full of pride and ancient tradition. I don't flinch at danger or blood. A warrior like me is always ready for battle.

But even though I'm shirtless and driving with the windows down on a cool October evening, my palms are sweating. When Lily left the house, I was sprawled on the sofa in my sweats and hoodie. Ten minutes later, I had my kilt buckled, my hair sorted, and my sporran most definitely full. Then, I raced out to my car so I could get there on time. Thank god she's the kind of sensible person who drives no more than 5 miles over the speed limit. That means I can flood the engine and absolutely floor it, which takes just a hint of edge off my nerves.

It's not that I'm nervous, per se. It's just that I want this to be perfect so badly that I have literally torn the cuticle off my thumb from planning it.

My phone rings on the Bluetooth, jolting me out of intense focus. Adrenaline shoots my gut when I see the caller is "Professor."

"Everything alright, love?" I say when I tap the dash.

"Yeah. I don't know, I just wanted to hear your voice."

I laugh. "You heard my voice not half an hour ago."

"Are you suggesting I shouldn't have asked for what I want?" Her tone is saucy, but I can hear her smile.

"Now, Professor, you know I'd never do such a thing. I take it back. Shall I read to you, then, so you can continue to hear my voice?"

Her musical laugh breaks through. "No, and I know it's silly. Just, I don't know. I'm excited to be going out with the girls, but part of me just kind of wants to be snuggling you on our couch—like we do basically every night."

"Mm, aye, before we go do a very different kind of snuggling on the bed."

"Exactly," she grumbles.

Another laugh rumbles in my chest. "Don't you worry, love. There will be plenty of time to paint and drink with the girls, then be worshipped until late into the night, I promise."

"I knew there was a reason I needed to hear your voice."

"Because you love me."

She giggles again. "Because I love you. And not just for your body. Or your tongue. Or your..."

"Sense of humor?"

"I was going to say kilt."

We both laugh at that, and then Lily says, "Are you driving too? It sounds like you're in the car."

Shit. Just when this silly banter had started to relax me and make me believe this was a good idea, I'm on the verge of spoiling it all. "Eh, thought I'd go to Billy's and watch the replay of the match since you're out. Cry into a pint that the most beautiful girl in the world isn't beside me, but better than crying at home, now innit?"

"Sounds like a good night. Enjoy—but, um, I want you

to be home before me. Please. Is it okay that I—ugh, I'm still working on the bold thing, I guess."

"Try again then."

She clears her throat. "Enjoy your night, Calder, but I want you to be home and ready to throw me on the bed when I text you. Got it?"

"Yes *ma'am*."

"God, I love you," she says through her giggles. "Okay, see you later."

"Hopefully sooner." Now, I can tease about it. She has no idea, and dammit, I think this is the perfect plan.

Lily hangs up as I pull into the shopping center and park beside the restaurant two shops down from my destination. My car is noticeable; best to avoid being seen.

Morgan is on the corner, just apart from the outdoor diners, and she beams when she sees me. "Hurry, she'll be here soon!" she shouts.

And so I adjust my kilt and break into a jog. The patrons drop their forks and jaws at the sight of a shirtless highlander running down this little strip mall, but I just grin and wink as I go past. Ladies blush, men chuckle, and I am so damn ready to make this happen.

30

EPILOGUE

LILY

"So. How's life with your hunky model boyfriend?" Morgan's question comes out in a huffy breath.

I squint at her as she settles in next to me at the sketch table, wondering why it sounds like she went for a jog instead of a quick trip to the bathroom to wash her hands like she said.

I'm about to ask her why she's so out of breath when an image of Calder lounging on our sofa in sweats, looking scruffy and delicious, flashes in my mind. I'm instantly distracted.

Life with Calder Ross has been a fantasy come true. Sure, we argue and disagree like any other couple. It turns out that Calder doesn't care about making the bed or unloading the dishwasher right away like I do. He turns the volume on the TV way too loud. And it's near constant shouting in the house every time his beloved soccer team plays. I can never remember the name, which drives him crazy when he's screaming himself hoarse over whatever is going on.

But all of that is trivial. Because I've never been so happy.

It doesn't matter if we're cuddled up on the couch watching Netflix. Or hunched over my potter's wheel as I'm trying to teach him how to sculpt properly while he's cracking jokes. Or I'm ogling him shamelessly whenever he lets me sit in on a photo shoot. Or we're enduring a long family dinner at my parents' house. Or we're Skyping with his parents and sister, and he's trying his best to translate their crazy thick Scottish accents for my American ears.

It's all bliss.

Joy surges at the center of my chest. "So happy," I whisper to myself.

Morgan smirks while shaking her head. "You're so smitten, it's sickening."

I chuckle, and she nudges me. It feels good to have my best friend back. I missed her good-natured teasing the months she was gone. Now that her grandma's recovered from surgery, Morgan and I are back to hanging out every other day.

I glance around the space. "Is it weird that we've never done a class like this before?"

"Yes. You're an art professor. I'm a model. This stuff is our bread and butter. I figured now is as good a time as any to try a wine and art class, on our first proper girls night since I've been back home."

Morgan checks her phone for the millionth time since we arrived. For a second, I wonder if there's something up with her grandma.

"Everything okay?" I ask.

"Yeah, fine. Just wondering if Harmony's ever going to show up."

I sip my glass of white wine, given to us by the woman who owns the studio. Strange, but she hasn't been back to check on us since dropping off our drinks. Even stranger, I suddenly notice, is the room is completely empty. We're the only ones signed up for tonight's class.

"Oh wait, she's about to walk in," Morgan says with yet another glance at her phone.

Never in a million years did I ever think I'd be friends with Harmony. But we are. And to my surprise, she's a pretty amazing friend. We're not besties—Morgan would kill me if I ever considered anyone other than her my best friend. But ever since she and Marco broke up, we've hung out a handful of times, and it's been a blast. We've clocked in two yoga classes and one bar crawl together. Even Morgan—who hated Harmony because of how she treated me as a kid—has warmed up to her.

Just then, Harmony walks in the door clad in skin-tight leather pants and a shimmery top, her long blonde hair styled into perfect barrel curls. Morgan and I, in our jeans and plain shirts, look slovenly in comparison.

"Sorry I'm late!" she announces with a wave of her arm. "My date ran a bit late."

She plops down on the other side of me and gives me a kiss on the cheek.

"With that hot chef?" Morgan asks, her eyes on her phone yet again.

Harmony bites her lip as she smiles. "Yup. He cooked for me at his restaurant before the dinner service started. It was just us two in the whole place. He even lit candles."

"That's so sweet. And super romantic," I say. "He's so into you."

Harmony's peaches-and-cream complexion lights up bright pink. "I hope so."

I pat her arm and reassure her that he absolutely does. I've only seen them together once, when he stopped by to say hi to Harmony after his shift while we were out having a drink together. But even in that short interaction, I could tell the guy had serious heart eyes for Harmony. He looked at her like she was the only woman in the room.

Harmony twists around me to look at Morgan. "I'm so hooking you up with his sous chef. He's single and ridiculously handsome."

"I don't date restaurant guys," she says sternly.

I recall just how heartbroken Morgan was a year ago when she found out that her restaurant owner ex-boyfriend of five years was cheating on her. Since then she's sworn off all guys in the industry.

Harmony's frowns. "Why not? He's, like, crazy hot. And tall. He's got muscles for days. And he volunteers at this after school program for elementary school kids on his days off."

Morgan swallows, and I think I see a bit of her resolve melt away. I nudge her softly.

"No restaurant guys," she says.

I know better than to argue with her, so I pat Harmony's hand. "I'll explain later. Are we seriously the only ones in this class? I thought it would be packed."

Harmony stutters just as Morgan clears her throat.

I twist my head from side to side, eyeing them both. "What is going on with you guys?"

Just then, the door to the studio creaks open. My jaw drops.

There stands Calder, dressed like he stepped out of a Scottish highlander romance.

I stammer as he takes his time walking up to me, his signature smirk plastered on his smug face. He's wearing nothing but a kilt, boots, and that little waist bag thing that I can never remember the name of. His bare, broad chest shines beneath the fluorescent lights.

His foot falls are measured and deliberate. It's like he knows I'm in shock at seeing him looking like a romance novel hero come to life, and I need an extra moment to absorb it all.

I choke on a breath. Even after seeing him naked countless times, his physique forever slays me.

"You're so... shirtless."

"Indeed, professor."

He stops right in front of me as Morgan and Harmony muffle squeals, giant smiles on their faces.

I flit my gaze between my girls. "Did you... did you plan this?"

They nod, still grinning.

"Surprise!" Morgan says, her eyes glistening.

"So wait. Calder's the model we're supposed to sketch? But..."

I trail off when Calder drops down on one knee.

"Oh my god," I manage to whisper, even though there's no air in my lungs.

Tears immediately flood my eyes. My heart flies to my throat. I cover my hands over my mouth as Calder digs a black velvet jewelry box from that man-purse thing hanging at his waist.

I try to focus on his eyes to steady myself, but when I see that he's tearing up too, I let out a sob. Calder isn't a crier. But for this moment—when he's proposing to me—he can't hold it together. And that shatters me in the most amazing way.

"Lily," he says, his voice shaky. He clears his throat. "This past year has been the happiest of my life because I've spent it with you. I want to spend the rest of my years, my months, my days, my everything with you. Will you marry me?"

A tear tumbles down his cheek. He wipes his nose with

the back of his wrist. A shaky laugh falls from both of us at the same time.

"Of course I'll marry you."

Cheers erupt from Harmony and Morgan as Calder jumps to his feet and rounds the table over to me. I stand up to meet him, and, with his hands cupping my face, we kiss.

I'm breathless when he lets go. I cuddle into his bare chest, relishing how his heart races. For me.

"You're so wearing this to the wedding."

"So commanding. I like it." He chuckles, tucking my head under his chin. "Anything for you, Professor."

Behind me Harmony squeals something about the ring. Calder leans away to reveal the open box in his hand.

My eyes bulge at the gigantic cushion cut diamond in the center of a bedazzled white gold band. "Holy..."

"It's my gran's. She wanted me to give it to you. I know I didn't ask you what kind of ring you wanted, but I hope this is okay."

I lean up and press a kiss to his lips. "More than okay. I love it."

He slips the ring on my finger, and that's when I spot Morgan a few feet away, aiming her phone at us.

"Sneaky." I smile at her.

She wipes a tear from her cheek. "Not even one bit sorry. You deserve this, Lily. A crazy awesome love and crazy romantic proposal."

I walk over to hug her. Then Harmony runs over and hugs us both, squealing and sniffling. When we finally let go, we're all wiping our eyes.

"We'll leave you love birds," Morgan says as she and Harmony step back and walk out of the room.

"Have fun!" Harmony squeals as she shuts the door behind them.

And then it's just Calder and me. In an empty art studio. Just like the day we met.

He walks up to me and gently grabs my hand. I melt at his touch, just like I always do. Joy still lingers in the center of my chest, now shrouded in comfort.

"This is a lot like the day we met."

I smile up at him. "I was just thinking that."

"Except I believe I was wearing fewer clothes."

I kiss his smiling mouth, then tug at his kilt. "We can fix that."

The heavy fabric lands with a soft thud on the floor.

"Are we really going to shag in an empty art studio?" He lifts a playful eyebrow. "I thought you wanted me to throw you into bed later."

"Screw the bed. I want you now." My tone is sure as a smile curves my lips.

"Your wish is my command, Professor."

ACKNOWLEDGMENTS

We have so many lovely people to thank for helping us make our very first book together possible!

Thank you Stefanie Simpson and Lauren Cosby for beta reading early drafts of *Sips & Strokes*. Thank you, Elle Maxwell, for designing the most gorgeous cover ever.

Thank you to our family and friends for loving us and supporting us through the wild and amazing journey that is writing and publishing.

Thank you to our fur babies for giving us endless cuddles through the writing/editing/revising process.

And last but never least, thanks to all of our amazing readers for your support. We love you!

ABOUT THE AUTHOR

Sarah Skye is the nom de plume of Sarah Smith and Skye McDonald. Sarah and Skye met on Twitter as fledgling authors seeking critique partners. That turned into a brilliant friendship, a joint podcast (Quick & Dirty Romance Podcast), and now a novel.

Sarah Smith is a copywriter-turned-author who wants to make the world a lovelier place, one kissing story at a time. When she's not writing, you can find her hiking, eating chocolate, and perfecting her lumpia recipe. She lives in Bend, Oregon, with her husband and adorable cat Salem.

Skye McDonald is an author, teacher, and personal development coach. When not writing sexy books or working with clients on fitness & self-love, Skye can be found out on a new adventure, usually with her pup at her side.

ALSO BY SARAH SKYE

Sarah Smith's Books:

FAKER

SIMMER DOWN

IF YOU NEVER COME BACK

Skye McDonald's Books

NOT SUITABLE FOR WORK

OFF THE RECORD

NEMESIS